A truck stopped for suspicious cargo. Then all hell broke loose.

WHEN HE GOT to her, Larae was still on her knees, staring at nothing in particular, just staring.

Bud dropped to his knees beside her and wrapped his big arms around her shoulders. "I've got you, darlin', I've got you."

She refocused for a time and croaked, "That you, Bud?"

"Yeah. It's me."

He felt her go slack as Maretti came sliding in beside him. "Oh…hell of a mess. She pass out?"

Bud just shook his head. "I don't know."

Maretti swatted him on the back of the head. "Pull it together, Bud. She don't need no weepies. She needs your help. You can be heart-broken later."

Bud pushed hard on his emotions and gathered himself.

"Lay her down, Bud. Keep her head turned so she can breathe. Check her pulse."

Bud gently lowered her stomach down on the ground, her face sideways, and then grabbed a wrist. It took several agonizing tries, but he found her pulse. "She's alive! Damn, she's alive."

WORKS BY ROD COLLINS

FICTION
The Sheriff Bud Blair Oregon Mystery Series
Spider Silk
Stone Fly
Bloodstone
Mariah's Song
Not Before Midnight

~

The John Bitter Post-Civil War Series
Bitter's Run
Abiqua

NON-FICTION
*What Do I Do When I Get There?:
A New Manager's Guidebook*

STONE FLY

Rod Collins

**The Sheriff Bud Blair Oregon Mystery Series
Volume 2**

BRIGHT WORKS PRESS

STONE FLY

Bright Works Press
Redmond, OR 97756
brightworkspress.com

© 2009 Rodney D. Collins
All rights reserved

This is a work of fiction. Names, characters, places, and incidents are the product of the author's imagination and are used fictitiously. Any resemblance to actual persons, living or dead, or events is entirely coincidental.

Print ISBN: 979-8-9895768-2-1
eBook ISBN: 979-8-9901364-1-0

Book Design by Jeffrey W. Duckworth
duckofalltrades.com

Cover Design by Val Stilwell and Anne Starke
Growth Collaborative • Eugene, Oregon
growthcollab.com

Editing & Book Production: Long On Books / Eva Long
longonbooks.com

Printed in the United States of America

to Vi

ACKNOWLEDGMENTS

My thanks to Peter Flowers for encouragement and honest feedback; to Eva Long, editor and friend, for keeping me at the keyboard; to Jeff Duckworth for his book design and to Val Stilwell and Anne Starke for their cover design; to Shelley Blumberg, proof reader extraordinaire, my catcher of nits, warts and bumps; to Vi, my wonderful lifetime companion, for her insight, guidance, encouragement and patience with the long discussions that carried us through the last three books; and finally to Alex Lafollette, who helped keep life interesting. Rest in peace, old friend.

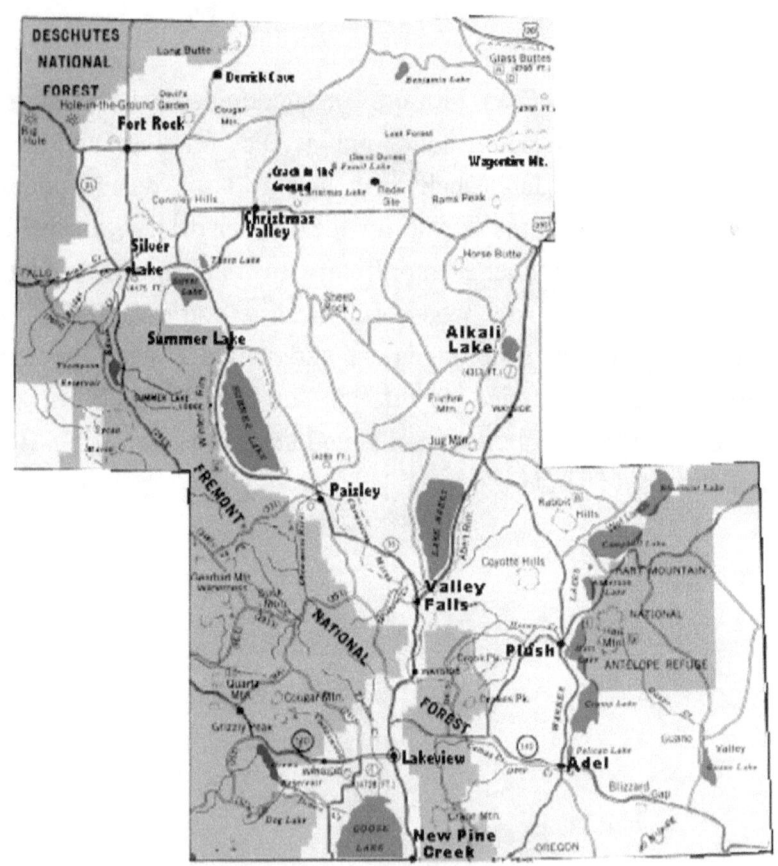

Lake County, Oregon Map

Chapter 1

A FULL MOON FOUND the man known only as Gar settled on his belly under the low-hanging branches of a juniper tree at the edge of Cowboy's barn lot. Dressed in desert camo, face and hands hidden under a coating of black and green face paint, he watched Cowboy's bunkhouse through night vision binoculars. The range was just over one hundred meters. Crazy Charlie was sitting on the front stoop sipping a beer, the glow from his cigarette a bright green dot on Gar's viewer. The sudden flare of light from the bunkhouse door caused Gar to wince and look away from the eyepiece.

He could hear a low murmur as Crazy and another man discussed something. The second figure stood on the porch for a few seconds, said something to Crazy and went back in the bunkhouse. Gar could see the flare and flicker of TV light through the windows.

That's two.

A light breeze drifted from Gar to the barnyard. An Australian shepherd crawled from under the porch, sniffed the air and barked, a short friendly yap. Gar froze and waited to see if the dog would identify him as friend or foe. The dog stretched, turned, and put his muzzle up to Crazy for a friendly pet and a scratch behind the ears.

Gar grinned to himself at the thought of all the dog biscuits he'd fed to barking dogs on his bottle hunting expeditions. *Yep, dog biscuits will do it every time.*

A coyote yip-yipped. The shepherd barked back, a challenging tone this time, and Crazy muttered, "Knock it off." The shepherd barked one last time and crawled back under the porch. Crazy stood and ground the stub of his cigarette in the dirt, stretched and went into the bunkhouse. Gar looked away in time to avoid the flash of light in the binoculars. The flicker and flare from the TV stopped, a light went on in the bathroom, and in ten minutes went off. A reading lamp in the last lighted bedroom was turned out and the bunkhouse was dark.

Gar didn't move. In thirty minutes he saw the bunkhouse door open a few inches and stay that way for another thirty. And then it slowly closed.

You know I'm here, don't you, Crazy? You always had that sixth sense when someone was watching.

Gar waited another three hours until the moon set and the only light was desert starlight. Slowly he rose and then walked quietly and directly to the bunkhouse porch. The shepherd came out from under the porch. Gar fed him a dog biscuit, patted him on the head and then placed a small, round river stone on the porch directly above the steps.

***

Homicide Detective Gino Maretti slammed the handset back into the cradle. He always slammed the phone down, and he always looked angry—which he was most of the time.

"Grandfield," he growled, "grab your coat. We got another one."

Grandfield, Ronald G., Detective Sergeant for the Bremerton Police Department, grimaced, closed the screen on his computer monitor and pulled his navy blue blazer off the back of his chair. He slipped the blazer on as he followed the slap-slap of Maretti's penny loafers down the hall.

After three years he still wasn't used to Maretti's profanity or his brusque ways. "But he's a good investigator," he always concluded when he told his wife about another of Maretti's tantrums. Grandfield's wife always countered with, "Maybe, but I can see why his wife left."

They slid into the unmarked dark blue sedan, Maretti behind the wheel, always behind the wheel. Grandfield wondered if Maretti was ever going to let him drive.

"What do we have?"

Maretti threw the car into gear and stomped the accelerator. "What we got is another body in the same damned dumpster. The one where we found the Bernard girl. That's what we got."

"The same dumpster? The one behind the High Hat?"

"That's the one. It's getting to be a popular dumping spot. Get it? Dumpster, dumping spot."

"Yeah, I get it, Gino. And it isn't funny." He braced as Gino turned left onto Washington and accelerated. "Dang it, Gino. Slow down. The body isn't going anyplace."

"This one's a sailor. I want to get there before the Navy does."

A uniformed police officer was keeping the curious and the ghoulish away from the dumpster when Maretti slid the car to a stop in the alley behind the High Hat. Maretti was out of the car before the engine died. Grandfield—Maretti never used Grandfield's first name—right behind him. A uniformed cop pointed at the battered brown dumpster and went back to crowd control.

Give him credit, Grandfield thought. *He's methodical at a crime scene.*

Maretti approached the dumpster slowly, looking at the worn, buckled pavement, and at the back door of the High Hat. Just looking. Looking for anything that wasn't where it belonged. He peeked over the high sides of the dumpster. "Hey, Grandfield. You better get the lab boys down here. And come look at this."

Grandfield tapped a key on his cell phone, hit Send, and walked to the dumpster. He peered over the edge. A Caucasian male in Navy whites was sprawled on a pile of black garbage bags, his trousers soaked with blood. A voice answered his call.

"Forensics."

"Hey, Dave. This is Grandfield. We got another job for you at the High Hat."

"Okay, we'll be there in fifteen."

Milo Jackson, Maretti's partner in an earlier life, flipped his notebook shut as he walked out the scarred steel back door of the High Hat. The nametag on his shirt pocket identified him as Sergeant Milo Jackson.

"Yo, Milo," Maretti greeted in a surprisingly friendly tone and stuck out his big hand.

Milo pumped Maretti's arm, and grinned. "Hey, Gino. How's it goin', pard?"

"Stayin' busy. You?"

Milo shrugged. "Same old shit."

Gino tilted back to look up at more than six feet of Milo. He nodded his head at an officer working crowd control. "How's your new partner working out?"

"Matt Brandt. Good kid. He'll do okay. Hell, he might even make detective. You did."

Maretti laughed. "I think I had more fun as a sergeant. Meet my partner, Ron Grandfield."

Grandfield and Jackson shook hands in a disinterested perfunctory way, none of the let's-see-who-can-crush-a-hand stuff. Grandfield nodded at the door. "Anything?"

"Nope. Nobody saw anything. Nobody heard anything. Nobody even saw him come in last night. The barmaid found him when she was dumping the trash this morning. Said she recognized him, but didn't know him except as Pike."

Grandfield shook his head. "Yeah, right. Somebody just brought him here and stuffed him in this convenient dumpster. I don't know, Gino. Maybe you're right. It's just a popular dumping site."

"I told you." Maretti looked at Milo. "Did you pick his pocket?"

"Just his wallet. The barmaid, Ms. Twyla Eubanks, had 'Pike' right. According to his driver's license, he is Harold Leroy Pike. He has a military drivers license, and he was obviously a sailor." Jackson flipped open his notebook, tore a page loose and handed it to Maretti. "Here's a physical address."

Maretti stuffed the page in his shirt pocket. "You sticking around until the lab boys and the coroner finish up?"

"We can do that."

"Okay then. We'll check out his house, and then Grandfield has a report to write, so I think we'll head back."

Milo grinned at Grandfield. "How do you put up with that? Nice seein' you again, Gino."

"You, too, Milo. Tap it light."

As Maretti pulled the sedan out of the alley, an NCIS sedan, lights flashing, turned in to park where Grandfield and Maretti's sedan had been.

Maretti grinned. "Too late, boys, too late."

"What you got against our boys in the Naval Criminal Investigative Service?"

"Nothing really, except those arrogant turds always want to stonewall any investigation involving military personnel, and it's my town, not theirs."

The address on Pike's driver's license turned out to be a run-down duplex and south of the city limits. The neighbor, a road-weary woman wearing a faded pink housecoat, who could have been forty-five or sixty, turned out to be the owner of the duplex, and Pike's landlady. She knew nothin', ain't seen Leroy for a couple of days, no, he ain't had no visitors, and she didn't know any of his asshole friends. But she did unlock the door to Leroy's apartment for them, then shuffled her slippers back to her share of the duplex, muttering something under her breath about "damned cops" before she slammed the door.

Leroy turned out to be a tidy housekeeper, too tidy it seemed. The place had been sanitized. No trash, no empty beer bottles, no paper, no bills, not even any junk mail.

"A pro?" Grandfield speculated.

"Well, for sure somebody beat us to it." Gino said in disgust. "Why put the body in a dumpster and then sanitize his apartment?"

***

Three days later Maretti walked by Grandfield's desk in the bullpen, flipped the autopsy report at him and growled, "Read this damn thing."

Grandfield scanned it. Harold Leroy Pike; age 29; occupation: Navy; military rank: Chief Petty Officer; weight, height, hair color, eye color, et cetera. But the listed cause of death stopped him.

"Holy shit!"

Several heads turned and looked at Grandfield. Maretti poked his head out of his office. "What the hell is going on, Grandfield? I never heard you cuss before."

"It's your bad influence, Maretti. Now I gotta go to confession."

"Well, if you get any Hail Marys, say a couple for me."

"Gino, did you read this?"

"Nope. I knew you'd fill me in."

Grandfield shook his head in disgust. "Okay, so here it is. This guy died from a broken neck. And somebody castrated him. According to the pathologist, he was probably alive when he was separated from his private parts."

"Damn, I'll bet that hurt. So what do you think?"

"Gino, did you ever have an original thought in your life?"

"Yeah," Maretti growled, "I listen to you, you come up with an idea, I correct your mistakes and *voila,* I got a new idea."

"Okay, this is ghoulish, but I don't think it's the work of a sex fiend or a psycho. My gut tells me it ties in with the Bernard murder."

Maretti nodded. "We'll have the lab boys get us a DNA comparison. Maybe this is one of the guys that raped her. And let's go find out who he was hanging with. Maybe those Navy cops will know something." He stopped. "What do we know about the Bernard girl's family?"

"No husband. A brother in the Marines. A mother living in North Dakota. Father deceased."

"See if you can find out where the brother is."

"I'm on it."

Chapter 2

SHE DIDN'T LIKE jails, and that included this one. Not on a trumped-up charge of speeding through the rural high desert of Lake County. When she suggested bail and offered a credit card, the sheriff just shook his head no. "We only take cash, local checks or debit cards," was all he said.

At least Lake County's jail was clean. The bedding was fresh and the bathroom was scrubbed and disinfected. Deputy Karen Highsmith brought her soup, salad, and hamburger steak at dinner. She watched Monday Night Football for a while, a preseason game that was pretty dull, read a magazine, and then had a good night's sleep.

At nine o'clock she was released.

She took a deep breath of air while Sheriff Bud Blair unchained the Harley. "Who paid my bail, Sheriff?"

"Let's just say that the record will show that your bail was paid by a Mister Owen MacDougal, a rancher from Christmas Valley," Bud answered. "You should also know he made the arrangement for your employment at the Christmas Valley Lodge."

She didn't say anything, just nodded. He patted her shoulder, locked eyes with her, and frowned. "You be careful, Ms. Holcomb. And watch for deer up through the Crooked Creek Canyon."

Larae stowed her gear in the saddlebags, zipped up her black leathers, strapped on the helmet, and headed north on 395. The jacket had a skull stenciled on the back. The black helmet carried a Darth Vader shield.

She liked the cool morning air and the solid feel of the Harley. And she liked being out of jail. *Jail time certainly interferes with my plans.*

She rode at an easy sixty miles an hour north through Crooked Creek Canyon. A driver in a blue and white Ford pickup passed her on a straight stretch through a little valley of meadow and pastureland hemmed by juniper and pine-covered ridges.

Four deer trotted across a freshly-cut alfalfa field beyond a ranch house shaded by a tall row of Lombardi poplar. *Girls*, she thought. Cold diesel smoke columned above a green John Deere tractor as a ranch hand warmed the engine.

She goosed her speed to sixty-five as she left the canyon. Abert Rim, the massive cliff to her right, rising some two thousand feet above the valley floor, was almost black in the morning shade.

Clyde Whittaker, proprietor of the stage stop store at Valley Falls and yarner of local fame, watched the black rider pass his store. "The damned outlaws are everywhere," he said to no one in particular. "Hell, that one even looks like a girl."

Chapter 3

BILLIE THOMPSON, OWNER, manager, bartender, and sometimes chief cook and bottle washer, was behind the short counter in the Christmas Valley Lodge dining room. She was refilling Wally Pidgeon's coffee cup when Larae swung the Harley around and backed it up on the kickstand.

Wally saw Billie staring and turned to look. He said, "My gawd. Look at that. What is it?"

"I think it's my new bartender."

"Judas Priest, Billie. Can it talk?

"I guess we'll find out. Here she comes."

"She?"

"Yep. She. Owen MacDougal asked me to give her a job. And since he owns a share of this place, I didn't think I could say no. Besides, I'm tired of working seven days a week."

Wally nodded but gave her a skeptical look.

Larae took off her helmet and shook out her short ash blond hair. She stretched and looked around.

The lodge was an attractive, stone-fronted, single-story restaurant and bar with a modified A-frame central dinning room. And lots of high windows. Except for the trees and evergreen shrubbery around the lodge and around the motel next door, there wasn't much vegetation in Christmas Valley, just a scatter of runty juniper trees and lots of sage and rabbit brush and cheat grass—miles and miles of it in all directions fading to pine mountains west and north of the ancient lake bed. The rest of Christmas Valley seemed to be gravel lanes, a collection of small homes, a post office, a small but attractive motel fronting a man-made lake, a small golf course and RV park, and a grocery store-gas station combo on the highway.

"Holy smoke," she mumbled. "Christmas Valley? I wonder who thought that up?"

She hooked her helmet on the handlebars, walked into the lodge and smiled. "Hi. I'm looking for Billie?"

The plump, comely woman studied her for a brief couple of seconds, then walked around the end of the counter. "I'm Billie," she said holding out her hand. "And you must be Ray."

"Larae, actually." She smiled and added, "But I've been called lots of things."

"Well, Larae, honey, this poor excuse for a gentleman sitting here drinking my coffee for free is Walter Pidgeon."

The small, spare man who looked to be in his late sixties took off his thin, wire-rimmed glasses, and squinted at her. Then he smiled, stood, and held out his hand. "Call me Wally. My mother was a fan of the late Walter Pidgeon, the old-time film star." His voice was a surprising baritone.

"And since your last name was Pidgeon…?"

He smiled, revealing a gleaming set of false teeth, held her hand a little longer than necessary, his dark brown eyes crinkling in amusement. "That's it. But don't think pigeon as in bird; think French as in P-I-D-G-E-O-N. Or maybe it was British. European for sure." And he laughed.

"And you are French?"

He shrugged. "Lord, honey, this is America. Who knows what we are. Hell, even the name was probably given to an early immigrant ancestor because the Yanks couldn't spell the real one."

He released her hand and sat back down on the red vinyl stool. "Well, get out of those leather things and let me have a look at you."

"Wally, mind your manners," Billie scolded.

He ran his hand through his thinning gray hair and put his glasses back on. "I mean no disrespect."

Larae laughed. "I'm sure you didn't." She shrugged out of her leather jacket and spun in a circle. "What do you think?"

Wally snorted. "What the hell is that thing on your left arm?"

"My pet snake."

"Looks like a cobra. You aren't one of those biker babes?"

Larae gave him a hard stare. In a quiet, steely voice she said, "Past tense, Wally. Past tense."

Billie recovered from her surprise and said, "Well you can't tend bar in a tank top. Do you have anything else to wear?"

"No. My friend will ship my clothes when I have an address."

"Okay. You might fit into some of my things. This may be the sticks, but my bartenders wear white shirts or blouses and black skirts or slacks. And you need to keep that tattoo covered up."

She turned on Wally. "And if I so much as hear a whisper about this, Wally, I'll know where it came from, and I'll finish what Mother Nature has started. Got it?"

Wally laughed. "Now, now, Mother Thompson. I know I can get carried away, but I know when to keep quiet. If this nice young lady wants a fresh start, she's come to the right place. But what exactly do you think Mother Nature has started other than creeping old age?"

"You want to keep that nice baritone voice?"

"My gawd, Billie. You are a coarse woman."

"Count on it, Wally."

Larae started laughing and when they both finally joined in she said, "I think I'm going to like it here."

Billie showed Larae to a back bedroom with bath, TV, nightstand, dresser, and a closet. "You can bunk here for now. I'll get you some bedding and some clothing." When she saw the puzzled looked on Larae's face, Billie added with a chuckle, "From my thinner days, honey, from my thinner days."

"I have a kit and a few things in my saddle bags."

Billie paused, looked at Larae and asked, "You running from anything, honey? Gangs, the law, that kind of thing?"

"No, Billie. I'm not wanted by the law. My ol' man said it was time to get out, but the gang never lets you go…totally. Will they follow me and then give you a hard time? No, that's not what happens."

Billie suppressed a cold shiver. "I don't want to think about that."

Chapter 4

SHERIFF BUD BLAIR and tall, willowy, dark-haired Deputy Michelle Trivoli put in two hours Monday morning directing traffic and helping Trooper Charlie Prince, Lake County's lone state policeman, investigate a traffic accident between New Pine Creek on the California-Oregon border and the town of Lakeview.

The open spaces, light traffic, and miles-long straight stretches encouraged drivers to high rates of speed. Bud figured the technology built into the modern automobile was also a temptation. The black Cadillac upside down in the sagebrush had a speedometer that ran all the way to one-sixty, and it looked like the driver was bent on finding out if it really could go that fast.

Unfortunately, a small group of mule deer chose to cross the highway just beyond a slight rise in the road. Michelle speculated that the Caddy owner didn't see the deer until he topped the rise. The ABS system worked just fine, but the driver swerved to miss the last doe and left the roadway at a high rate of speed. That was working all right until the right front tire struck a rock about twenty inches in diameter. At that point the car left the ground, torqued in the air and slid on its top some two hundred feet before a power pole arrested any further forward progress, thereby protecting a barbed wire fence from destruction.

"Well," Bud said, "he got it stopped."

Michelle laughed. "And he didn't kill any deer."

They watched the driver of the tow truck winch the Caddy back over on its wheels. A small dusty cloud sifted over the car as it dropped heavily on its tires.

They walked to the state police cruiser where six-foot-six Trooper Charlie Prince was making notes for his report. Charlie powered the window down and Bud leaned over and said, " I think that's a wrap, don't you?"

Trooper Prince snapped his notebook shut. "Thanks for your help. I'm going to the hospital to get a statement from the driver. And to give him a citation for violation of the basic rule, reckless driving, and anything else I can think of. He's damned lucky he didn't get killed. If he'd hit another rock, it could have come right through the windshield."

"I don't suppose," Michelle speculated, "you can cite him for hunting deer out of season?"

Trooper Prince just shook his head. "Wish I could."

Michelle was suddenly irritated.

Bud sensed her mood. Even thought he understood it. Trooper Prince was a "comer," destined for bigger and better things. And totally invested in his career.

"Well, Charlie," Bud said dryly, "remember to dot the i's and cross the t's. And send us a copy of the report, please."

"Yes, sir."

***

Back in his office, Bud checked his messages and winced when he spotted a message from SCF, Services for Children and Families. He hated child abuse cases. He was good at interviewing children, but he still hated it. And he ducked those calls when he could.

He poked his head out of his office door. "Deputy Trivoli, I need to see you for a minute." Bud held the door open for her and then closed it behind him. "I need some help." He gimped over to his desk and sat down, motioning Michelle to a chair.

She plopped down in Bud's wooden visitor's chair, crossed her arms, and looked expectantly at him. "What? Walking?"

"I'll ignore that unkind cut. I just turned my ankle a little this morning."

"I didn't see you limping this morning."

He nodded. "Good."

"Are you going to have it looked at?

"You sound more and more like Nancy. What I want to talk about is the assignment of our esteemed undersheriff, Sonny Sixkiller, to the Central Oregon Interagency Arson Task Force. He starts working out of LaPine next week. And since Deputy Hildebrand is moving to Silver Lake, that leaves us to keep the peace."

"What are you going to do for an undersheriff?"

"Why, Sergeant Trivoli, until Sonny gets back, *you* are the undersheriff." He smiled, came around from behind his desk, and handed her a letter.

She read it carefully, blushed and then stood up and put out her hand. "Thank you, Bud."

"My pleasure. You earned it. Tomorrow at 0900 there will be a ceremony in the Courtroom. Judge Lynch wants it that way, so look sharp."

He studied her for a minute, this tall, willowy dark-haired deputy sheriff. A sudden picture flashed through his mind of Michelle, pistol out and up in a shooter's stance, banging away in a cold rage because she thought Bill Casey had shot her sheriff. Casey did manage to kill Bud's horse, which then had the unmitigated gall to roll on Bud's right leg and prove that the human ankle is no match for twelve hundred pounds of dead horse.

He shook off the thought, smiled and added, "And no blushing."

Then he handed her the note from SCF. "And call this caseworker back."

Karen Highsmith, a technical deputy seven years Michelle's senior, was standing by the door when Michelle came into the booking area with a big smile on her face. "Congratulations, Sergeant Ma'am."

Michelle stammered, muttered thanks and then stopped.

Karen understood immediately. "Don't fret. The sheriff always gives me a bonus at the end of the year, and I like running the jail. I'm not a road warrior. You earned it."

"Karen, you are one of most generous people I know."

Deputy Highsmith laughed and impulsively hugged Michelle. "Try telling that to my guests."

***

Bud's small police force, D.A. Howard Finch, and three reserve deputies lined the walls of the courtroom. They were joined by Augustus Hildebrand, father to Deputy Roger Hildebrand, and longtime chief of police for the city of Lakeview, population three thousand or so.

At nine that morning, Deputy Trivoli stood straight and tall in her blue dress uniform, black Wellingtons mirror polished, as Judge Tom Lynch read the citation "for outstanding community service, for courage in the line of duty...."

When he finished, the silver-haired rancher and chief county administrator handed her a plaque, her new stripes, and a gleaming new badge that said "Sergeant Trivoli, Lake County Sheriff's Department." The onlookers applauded enthusiastically.

Judge Lynch shook her hand and beamed at the camera. Carol Connor, the blond haired, thirty-year-old daughter of Asa Connor, owner/editor of the *Lake County News*, took a half dozen photos and then said, "Thank you" as a signal that she was through. Bud saw Sonny smile and nod at Carol. It was no secret that the handsome Sonny Sixkiller and the petite blond were special friends.

Bud caught Sonny and Roger grinning at him and he winked. Then he leaned over and whispered, "Lynch has turned into a politician."

Sonny whispered back, "Nothing like a camera and a reporter to get him going."

When the judge finished, they all crowded around Michelle to offer congratulations. Bud grinned. "Well, Trigger Trueshot, you didn't blush until the judge was finished. Why don't we all have a little celebration this evening at my place out on the highway? I'll put some steaks on and whip up a salad. And if you feel like it, bring whatever else you want to eat...or drink. And no shop talk. This is strictly for fun."

He turned to Lonnie Beltram. Lonnie was a home-grown reserve officer who had paid his own way to the Monmouth Academy. He had graduated in the top quarter of his class, but he was only willing to work in eastern Oregon, and no eastside jobs had come open in the two months since graduation. Bud had put him to work two days a week as the quasi-leader of the Lake County Reserves. "Lonnie, be sure and invite the reserve officers."

"You got it, Sheriff. We'll be there!"

"Chief," Bud said, "that invitation includes the City."

Gus gave him a wry smile. "Good thing, I'd say. Otherwise you'd never get through town without a citation for reckless eating."

"Reckless eating?"

"Yep, for having a party without us."

"But, Gus, we control the county roads." That brought the expected chuckles.

Bud waved at Howard, Gus and the judge, and then said to the officers, "Let's have a short meeting before you all scatter."

Bud stuck his hand out to Lonnie. "Thanks for coming, Lonnie." And Lonnie understood he was dismissed.

***

Karen punched the lock release when Bud rang the call button. "Get yourselves some coffee and let's meet in my office. You too, Karen. Forward calls to my phone."

The top half of the solid wall behind Bud's desk was corkboard that he had personally installed out of his own pocket. It was covered with a large Lake County map. Red pins marked the location of each major crime scene. Green pins matched those locations where crimes had been solved.

Karen, pulling her chair behind her, noted once again there were no personal or family photos in Bud's office. A bookcase held an eclectic array of titles on forensic science, criminology textbooks, magazines, novels, and a rumpled pile of quarter-folded newspapers. Tacked to the upper right corner of the map were wanted posters that Bud either thought to be the most interesting or of people likely to come to come through the county.

When everyone was settled, Molly, Bud's little black Lab, started to get up off her pad in the corner, but Bud just looked at her and she laid back down.

Bud said, "I want to take advantage of the fact that we are all here at the same time. Sonny, when are you heading for Bend?"

"Our first meeting as a task force is next Monday at the Deschutes National Forest Office. I'll drive up on Monday. I'm booked in the Best Western, but if it looks like this is going to last very long, I'll hunt a cheap apartment."

Frowning, Roger said, "Boss, I don't understand why you're loaning Sonny to the task force. We're understaffed and underfunded as it is."

"I know, but the feds are paying his salary and per diem, and some of the arson fires have been set inside the county boundaries. We'll get Lonnie to handle the security for the county fair, so that will help some. Forest Service Special Agent Wires asked for Roger, but we need Roger in Christmas Valley. It was either Michelle or Sonny." He turned to Sonny. "Do you know Wires?"

"No, but Tom Johnson, the Forest Service LEO in Paisley, thinks highly of him." Sonny looked at Roger. "Any word on Tom's transfer?"

The wooden chair creaked as Roger tipped it back and looked disgusted. "You'd think the feds could come up with a better plan than centralizing the Forest Service law enforcement officers. Tom thinks he'll be out of here by October 1."

Bud interjected. "Any chance we can influence things?"

Roger shook his head. "I don't think so. Even the regional forester couldn't budge her Washington office on this one."

"Okay, then we'll have to live with it," Bud answered. "Have you found a place to bunk in Silver Lake?"

"As a matter of fact, I found a nice house to rent, small but really nice. I'll move up there next month."

"Good. Michelle is going to be the acting undersheriff while Sonny's gone." Bud fished through a stack of papers on his desk, found what he was looking for and held up an Alert from Homeland Security. "Guess what? Homeland Security has it, quote, on good authority, end quote, that the Mexican Mafia is smuggling Middle Eastern types into the country in exchange for good Afghani opium. They suspect, for undisclosed reasons, Highway 395 may be the conduit for these possible terrorists.

"I'm not privy to any information beyond that. My inclination is to give the story to Asa, but that might scare the hell out of the people in the county. And it might get some innocent citizen of Semitic origins shot. My instincts say sit on it and ask our police officers—city, county, federal and state—to stay alert. But I'm open to any ideas on the subject."

The room was quiet until Michelle said, "It just doesn't seem real. I mean this is so far off the beaten track. Terrorists don't target small places, do they?"

Sonny shook his head. "No, they don't. No media splash, but we've been hearing rumors about Highway 395 being the heroin route into the northwest. So I guess it could be true."

Roger said, "I've been hearing that since I was a kid, but there's really no hard evidence. It's like a myth, or a folktale. It's always one of those stories where someone knows a person who's second cousin heard from the third cousin of somebody else."

"What do you think we should do, outside of sharing with other law enforcement agencies?" Bud asked. "Do we need more eyes and ears on the job?"

The deputies all looked at each other and then back at Bud. Finally Sonny spoke. "Given the kind of profession we're in, information is pure gold, and I suspect we go overboard to protect our information. It could be helpful to have our citizens keeping an eye out. But I think if we go to the paper, and word gets out that we are watching, and assuming the alert to be accurate, these guys will stop coming this way and pick another route. No, we should tell Chief Hildebrand and maybe Trooper Prince, but we need to keep this quiet…for now."

Bud raised his eyebrows. "Anybody else?"

Roger swore quietly, "Damn it. This is a democracy. At least I think it is, and in a democracy the people have a right to know what's going on. We're in a war we didn't choose, but it's real. The television pictures of 9-11 are still vivid in my mind. No…I think we need to share it. The only question in my mind is how."

"So what do we do?" Michelle asked. "Stop every Semitic-looking person that comes through the county?"

Bud frowned and shook his head. "No. We still need probable cause. We uphold the law; we don't break it. But that doesn't mean we get stupid either. What we have here is somebody's guess based on information they didn't share. I can just see a newspaper article that reads, "The Lake County Sheriff's Office, acting on unconfirmed information, is stopping all Arab-looking people passing through the county to determine if they are terrorists."

Because she had never offered any opinion in any setting unless it was about operating the jail, they were all surprised when Karen, arms folded across her ample bosom, shook her head.

"This is what I think. The information is out there in the open already. Someone, somewhere will leak it to the press, and then we'll all look like fools when the people here in Lake County discover we knew it but didn't share it. They'll think we don't trust them, and then they won't trust us."

Bud nodded his head and then looked embarrassed. "Ouch! You nailed it, Karen. We're thinking like cops."

Roger nodded. "You know, in an earlier life, my team had to figure out who to trust and who to avoid. Those we trusted brought us good intelligence and we made better decisions from that intelligence. What we have here is unsubstantiated intelligence, but what if we treat this info as maybe true? And then bring those people likely to see any terrorist suspects, aka Arab-looking people, to our attention. They don't do anything but watch and keep us informed. I'm thinking of people like Clyde Whitaker at Valley Falls, Amy out in Adel—folks like that who run stores and gas stations, places where travelers are likely to stop. You know…for gas, food, lodging."

Bud nodded his head. "I like it. Let's plan it. Karen, take notes."

At the end of thirty minutes they knew who would contact whom in the county on a "just in case you see anything suspicious" basis, and a "keep this quiet…it's not a secret…but we don't want to scare off the bad guys" basis.

Bud was assigned the task of filling in D.A Finch, Judge Lynch, Trooper Prince, and Chief Hildebrand. He also chose Clyde Whittaker to be his informant. Michelle had New Pine Creek, Adel, and Plush. Roger took Tom Johnson, and had Paisley, Summer Lake, Silver Lake and Christmas Valley.

"Okay. Work this into your patrol schedules…soon," Bud advised.

Michelle decided Bud was enthused and pleased with their planning, and again she wistfully thought it was too bad this almost handsome, rugged looking man was in love with Nancy Sixkiller.

Chapter 5

IT DIDN'T TAKE very long for the word to get around that Billie had a new, good-looking, female bartender. During the first week every lonesome cowboy from forty miles around stopped in for a cold beer and a chance to get acquainted. There was a lot of daydreaming and wishbooking going on over Larae's quick smile, soft brown eyes and warm welcome. A couple of the cowboys who stopped weren't quite as single as they let on.

She deflected their passes with easy good humor. Billie was impressed, and Wally was in love again. Every evening he sat at the end of the bar and made small talk with Larae. She teased him about being her bouncer, and he started calling her Sweet Mama.

Wally was also a fountain of information. "Watch out for that one," he'd say, "He has a reputation for starting fights." Or, "That one owns a nice ranch this side of Fort Rock." Or, "That one isn't from around here."

Larae was having fun. She had a good memory, and as jobs go, this was a dream.

By nine Saturday night, the place was overflowing, and even though it was a cool night, Billie opened the big slider near the end of the bar so patrons could use the patio. Both Billie and Larae had their hands full filling pitchers of beer, popping bottle caps and mixing drinks for those few who liked the harder stuff. It was noisy, but it was happy noise. The gamblers were playing the video poker machines and the jukebox was playing Willie

Nelson, singing in his distinct nasal twang, "Of all the girls I loved…" A couple of happy cowboys, Stetson hats over their hearts, joined in until some one told them to knock it off "cause we want to hear Willy."

Billie checked the restaurant. Half the tables were still full, and her waitress, Carla Winkle, had an armload of steaming prime rib on the way to two middle-aged couples sitting near the back. Chef Peter "Rocky" Gunn, set another dinner plate on the service counter and rang the bell. "Not a bad night," Billie thought. "I wonder if we should hire a small band?"

At ten Carla and Rocky closed the restaurant and did a weary but thorough job of cleaning up. The hardcore drinkers were still at it. Those freezing on the patio moved into the bar. The rest of the partygoers drifted away. At midnight Billie announced last call. Some of the younger men grumbled about just getting started, but they all started putting on hats and coats, saying good night and leaving a last tip on the bar or table.

Larae started clearing the tables, emptying ashtrays, gathering empty bottles, wiping down the bar and filling the dishwasher while Billie counted out the till. "Not bad, honey. This is the best night we've had in a long time." She laughed. "No, that's not true. It's the best night we *ever* had." Billie bagged the money, checks and credit card slips and took them to the safe in her back office. When she returned, Larae had almost finished mopping up, and the dishwasher was running.

"Why didn't you leave that until morning?"

Larae looked puzzled. "Do you?"

"No."

"Well, I don't wait until morning either. Never." She pushed the roll-around mop bucket to Wally, handed him a roll of paper towels and two spray bottles, one with window cleaner and the other with disinfectant. "Even the bouncer has to earn his keep, Wally." She pointed in the direction of the restrooms.

"Judas, Sweet Mama, I was only kidding about being the bouncer."

"You drink our beer, you work."

Billie chuckled. "You been called, Wally. Fish or cut bait."

Grumbling about not getting any respect, he rolled the mop bucket into the short hallway and out of sight.

Billie split the tips and then put an extra $20 on Larae's pile. When Larae protested, Billie said, "No, you earned it."

Larae looked surprised, and a little troubled. She wondered what her employer would say if she knew Larae was traveling under false colors.

***

Larae was sitting at the counter eating a breakfast of toast and orange juice when Wally wandered in for his morning coffee. Billie poured a cup of coffee and set it in front of his usual stool. "Morning, Sunshine," she said.

"Morning, Billie." He pointedly ignored Larae. The two women glanced at each other.

Larae winked at Billie. "Are we grumpy this morning, Mr. Pidgeon?"

"Yes, Miz Holcomb. Yes we are. Cleaning latrines, no less! I haven't cleaned a latrine in almost fifty years. That was a dirty trick."

"You do have a toilet in your house, right?"

"That's a whole lot different than cleaning up after drunks who get more on the floor than in the pot."

Larae put a twenty under his cup. "Here, darlin', this is for cleaning the bathrooms."

"You trying to buy good graces?"

"The laborer is worthy of his hire."

"You keep it. You earned it." He paused. "And I apologize for my rudeness. On second thought, however, we might just invest this in the video poker machine and split the profits." With exaggerated dignity he slipped the $20 bill into his shirt pocket.

"And I suppose you are now able to pay for your own coffee," Billie opined.

"That, my sweet Billie, I pay for by gracing you with my elegant presence."

They all smiled. Billie winked at Larae. Peace had been restored.

Larae finished her toast, sipped at her coffee and said, "I was curious about the big guy. I don't know his name. The one with the Dick Butkus look."

Wally said, "You mean the one in the Niners cap?"

"Yeah, that's the one."

Wally said. "Everybody just calls him Cowboy. You be careful of him. He's a mean drunk."

"Been here long?"

Billie said, "Well, he started coming in about a year ago. Claims to own the old Barry ranch."

Wally snorted. "He may be big and he may be called Cowboy, but he hasn't done a lick of work. He contracted to have his hay put up. Small place like that, you put up your own hay or you go under. Drives a big red Ford diesel pickup—big, big sticker price. Always has three or four guys hanging round the place. They didn't put up any hay either."

Larae just nodded and filed that away for future reference. The ex-biker babe had dealt with dangerous people before. "And what about the guy who sat in the back corner by himself? He nursed one beer all night, just watching, and never said a word to anyone. He has alert eyes. I swear he was cataloging every one in the room."

"The guy with the short beard, black sweatshirt, blue eyes? I noticed him, too," Billie added.

Wally laughed. "Do you have a romantic interest in that fellow, Larae?"

"No, Wally. Just curious. Everyone else was whooping it up and having a good time, and he was just sitting and watching."

"That's the type that women get all mushy over," Wally said disgustedly. "The lonesome, hangdog type."

"Well, he wasn't hangdog. He was sharp, alert, and watching all of us like a hawk."

Wally just waved it off. "Oh, I wouldn't take him too seriously. He's just the bottles-and-cans man."

"What does that mean?"

"It means he makes his living by riding his bicycle up and down the roads around here picking up bottles and cans. He cashes them in at the store for the deposit money."

Billie frowned. "Well, no wonder he only drank one beer."

"Maybe," Larae answered, "but he isn't someone who's been whipped by life."

"Maybe he's just a hippie," Wally offered.

Chapter 6

CLYDE WHITTAKER WAS pumping gas into a pickup and camper combination with Idaho plates when Bud pulled in beside the stage stop store in Valley Falls. He returned Clyde's wave and then let Molly out for a quick run in Clyde's little RV park. An older couple in lawn chairs, wearing white matching sweatshirts, sat next to a large fifth-wheeler, a white Dodge diesel pickup still connected to the trailer. Bud waved, and the woman pointed to Molly and asked, "Does she bite?"

"Never happens, but she might beat you to death with her tail. You folks waiting on the sun?"

The man rose stiffly from his chair, a tall, spare grey-haired man Bud guessed to be in his late sixties or early seventies. The man wandered across the narrow strip of lawn, while Molly had her ears scratched and her head petted by the older woman.

"How'd you know that?"

Bud pointed at the high cliffs of Abert Rim. "Just guessing. The rim blocks the morning sun. And at this elevation, even the desert can get pretty cool at night."

"Well, you nailed 'er. Here it is August and I had to run the furnace to stay warm last night." And then he offered, "I'm Warren Winslow. That's my wife, Betty. We're from Port Angeles, up in Washington. We always make a stop here on our trip through. Can't miss a chance to hear Clyde tell us some more whoppers."

Bud smiled and held out his hand. "Bud Blair. Does Clyde charge you for two drinks when you only ordered one?"

Warren's blue eyes smiled. "Pulled that one on you, did he?"

"Yep. On my first stop here."

"But he did buy the next round?"

Bud laughed. "Yes he did. That's gotten to be one of my favorite stories."

Warren chuckled. "He's a character all right. The first time we stopped, I asked him why this place was called Valley Falls. He wouldn't tell me. Just said it had nothing to do with water, and he didn't drink water anyway, and he had some nice cold beer inside."

"Pulled that one on me, too. Actually there *is* a small waterfall on the Chewacan River. Just over there." Bud pointed north towards the sage covered hills a couple miles across the flats. "According to my copy of *Oregon Geographic Names*, that's how this spot got its name, but the book says it's a couple feet high."

Warren grunted. "I guess that could spoil the fun for Clyde. He just hints that some Indians chased a troop of cavalry to the edge of the rim and a trooper fell off the cliff. He hints that is why it's called Valley Falls."

Bud laughed. "In truth, there is a story that someone found an old cavalry saber and a breastwork on the edge of the rim someplace up there, a place where an officer and a couple of troopers fought with the Indians. That part might be true, but the name comes from the waterfall on the Chewacan River."

Warren laughed. "I think I'll not disabuse him of his notions. Better story that way."

Bud heard the Idaho pickup start and turned to watch it pull away from the pump. Clyde waved and hollered, "Howdy, neighbors."

Bud nodded and Betty shouted, "Breakfast on yet?"

"You bet. Come on in."

Bud turned to Warren and asked, "Would you mind waiting a couple of minutes? I've got some personal business with Clyde."

"He in trouble?"

"No, nothing like that. I just need to ask him for a favor."

***

Ten minutes later, Bud called Molly to get in the pickup, waved at the Winslows and pulled out of the parking lot headed south back to Lakeview.

"Molly, I hope Clyde can keep a lid on it. Terrorism is pretty juicy stuff. Knowing Clyde. he'll have to tell someone. But that might not be a bad thing. Guess we'll see, huh?"

Molly pulled her head out of the window and looked in his direction before sticking her nose back into the wind, testing the air for the scent of birds and other critters.

Chapter 7

WESLEY WELLINGTON, A law student at the University of Oregon and an avid fly fisherman, sat in his float tube on the flat, glass smooth surface of Anna Reservoir. The cliffs of Summer Rim reflected back in a perfect mirror image.

He had fished the morning away for the few remaining striped bass in the reservoir without success. "Maybe the stories of striped bass are just rumors after all," he muttered as he clipped the streamer fly from the ten-pound test tippet. He scanned the open fly box and selected a big stonefly pattern, one to inch slowly across the bottom.

He worked the line out in a series of casts and let the fly settle to the bottom. Then he began a slow retrieve. Nothing. He kicked his flippers, working the tube slowly a few yards down the reservoir and tried again. As the stonefly settled, a nice rainbow struck and Wes set the hook. The fish raced across the lake stripping a bit of line, then jumped and tail-walked before driving deep again. He kept a taut line and slowly worked the fish into his net. He laid the trout on the mesh of the float tube and measured it. Eighteen inches. He slipped the barbless hook from its jaw and cradled the fish, gently rocking it back and forth in the water until it gave a twitch and slowly swam away.

"Well, that certainly makes this trip worthwhile."

He kicked the float tube a few more yards down the reservoir, enjoying the quiet and the morning sun. The fly lay quietly on the water at the end of a long cast. As he started a retrieve, he felt the solid resistance of a big fish and set the hook. Only there was no sudden rush.

"Dagnabit. I'm hung up." He worked the tube to where the line was snagged and tried to pop the hook loose. No luck. He tried a steady pull.

"It's probably a waterlogged limb," he mumbled. "But it sure is heavy."

He kept the pressure just short of the tensile strength of his tippet, and slowly, ever so slowly, it rose to the surface.

***

When he answered the phone, Bud recognized the voice of Jack Henderson, a 911 dispatcher. "Sheriff, we just received a call from a guy at Ana Reservoir. He said he was fishing and snagged a body. Said it scared the devil out of him. Apparently he tried to pull it in, but his leader broke and the body sank back in the lake. He did have the presence of mind to mark the location."

"Okay."

"He identified himself as Wes Wellington. And he was calling on a cell phone. I have the number."

"Okay, Jack, give it to me, and have Control get Roger moving in that direction. I'll call Mr. Wellington."

When Jack rang off, Bud keyed his lapel mike. "County Two, this is County One."

"County Two. Go ahead."

"Sonny, I just got a report of a body in Ana Reservoir. Roger is en route from Paisley. We'll need the sled. I'm heading that way. Do you want Michelle as well?"

"Boss, she's out at Five Corners with an SCF case worker.

"Roger that. She'll have to cover the home front. County One out."

Bud dialed Wellington's cell number. "Mr. Wellington? This is Sheriff Blair. How you doing?"

"I was having a really great day 'til this guy came floating to the surface. I've never been so startled in my life."

"Can you describe the body?"

"Well, ah…it looked like he was wearing a flannel shirt, red-checked pattern. Uh…dark hair. Definitely a man. And, Sheriff, he was puffy and…"

"Decomposing?"

"Yeah."

"Okay. I would like you to stay put. I have Deputy Hildebrand en route. It might take him the better part of thirty minutes to get there, so have patience. Where are you right now?"

"I'm at the boat ramp. I drive a green Subaru Forester."

"And you marked the body?"

"Yeah. I used a small lead ball and some light nylon rope. I tied my life vest to the line."

"Good thinking, Mr. Wellington. That's terrific. Are there any cars parked at the lake? Any sign of a boat or someone fishing?"

"No, no cars, no boats, nothing." He gave a short tight laugh. "I skipped class so I could have the lake to myself."

"Understood. Now I'm going to give you my cell number in case you need to call me. It will take me about an hour to get up there, so please stay put. And if you can't reach me on my cell phone, don't hesitate to call 911. They can always raise me on my radio. So stay put."

"I will. I might run over to the store for something to drink, but I'll be at the boat launch when your deputy gets here."

"Thanks. You ready for my cell number?"

When he hung up, Bud looked at Molly. "Well, old gal, we have to head north." The little black Lab got up off her pillow in the corner of the office and padded to the door, tail wagging. The phone rang. "Blair."

Doc Loeffler, a retired M.D. who moonlighted as the county's coroner and medical examiner, said, "Bud? Do you have something for me?"

"Hi, Doc. We have a report of a body in Ana Reservoir. Why don't you wait for me at the Summer Lake State Park and then follow me on over to the boat ramp? I should be there in about an hour."

"I'm on the way."

Bud grimaced as he thought about the phone call. *An hour. Damn big county to cover with four people. No, five.*

Lake County *was* big, about 8,000 square miles. The latest census figures ran about 7,000 people in the county, a population "density" of almost one person per square mile. As Bud put it, Lake County ran long on cattle, timber, and high lonesome.

He spoke out loud. "Molly, Nancy wants to meet us at the cabin tonight. That's the good part. But I have bad feelings about this. She keeps putting me off about a wedding date, and I don't know why. Hell, dog, I'd head for Reno in heartbeat if she would agree."

He smiled as he pictured Nancy, the competent manager of the Lake Country Emergency Services Center, a beautiful Yakima woman with startling green eyes, faint hints of auburn in her hair. The woman he loved. But he didn't understand his growing uneasiness, only that something wasn't right between them.

Bud's white Dodge 4x4 pickup eased in behind Doc Loeffler's maroon Suburban parked in the small, tree shaded state park across the highway from the Summer Lake store.

After a fifty-minute ride, Bud slid from behind the wheel and almost ran to the restrooms, hollering at Doc, "I'll be right with you." Molly jumped out the open door and started a tail-wagging hunt along the park fence sniffing for interesting odors.

Sonny in his white Dodge 4x4 extended-cab diesel pickup with a boat in tow pulled in and parked on the edge of the highway next to the entrance of the little park.

Doc waved and walked over to inspect the brown twenty-foot sled, complete with center console, light rack, and "Lake County Sheriff" in bright yellow decals along each side. He eyed the big Honda 150 jet pump thoughtfully.

Doc pointed at the boat and said, "I didn't know the county owned any boats."

"Well," Sonny said as he walked up to Doc, "we don't use it much, but once in a while we need one. Mainly for drownings. This old boat has been around for about thirty years, but it can still get up and move if we need it to."

"I hear rumors you are engaged, Mr. Sixkiller."

"Just rumors, Doc." Sonny said ruefully. "I think the girl of my dreams is more interested in running the newspaper than in marriage."

"Oh."

Bud whistled Molly up. She jumped into the cab and sat up on the passenger seat, unwilling to miss any of the excitement.

***

When the caravan reached the boat ramp, a collection of cars, pickups and gawkers were already gathering, small knots of people along the bank talking or just staring out across the reservoir.

Wide-bodied Deputy Roger Hildebrand and a slim, brown-haired young man wearing blue jeans and a green sweatshirt with a yellow O were standing on the floating dock. Roger was in a wetsuit. Flippers, tank, mask, and a steel mesh rescue stretcher were laid out the dock.

When the boat was snubbed to the dock, Bud looked at the scuba gear and back at Roger, who only shrugged. "A little something from my military days. I figured we might have a better looking corpse if I dove for it."

"Did you swim to Kuwait?"

"Something like that."

Bud eyeballed Roger thoughtfully and Sonny just grinned. Bud held out his hand. "You must be Mr. Wellington."

"Yes, sir, I am."

"This has been quite a fishing trip for you."

"Oh, man! You can say that again. But I'm glad in a way. You might never have found this guy otherwise."

"Well, if you've given Deputy Hildebrand a statement, you don't have to stay."

"I'd sort of like to. That's my life vest out there, so I'd like to have it back. And I'm interested."

Sonny walked across the gravel parking area to a small group of people gathered near the restrooms, a strategic spot with a good view of the life vest out in the lake. "Hi," Sonny said. "I'm Deputy Sixkiller. I'd like to ask you a few questions."

Bud waved Doc into the boat, handed him a lifejacket, and then helped Roger load the scuba gear and the rescue stretcher.

Bud slipped on a lifejacket, hit the starter, cranked the engine for a few seconds and then heard the healthy cough of the engine as it caught and then smoothed out in an idle. He grinned at Roger and Doc. "There's nothing like a four-cycle outboard for reliability."

He eased the boat back away from the dock, spun the wheel and headed for Wellington's anchored life vest about a half mile up the lake.

"Wes told me this guy looked rubbery," Roger said over the noise of the engine. "So I'm thinking we can bring him up in the basket without tearing the body up too much. I don't normally dive alone, but this is clear, fairly shallow water, so I don't see much risk. And I'll have a line if there is trouble."

"Well," Doc said in his dry tone, "it would be nice to have an intact corpse."

Bud pulled back on the throttle and shifted the boat into neutral as they neared the marker. When the boat had lost headway Roger flipped over backwards off the rail into the water, turned and swam down the slim nylon cord to Wesley Wellington's cannon ball.

Thirty minutes later the remains of one "John Doe" zipped into a black body bag, was resting in the back of Doc's station wagon. The small crowd of people was drifting away, and Wes, his life vest once again his own, waved and drove away.

Sonny backed the trailer down the boat ramp while Roger peeled out of his wet suit, and Bud eased the sled onto the trailer. When the boat was tied down and the gear stowed, Bud let Molly out of the pickup for a run. Tail wagging and nose to the ground. she started hunting the sagebrush along the bank of the reservoir. A Chinese pheasant cackled and took to the air, and Molly looked back at Bud as if to say, "See? I told you so."

They congregated by Doc's vehicle. Bud passed out paper cups and from a thermos, poured coffee for each of them.

"This is when I used to have a cigarette," Bud growled.

Roger nodded. "I could use a chaw and a drink right now."

Sonny was quiet, just staring across the lake at the high cliffs of Winter Rim.

"Well, Doc?" Bud asked.

"Guessing...the bailer twine on the left leg suggests he was weighted and dumped in the lake. I have no idea how long ago. His clothes are about the only thing holding him together. I'm not sure I've ever seen anything that gruesome.

"We'll need an autopsy. And we might not know how long ago he died even then. I know a pathologist over on the coast who has a reputation as an expert on drowning. He claims you can make a pretty good estimate of how long someone has been in the water by the extent of decomposition and water temperature."

"Fifty-one degrees. That's how cold it is on the bottom." Roger volunteered. "My temp gauge read fifty-one."

Doc nodded. "That might be very helpful. Well, if there's nothing more, I'll get our friend to town and put him on ice."

"Thanks, Doc," Bud said.

They watched Doc's vehicle pull away.

Sonny broke the silence. "I worked the crowd. They said high school kids sometimes come down to the landing to have parties, so nighttime activities are not all that unusual. And none of them know of anyone who is missing.".

"Except my snitch," Roger offered gloomily.

"Snitch?" Sonny queried. "The one who called about a meth operation?"

"Yeah. It's been almost a month. He said he would call back, but...he seems to have gone missing."

"So, this could be your guy?" Sonny asked?

"Maybe," Roger said, "but we don't have a report of anyone missing from Christmas Valley. So...what do we have here?"

"Suicide," Bud suggested. "He just walked here, tied a weight to his leg, swam to the middle of the lake, and drowned."

Sonny arched an eyebrow and grimaced. "You sound cynical, Bud."

Bud whistled up Molly and opened the passenger door for her. He turned back to his crew. "Good job. We'll know more, I hope, when we have the autopsy report. I have to get back to town."

"Date night?" Roger asked.

"Well, I'll be at the cabin this evening, but thanks to the phone company my peace and tranquility can be disturbed. I'll have my cell phone on."

The tension broke and Roger and Sonny smiled for the first time a couple of hours.

"Oh, we'll find you if we need you, Mr. Sheriff," Sonny said.

Bud frowned, but didn't say anything. He whistled Molly up and opened the passenger door for her.

"Oops!" Roger said as Bud drove away. He darted a glance at Sonny. "Is there trouble in paradise?"

Sonny looked out over the lake. Finally he said, "What goes on between my sister and Bud is their business."

"So it is, Sonny. So it is."

Sonny nodded, then added, "No way to know. Bud doesn't talk about it much and Nancy hasn't said a word to me. My last information was Bud proposed and she said yes."

"Sorry," Roger said. "Just teasing. Didn't mean to pry."

Chapter 8

Bud grumbled at himself for being short-tempered. The drive to Lakeview seemed interminable. Nothing in the landscape interested him. On a "normal" day he and Molly would drive into the wildlife refuge at Summer Lake and try for some good waterfowl pictures, but that had no lure for him today. A rancher standing in front of the Summer Lake Café waved as Bud sped by.

He accelerated to eighty on the straight stretch beyond the Narrows and passed Doc's vehicle, telling himself that he was the sheriff and he had important business to attend. Besides, the only one who would dare write him up for speeding was Charlie Prince. Everyone else would just figure he was on a call.

He slowed to a reasonable sixty when he popped over the rise out of Crooked Creek Canyon. He listened to Control talking to someone he couldn't pick up on his radio about an injury accident somewhere in the Silver Lake country. He scowled, but keyed his mike. "Control, this is County One."

Nancy's voice answered through the speakers. "County One, Control. Go ahead."

"I can't read the last caller. What can you tell me about an injury accident?"

"County One, we have a report of a shooting. We have an ambulance en route from the Silver Lake fire station."

Sonny's voice broke in. "We're on it, boss."

"Control, County One. Did you copy?"

"I copy that."

Bud listened while Nancy Sixkiller, the love of his life, gave clear, precise directions to the scene of the shooting. He marveled. She never made mistakes, she never got rattled, and she never overlooked a single detail. The only mistake anyone could point to was her prior marriage to "old what's his name" as she referred to her ex-husband.

From what he could hear over the radio, the shooter was a fifteen-year-old boy who was being held by his father until the police arrived. The victim, a middle-aged woman, had a .22 caliber slug in her leg, but wasn't in crisis.

Bud pulled into his reserved parking spot behind the courthouse and keyed the mike. "Control, County One."

"Control, go ahead."

"County One out of service in Lakeview."

"Copy that."

"County One, clear."

"Well, Molly, let's go see what alligators are lurking in the swamp."

***

Karen Highsmith, only the top of her curly light brown hair visible behind the booking counter, looked up. Bud had to move up to the counter to actually see her face.

"Afternoon, Bud. It's been quite a day, hasn't it?"

"Tell me there isn't more," he pleaded.

"Can't do that, I'm afraid."

"Will it keep?"

"Nope."

He ignored the expectant look. "What are you working on?"

"Sergeant Trivoli arrested..." she glanced at the report on her desk "...a Mr. Harlon James Scott for child molestation and child abuse, and a Ms. Loretta McBride, Mr. Scott's girlfriend, for child abuse and child neglect. I have them in two of our guest rooms. And Michelle is talking to our esteemed D.A. right now. She wants you to join them as soon as you can."

"I'd better head for Howard's office."

"Aren't you going to call Nancy back?"

"Okay, let's have it. What's going on?"

"Nancy wants you to call."

"That's it? Just call? That's the whole message?"

Karen just nodded and went back to pounding out her booking report. She heard him whisper a soft "shit" just before he slammed the door to his office.

He hit the speed dial, listened, and then heard Nancy's sweet voice. "Is that you, Bud?"

"It is indeed. The summoned. So what's up?"

"A Miss Linda Blair is in town and is trying to find you. She is currently having coffee at the Indian Village and would like to see you."

"Well, I'm sort of busy right now."

"May I tell her that?"

"Be my guest."

"You were once married to her, I'm told."

"Yes, but now I'm going to marry *you*. So tell me, what is this ominous 'we need to talk' business?"

"I'll see you at the cabin about seven tonight. We can discuss it then." She paused and then in a quiet voice added, "I love you, Bud."

She hung up before he could tell her that he loved her, too.

Chapter 9

HOWARD FINCH, CHIEF Hildebrand, Deputy Trivoli, and a young, attractive SCF caseworker were crowded around Howard's small conference table when Bud knocked.

The young caseworker opened the door and said, "Yes?"

"Sheriff Blair to join you."

"Oh." She opened the door and waved him in. "We haven't met. I'm Deanna Baker. I'm with SCF." She held out her hand.

"Welcome to the outback," Bud replied.

She pushed another chair into an already tight circle, sat down across from Bud in the only other empty chair and picked up her pen, poised to continue taking notes on a yellow legal pad.

Bud ran a quick profile on the on the young caseworker. *Tall—five-six or -seven. Maybe twenty-four or five. Dark hair. From a bottle? Blue eyes. Not bad looking. A bit on the thin side. Nervous tic. New to the job.*

Bud shook hands with Gus, and mumbled "howdy" in spite of himself. There was something in Gus's laid-back style that brought out the "country" in Bud.

Howard leaned forward and tapped the table with his right index finger. "Thanks to Ms. Baker and to Sergeant Trivoli, we have in your jail two of the most miserable, abject, evil human beings I have ever had the joy of prosecuting." And then he proceeded to describe in graphic detail the beating of a four-year old boy.

Bud felt his stomach contract and a hard knot of anger in his throat, and glancing at Chief Hildebrand and Michelle, he knew they were feeling the same. "Are those two in my jail married?"

"No," Michelle said. "He's her live-in boyfriend."

"Damn!" was all Bud could say. "Where's the boy?"

Chief Hildebrand said, "He's at the hospital getting a cast on a broken arm and his other injuries looked at."

Bud looked first at Michelle and then at Howard. "Witnesses?"

Michelle flipped open her notebook. "A neighbor, Candice Brown, called in the incident. She saw the boyfriend out in the backyard beating on the little boy."

There was strained silence. Finally Howard muttered, "Vengeance is mine, saith the Lord."

"The Lord works in mysterious ways, his wonders to perform," Gus added.

Gus rose, put his black Stetson on his graying hair, pulled in a gut that was beyond paunchy, and said, "Sergeant Trivoli, you mind if my department trails along behind on this one? Your gal has a mother and a sister livin' here in town. I'll have to check, but I think they're takin' care of a little girl that belongs to Loretta McBride."

Michelle had known Augustus Hildebrand for over a year, but he was still something of a mystery to her with his "countrified-good-old-boy" demeanor. Still, the town was well served by the small, city police department. "I'd appreciate that, Chief. Should I coordinate with you?"

Gus nodded, a grim look on his face. "Yep."

Deanna nodded. "Good. I didn't get that kind of help in my last job. I haven't had time to check, but I'll pull the files on McBride and see what we can find."

Howard launched his five-foot-six-inch frame from his chair. "Thank you all for coming." He held out his hand to Deanna. "It's nice meeting you, Deanna. Welcome to Lakeview."

Bud waited until the room cleared and closed the door. "Howard, I wanted you to see this and let you know what we have planned." He slid a copy of the Homeland Security bulletin across the desk.

***

Back in his office, Bud turned his computer on and got down to the business of writing his "John Doe" incident report.

Karen knocked and brought him a cup of coffee. "It's fresh and there's a leftover donut if you want it."

He murmured thanks without looking up and continued banging away on his keyboard.

Chapter 10

LARAE'S SECOND SATURDAY as bartender at the Christmas Valley Lodge was a repeat of her first, complete with drunk cowboys singing off-key with Willie Nelson, and optimistic gamblers pumping money into the video poker machines. She kept half an eye on the gamblers trying to decide who was addicted and who was just having some fun.

Cowboy sounded the only discordant note with his crude pick-up lines. When she politely but firmly rejected his offer, Cowboy tried to pinch her butt. What he got for his troubles was a quick thumb-lock that had him wincing in pain. "Don't ever touch me again, Cowboy," she whispered in his ear.

"Or what?" he bluffed.

"Or I'll break more than your thumb. Now you be a good boy, and we'll forget this ever happened. Got it?" She increased the pressure until he finally nodded.

It had happened so quietly that the only people who noticed were Wally and the bottles-and-cans man. What Wally didn't see was the quiet man at the back table start to rise from his chair and then settle back down as Larae handled Cowboy. The watcher eyed Larae speculatively as she walked behind the bar to fill another pitcher for a table of thirsty young men.

"Nicely done, Ms. Holcomb," he said quietly to himself.

Wally just stared. Larae tried to appear innocent, but a small grin twitched the corners of her mouth.

Cowboy left her alone the rest of the evening, except for muttering "bitch" under his breath. He sulked for an hour and then left without paying his tab.

The bottles-and-cans man dressed in his black sweatshirt and blue jeans, sat in the rear of the room nursing a beer. Wally tried to squeeze in some conversation with Larae and Billie while they mixed drinks and drew mugs and pitchers of beer for a thirsty crowd.

It was past midnight when Billie announced last call and the crowd of cowboys, local retirees, and tourists drawn to the noise of a good time began drifting out the door with a chorus of "good-night" and "drive carefully" trailing into silence. The last to leave was the bottles-and-cans man.

Billie locked the door, turned out the porch lights and began counting the till. Wally sighed and rolled the mop bucket into the short hallway, muttering "latrine duty again," and Larae began cleaning mugs, bottles and ashtrays off the tables. She fished a plastic baggie from the pocket of her black slacks, looked to see if Wally or Billie noticed what she was doing, and, using a pencil, she dropped a beer bottle from the back table into the baggie.

"I'll be right back." She hurried down the inner hallway to her room and hid the bottle in a dresser drawer, and then hurried back to the bar.

"Billie, Larae asked, "where does he live?"

"Who?"

"The bottles-and-cans guy."

"You still interested in him?"

"I can't peg him is all."

Billie said, "I think he lives in a little trailer on the Horse Ranch, that RV park out on the main highway."

"And he peddles here? That's a long way."

"About thirty miles. But he drives an old pickup on Saturday nights."

"Hmm," Larae mused. "There can't be that many bottles and cans along that stretch."

"Well, it takes all kinds I guess."

Larae smiled at that and then asked, "How long has he been here?"

"Oh, I don't know. Four or five weeks, I guess."

Chapter II

BUD PARKED IN the gravel driveway of his small tree shaded house in a quiet neighborhood just north of town and let Molly roam the cedar fenced backyard while he changed into blue jeans, short sleeved denim shirt and Wellington boots. He switched on the CD player and listened to the Eagles while he prowled the kitchen, trying to decide what he needed in the way of food at the cabin. When the Eagles started in on "Get Over It," he just stared into the refrigerator, and the old tape ran again… the one of Linda, his ex-wife, telling him she was leaving him that night…their jobs seemed to have become more important than their marriage…her packed bags at the front door and he'd never even noticed…his panic and fear…and how quickly their marriage was just…over.

Bud shook his head and growled. "Enough of that." He closed the refrigerator door, shut off the CD player, grabbed a paint-spattered green UO cap from an overloaded coat rack on the back porch, and called Molly. "Molly, let's go buy some steak and make a nice evening out of this."

Twenty minutes later two T-bones, the veggies for a tossed salad, a bottle of merlot, and big bouquet of pink carnations rode securely in the space behind the seat of his pickup.

The twenty-five mile drive to his A-frame cabin on Dog Lake always worked its magic for Bud. And when a big mule deer doe and her fawn hurried to cross the road near Drews Reservoir, some of his normal enthusiasm returned. "You know Molly, I think I sometimes worry too much. Nancy says she loves me, so I'll just hang on to that. I think the divorce from Linda might have made me a bit pessimistic about women. What do you think?"

The little black Lab pulled her head back out of the window, looked at him and then stuck her head back out the open window, ears floating like floppy wings, nose twitching to catch any interesting odors on the juniper and pine-scented breeze.

His cabin sat with its back to the road on the north end of Dog Lake. Bud wasn't sure how the lake got its name. Maybe because it was roughly shaped like a dog's hind leg…sort of…if you had that kind of imagination. Bud's cabin was set on the end of those two miles of the dog's leg, the skinny end that sometimes—depending on water levels in the wet months—fed a small stream that always dried up in the summer.

Finding the property in his first year in Lake County was a blessing, a gift, sold to him on the cheap by the elderly owner who said he simply didn't want the bother of rebuilding the ramshackle vintage cabin that occupied the site before it burned down.

Though Bud felt a degree of antipathy toward organized religion, he thought there must have been some divine guidance at work. After a drinking binge that lasted almost a year, and after a fistfight with his old partner BB, the grace of his old captain eased him out of his job as a homicide detective in Portland, and landed him a job as undersheriff of Lake County along with a strong admonishment to "stop drinking or get out of law enforcement."

The year of weekends and evenings spent building the cabin had been absorbing and distracting. He took his lessons to heart and stopped boozing. And somewhere along the way the guilt and remorse had subsided. He stopped living the past and started looking to the future.

He parked next to the old one-car garage that served as boathouse, woodshed and general storage. The only changes made to the shingle- sided garage—the lone survivor from the fire—were a new sage green paint job and a new metal roof to match the cabin.

Molly loped down to the little floating dock to bark at the mud hens, the little black ducks that spent their summers on the lake.

He opened the windows downstairs to air the place out, and started a pot of coffee.

The vibration of the cell phone in his shirt pocket claimed his attention. He flipped it open. "Hello?"

"Bud, I'm running a bit behind, but I'll be out there in about an hour. Is there anything to eat at the cabin?"

"Ah…well, I brought out some frozen dinners."

"Shame on you, Bud. Why don't I bring out a couple of T-bones and we'll barbeque. Okay?"

He laughed. "Just kidding. I picked up some steaks in town. I'll start the barbeque in about thirty minutes."

"Love you, Bud."

"I know! I've got an idea. Let's get married."

"Okay, but only to each other."

"Deal!" He felt suddenly better than he had in days.

***

An hour later, Nancy turned off the main road into Bud's driveway. She just sat and watched for a few seconds, watching and marveling at the look of him. A compact five-eleven, weighing maybe one-ninety, square shouldered, with just a hint of a tummy bulge. He wasn't handsome in the Hollywood pretty-boy style, but he had tanned, regular features spoiled only by a small scar over his left eyebrow, dark brown hair, and the kindest hazel eyes she had ever seen. Body and soul, he was simply was one of the most attractive men she had ever known…or loved.

Sitting at the picnic table, an open book and a cup of coffee keeping him company, he was nervously aware of how long she sat there watching him. Her serious look when she finally got out of her pickup turned his stomach to ice. *This can't be good.*

"Hey, good lookin'" she called, walking up the drive.

"Hey, yourself."

"Steaks on?"

He looked at the lid and the steak fork next to the barbeque. "Not yet."

"Good. I want to cook for my man." She stepped close to him and then stopped when she noticed his confused look. "Bud, what's wrong?"

"Nancy, I don't understand what's going on. This 'we have to talk' business is killing me. I have never had a conversation start that way that turned out right. You're late getting out here. Your face is like stone. You sit and stare at me instead of getting out of the pickup. And now you want to 'cook for my man.' I simply don't know what to make of it."

She walked around the table, slid onto the bench beside him and put her sweet face against his shoulder. When he didn't put his arms around her, she said, "She really hurt you, didn't she? Well, know this, Bud Blair, I'll never do anything deliberately to hurt you, so put your arms around me and quit behaving like a little boy."

With a little show of reluctance he sighed, wrapped his arms around her, gave her a hug, and set his chin on top of her head. "Okay. But I need to know what's going on between us. You sat there and stared."

"Oh, Bud. I was simply liking the sight of you. As for what's going on, I'm just worried about my mother. I called Mama last night, and she started telling a story about her childhood, a really funny story, but ten minutes later she was telling the same story again. When I said she had just told me that story, she said she hadn't either. I didn't argue with her, but I'm worried that she's had a stroke or something. I called Verna, one of her friends, and asked her to check on Mama. Verna called back and said she thought Mama was all right, just tired and that she was on her way to bed. But I need to go see her for myself."

Bud squeezed her again. "I'm sorry about your mom. And I feel damned foolish."

"Couldn't have had anything to do with Linda wanting to see you?"

"No! Well…maybe. I get to worrying some, and then I get to thinking that no woman in her right mind would marry me and that you'll come to your senses and run."

"Not a chance. You stuck, boy."

"Well, then." He hurried into the cabin and emerged with the bouquet of carnations. "Here."

She took the carnations, smelled the blossoms and smiled her thanks. "Thank you. We'll need something for a vase."

"How about a fruit jar?"

"Definitely *avant garde*." They both laughed.

Just as he reached to give her another hug, Bud's cell phone began vibrating in his shirt pocket. "Damn. My timing is off today." The screen showed a 503 prefix. "Hello. This is Bud."

A familiar voice growled back, "That you, Honky?"

"BB, you old swindler! How the hell you doing?"

"Been suspended for thirty days, so thought I'd make the pilgrimage to Hicksville and maybe help you lasso a fish or catch a doggie or some such thing. That all right?"

"Damn right. I'd love to see you. But what did you do to get suspended?"

BB laughed. "Well I mighta gotten a little rough with this street bum cause he was sassin' me and callin' me names. Now I didn't mind being called a pig. You know I've gotten used to that, and there ain't that many old hippies left, but when he challenged my sexual orientation, I took offense. Next I know, there's an internal investigation going on, this guy's drivers license is laying in the middle of my garage floor to be found by some pasty-faced dude from Internal, and I'm on thirty days administrative leave. Turns out the guy I rousted was undercover. I deny taking his license, but his missing tooth and my scraped knuckles just wouldn't go away. Anyway, he set me up. He won this round, but don't bet on him a second time."

By the time BB had run the scenario, Bud was laughing. "Well, you're just like the habitual speeder who finally got caught, but it was for something he didn't do. Why don't you come on down. I can put you up. Might even put you to work."

"What you got that might interest a high-powered investigator like me? Bull doggin' or tail twistin'? Cow rustlin'?"

"Nope, just an ordinary everyday run-of-the-mill homicide."

"Murder…in the middle of the desert…in the middle of nowhere? Come on, Honky, don't crap on me like that."

"Serious, BB."

"Now you talkin'. Somethin' I know about. How 'bout I come down day after next Monday?"

"Good. My office is in the courthouse smack dab in the middle of town. Call me when you get in. And, BB…"

"Yes?"

"When you get down here, how about knocking off that inner city gutter talk. You talk that way down here, you just confirm what people believe—and you with a Masters in criminology."

"Yassuh, boss."

"Enough, already. I'm hanging up, and you call when you get in. I don't want you getting lost and wandering into one of our dangerous neighborhoods."

He heard BB laughing as he shut down the phone.

Nancy was putting the steaks on the grill when he hung up. "I heard half of that. What's this about 'dangerous' neighborhoods?"

"Oh, just an old, tired joke between the two of us. BB used to warn me about being a honky on Williams Avenue at midnight. He always made a joke of it, but I think he was embarrassed by it, by the fact that the gangs took the streets away from ordinary people after dark. And the gangs were almost always black."

"Was it really dangerous?"

"Sometimes." He shook off the memories. "Let's open that nice bottle of Columbia Valley merlot while the steaks cook."

Seated at the picnic table with small glasses of wine, she asked, "Do you think I'm being foolish about Mama?"

"Well, my dad says that if you want to talk to older people, do it in the morning when they're rested. He says they have more enthusiasm and their minds are clearer in the morning."

"Okay then, I'll call Mama in the morning. Maybe I can get a better read on how she's doing then. But I still want to go up to see her. Bud, would you mind going with me? I think it's time she met you, and I think you would like her. And Verna. Verna's a kick in the pants."

"Okay. I'll hire Bruno to fly us up in his plane. He just bought a new twin-engine Apache that will have us up there in a couple of hours."

"This Saturday?"

"If he doesn't have any other charter work, I'll arrange it. Have you told Sonny?"

"No. I don't want him to worry until there is something to worry about."

***

Later that evening, Bud watched Nancy's tail lights until they disappeared behind the screen of trees beyond the lake. He called Molly, let her in to sleep on her cedar chips mattress by the woodstove, and called it a day. Tomorrow was going to be a busy one, but for now it was enough to know that all was right between himself and Nancy.

Chapter 12

TWO DAYS AFTER the discovery of the "John Doe" in Ana Reservoir, Doc Loeffler walked into the sheriff's office with a thin file under his arm. He was wearing his standard white shirt, red tie, dark blue blazer with dark trousers and shiny black oxfords. Even in his retirement, he never left the house without proper attire, yet somehow he managed to avoid looking stuffy in a town where most of the people favored blue jeans, cowboy boots, and pickup trucks.

Karen's brown hair was barely visible behind the high booking counter. She looked up and smiles. "Good morning, Doc."

"Good morning, Karen. How's Jenny doing?"

With a big grin, Karen said, "The baby is due in the next few days."

"Are you looking forward to being a grandmother?"

"You bet. I'm taking a few days off so I can be there when the baby comes."

"You tell her hello for me," he said with a smile.

"Thanks, Doc. She always loved you."

"She should. I delivered her."

He put the file marked Autopsy Report on the counter. "There's a copy for the D.A.'s office, and one for Bud."

"Thank you. He's in, but he's meeting with Sonny and Howard right now. He should be back in about an hour. Can he call you?"

"I'll be home most of the day."

***

Sonny, Bud, Judge Lynch, and Candice Miller, a large, overweight young woman who worked for Juvenile, were seated at Howard's small conference table. Sunlight filtered through yellowed Venetian blinds as Sonny briefed them on the Silver Lake shooting.

"Apparently Mr. Alva Pope and Mrs. Nadine Pope were having a picnic lunch at a little hot springs up behind their ranch house when Billy Simpson, son of a neighboring rancher spotted them. He shot at them from a distance of perhaps eight hundred yards with a .22 caliber rifle. The slug struck Mrs. Pope on the outside of the left upper thigh. At that distance the bullet didn't have a lot of oomph left, so it only penetrated about half an inch. Mr. Pope called 911 and Deputy Hildebrand and I responded. The Silver Lake ambulance was at the scene when we arrived approximately fifteen minutes after being dispatched. Mrs. Pope refused to be transported by ambulance, so Mr. Pope took her to the Silver Lake Clinic, a once-a-week operation run through our county health department. An RN licensed as a physician's assistant removed the bullet and bandaged the wound. We have that bullet and what we believe to be the shell casing. Mr. and Mrs. Pope did not want to press charges. I urged them to do so, but they kept refusing.

"Deputy Hildebrand and I then drove to the Simpson ranch. Mr. Donald Simpson had his son locked in a small feed shed. There was a single shot .22 leaning against the wall of the shed. Mr. Simpson told us he had taken a belt to the boy, but the shooting was really his own fault.

"He explained that the Simpsons and the Popes have been feuding for several generations over a grazing allotment. The feud went back to the original assignment of grazing rights by the Forest Service in about 1915 or so. The Simpsons thought the Popes had been unfairly given 'their' grazing allotment. Simpson said that some Pope cattle had recently broken through his pasture fence. He said in a moment of anger that the best thing they could do was 'shoot those sons-a-bitches.' The idiot son took him seriously. Hence, the shooting."

"A Hatfields and McCoys type of thing," Howard speculated.

"Exactly," Sonny answered.

"Well, Howard," Judge Lynch interjected, "what do you want to do? We can't let this go. That boy needs some serious correction."

Howard nodded and looked at Candice. "Agreed, but what I'm thinking is that Juvenile should handle it. If Mrs. Pope doesn't want to press charges, then I'm not inclined to prosecute. But Juvenile can get in the mix and see that he gets probation and some counseling."

Candice nodded, her lips pursed and her blue eyes glinting with anger at the decision.

Bud stated, "I had no idea there was a feud going on, but it's got to stop. How about a meeting between the parties, here, in my office, a sort of come-to-Jesus meeting?"

"Might work," Sonny said, "but it might not be necessary. Donald ordered us to arrest his son, which we did. Roger took the son to the Juvenile Detention Center in Bend. And when we left the Simpsons, Donald said he was on his way to the Pope's to see how Nadine was doing. He also said it was time to smoke the peace pipe."

Judge Lynch rose, slapped a palm on the table and said directly to Candice, who was known to have a curious blend of ambition and sloth, "I want him back down here for a hearing. And I want a clear case report to review, and I want your recommendations to help me decide what to do with this boy."

Candice flushed, looked at the silver-haired rancher-turned-judge, and said, "Yes, sir. I'll have a case report to you by tomorrow afternoon." She closed her notebook. Judge Lynch held the door open for her and closed it behind him as they left.

Howard grinned and said to Sonny and Bud, "I think the Judge is getting tired of her letting business slide and then blaming other people when things go to pot. Sonny, that was a good report. Thanks."

As they walked the inner hallway that led to the locked interior door to the Sheriff's office, Bud said, "Have Roger keep in touch with those families. If they make peace, good. If not then we *will* have a come-to-Jesus meeting. Damn! I hate these distractions, Sonny. I've got a homicide to solve."

Sonny nodded. "Understood. I sure wish I didn't have to take on this arson assignment right now."

Bud looked sharply at Sonny, and Sonny threw up his hands. "I know, I know. I'm going, boss."

***

Bud was deep in thought when he entered his office. Karen smiled, but he didn't notice, just walked into his office and shut the door. She sighed, rose and carried the autopsy file to the door. She knocked and Bud said, "Enter."

She handed Bud the file. "I have Doc's autopsy report."

Bud looked up at her. "Did you read it?"

She flushed and stammered, "Well I might have glanced it over."

"Don't get flustered. I'm hoping you can save me some time. What struck you as important?"

"Well…he'd been castrated."

"What?"

"Somebody cut off his dingus."

"You mean his penis? If you are going to brief me on these report, you are going to have to be more accurate. Words like 'dingus' won't do. What else?"

"His neck was broken. The report lists that as the probable cause of death."

"And did Doc hazard a guess as to how long John Doe has been dead?"

"Based on a formula he got from an expert on drowning and body decomposition, the estimated time of death was between four and five weeks ago."

"Any identification? Any distinguishing marks?"

"There was a chain-and-anchor tattoo on the deceased's left forearm."

"And deceased's size, race, age, weight, eye color, hair color?"

She picked up the report and read: "Caucasian male, light brown hair, twenty to twenty-five years old, about five-ten, not much fatty tissue in the body, so estimated weight at time of death was one-fifty-five, one-sixty." She put the report down and continued, "And no way to determine eye color."

Bud stared hard at her for a minute, and then his features loosened and he smiled.

"Well, Officer Highsmith, since you've decided to help me with my detective work, why don't you get on your computer and start looking for two things: One, which military service prefers a chain and anchor tattoo—think Navy; and two, a list of all military personnel who have been AWOL for thirty days or more."

"AWOL?"

"Absent Without Leave, Deputy Highsmith."

"Yes, I know. But *all* military personnel, sir?"

"All. But I'm especially interested in those west of the Mississippi. You run a good jail, Highsmith, but maybe you'd like a new challenge."

"I would, Sheriff, I would." And then she smirked. "Besides, I also know you don't like the computer much."

He grumped and reached for the phone. "And shut the door."

***

Chief Hildebrand had stopped by and both of the city cops—Ken Worth and Donnie Smith—each made a "patrol" to sample the barbeque, look longingly at the cooler of beer and the bottles of wine, only to settle for cans of diet Pepsi. Each toasted the new sergeant and congratulated Michelle.

Lonnie Beltram—dressed to the nines in new jeans, polished boots, a white Stetson and sunray dark glasses, his mustache neatly trimmed—put in an appearance, and after five beers made a half-hearted pass at Michelle, and embarrassed himself by apologizing.

She compounded his embarrassment by slurring, "For what?"

Nancy and Sonny had a chance to talk privately about their mother, and about Nancy and Bud's plans to visit her the coming week-end.

The reserve officers, all four of them—ages twenty to twenty-five, good, clean-cut citizens, and each sporting a moustache they thought of as the "flag"—ate platters of ribs, potato salad, and baked beans. They kept pretty much to themselves and drank sparingly, wanting to give the "regulars" the impression they were straight shooters, an impression that went unnoticed.

Old, polished stories were retold, the topper being Roger's account of Georgia Blackmon running around with a local cowboy and then knocking down her husband Wes down in the Paisley Bar because she didn't want Wes following her around.

All in all, Bud and Nancy judged it to be a successful celebration even if they had to call the Lakeview Taxi to take Karen Highsmith home. Conspicuously absent was Trooper Prince.

The only sour note was Bud's admission to Nancy that Bruno's plane was not available until the weekend after next. Their trip to Yakima would have to wait or they would have to drive.

Late in the evening Sonny and Carol Connor gave Officer Trivoli a ride home, stopping only once to let her be sick in the Forest Service parking lot.

***

At eight the next morning, Deputy Highsmith, nursing a near-hangover, set the coffee pot back on the warmer and hurried to her desk. She picked up the phone on the second ring and said, "Lake County Sheriff's Office. This is Deputy Highsmith."

No one answered back.

"Hello? Are you wanting the Sheriff's Department?"

A man speaking in a forced baritone said, "I understand you found a body in Ana Reservoir."

"Who is this, please?"

"It's been in the paper, and you can't identify the body. Check with the Navy in Bremerton. They can describe three people who have gone AWOL. One of them might just be your guy."

She started to say, "How can I contact…" And then all she could hear was a dial tone.

"Well, crap. I think I just talked to a killer. Or maybe not." At any rate it was a tip. Her inquiries to the military had met with more questions than answers. Why did she want to know?

How could they authenticate her identity? Did she have any information? The FBI was more polite, but not much more helpful.

She hung up the phone and sat thinking about the phone call. Her first inclination was to call Bud. She shook her head, her short brown curls bouncing. "No. He expects me to dig out the info on the identify of our John Doe," she said quietly to herself.

"Well, if the military and the FBI can't help, maybe we'll get lucky within the law enforcement community." She turned to her computer and began typing a bulletin to northwest law enforcement agencies describing her John Doe, where the body had been found, a description of the tattoo, estimated date of death, and the extent and type of injuries, and remembering to use the word penis. She read the bulletin, proofed it, then added "Sheriff Henry Blair, Lake County," and hit Send.

Chapter 13

CHUNKY WINONA PEEL, fifty-five-year-old wife of the town's only mortician, worked the night shift Saturdays and Sundays at the jail. She joked about the job being her "pin money." But the "Ol' Girl" network said it was because her tightwad husband was too cheap to give her an allowance. And he was rumored to be rich.

Winona, sitting at her desk reading *People* magazine, looked up at the clock as Karen, dressed in a tight-fitting khaki uniform, unlocked the front door and came bustling in, a cup of latte in one hand and a white bag that smelled suspiciously like a cinnamon roll in the other.

"Well, aren't you the early bird. Something up?"

"No. I just thought I'd see if I got any hits from my John Doe bulletin. Here, I brought you a cinnamon roll."

"I don't need that. I'm trying to lose some weight."

"Well, okay. I'll save it for later."

Grinning, Winona reached for the bag. "I don't suppose one will hurt. I don't want to be a bad cop." She had a bumper sticker pinned to a cluttered bulletin board that said, "Bad Cop, No Donut."

***

Karen munched on a cinnamon roll as the screen brightened. One-handed, she typed in her password and clicked on "e-mail."

Top of the list was a message from a Detective Maretti of the Bremerton City Police Department. *Re: inquiry. Phone number.*

She typed in *What phone number?*

The answer was almost instantaneous. *Yours. I want to talk re bulletin two days ago.*

She typed in the office number and hit Send.

Within thirty seconds her phone rang. She picked up and said, "Lake County Sheriff's Office, Deputy Highsmith."

"Hey, great! I hear you got a body on ice down there...out there...wherever in the hell you are."

"You don't have a map? Who is this?"

"Detective Maretti. I wanna talk to your sheriff."

"He's not in yet. You'll have to talk to me."

"Why should I do that? I don't wanna talk to you. I wanna talk to the sheriff."

"About what? I sent out the bulletin, so why not talk to me?"

"What's your job, lady?"

"It's Deputy Highsmith, and I'm a technical deputy in charge of the office and the jail. I'm also the sheriff's admin."

Winona put her half-eaten cinnamon roll down and swiveled her chair to look at Karen. Winona had never heard Karen use such a hard steely voice on anyone, not even her jailbirds.

Karen put one hand over the receiver. "Why don't you check on our guests."

Winona grinned and rose to exit via the locked steel door to the cellblock.

"Okay, this isn't getting us anyplace," Maretti said. "I want you to talk to my partner, Detective Grandfield."

Grandfield came on the phone. "Don't mind Gino, please. I read your bulletin this morning. We have a homicide case going here, two actually, that might be related to your John Doe. It's a stretch, but we are looking for three AWOL sailors in connection with this case. And the nature of your homicide matches one that took place up here. We're trying to track an AWOL sailor we suspect might have been involved in a rape-homicide."

Karen felt a tingle of excitement. It fit with the info from her tipster. What if she could give the sheriff the lead he needed? Wouldn't that be something.

"I had an anonymous phone call yesterday telling me to check with the Navy in Bremerton for three AWOL sailors. Said our John Doe might be one of them."

Grandfield asked, "Did you get a name?"

"No. He hung up." She paused and then asked, "So, how, ah, how long has your suspect been missing?"

"About six-weeks."

"Okay. Our guy was in the water for four to five weeks, so the timeframe is good. So, umm, uh, how do we check this out?"

"We have DNA samples we think belong to the guys we're looking for. Have you done any DNA tests?"

"No, not yet."

"Well, you get a DNA test and we compare. You got a lab there?"

"No. We use the state lab in Bend."

Maretti's voice came back on the line. "How long?"

Why you sneaky rat. You've been on the line the whole time.

"It takes us about ten days to get results back."

"Yeah, sure, why rush?" Maretti snarled.

"Listen, you jerk, I've about had enough of you. For your information the lab is a hundred and seventy miles away, and we courier samples to the lab, and we get in line for service just like everybody else."

She could hear Maretti chuckling, and then he said, "I deserved that." And Grandfield murmured, "not the first time," into the receiver.

Karen was beginning to smile and felt a giggle start to work its way to the surface. "Okay, okay. Let's get on the same side. You have a homicide. We have a John Doe homicide. Let's compare notes. I've had no cooperation from the Navy or from the FBI or anyone federal, so let's get our heads together and see what we can come up with."

When the conversation finished, Karen cradled the receiver and spun in her chair. Sheriff Bud Blair was standing a few feet behind her, a big grin on his face. Purse in hand, Winona gave a wave and left. They could hear her laughing as the door shut.

A blush colored Karen's face. "Uh, how much did you hear?"

"Well, now, I could only hear your half, so I had to make some guesses, but I did come in where you called Detective Maretti a jerk."

"Oh, I'm so sorry you heard that, but he was just being...a... an irritating...an..."

"Asshole," he finished for her.

"Yeah, he was."

"Okay, That's settled. What did you find out?"

When Karen finished going over her notes, Bud nodded. "Nice job, Karen. See Doc about getting some tissue samples up to the lab for DNA analysis. And when that comes in we'll call our Bremerton friends back. I just wish you had told me about your tipster sooner. Now we don't have any way to trace the call." He flipped open his notebook. "Okay, tell me what you can about our tipster. Young, old, accent, background noises, everything you can remember."

Chapter 14

LATE ON A Friday, Deputy Hildebrand moved to a motel room in Christmas Valley for a couple of nights while the owner repainted the interior of the small two-bedroom house he had rented just west of the lodge.

The owner was delighted to have an employed tenant, especially a cop. Now something would be done about the "hippie trash" that found Christmas Valley attractive. The owner let Roger park a utility trailer loaded with Roger's personal goods in the garage.

The Saturday morning air was cool when Roger slipped out of the motel as quietly as he could. Dressed in new jogging gear, he started a brisk walk down the dusty lane to a gravel street that led to the main highway. Larae, in a hooded sweatshirt, shorts, and wearing New Balance tennis shoes, was jogging a half-block ahead of him. He whistled and she turned, slowing down until he caught up with her.

"Morning, Ms. Holcomb. Mind if I walk with you?"

She grinned. "Nope, but I was thinking I would jog a little."

"So you think I might not keep up?"

She tilted her head back, looked down her nose at him. "You aren't exactly built like a runner."

He stuck his chin out at the challenge. "Any time you're ready."

She turned and began an easy, ground-eating lope, Roger right beside her. They turned left at the store and started east, down the straight two-lane highway, cutting through the rolling sage-covered hills. The first ten minutes were hard for Roger, who hadn't done any running for several months, but after the initial burn, he began to loosen up. "This ain't as bad I thought it was going to be," he puffed as they neared the half-mile point.

"Out of shape, are we Mr. Hildebrand?"

"Fat, soft and ugly, I am."

She glanced at the laboring figure pounding along beside her. "I agree on the first two. But 'ugly'? No. You have a nice face, Mr. Hildebrand." And then she picked up the pace and left him panting behind.

He watched as she ran loosely and easily down the edge of the black top, putting distance between them. *So that's how she maintains her nice figure...and makes me look bad at the same time.*

He slowed to a brisk walk, even that hurting a bit, his heart pounding along at about a hundred and thirty beats per minute. *Aerobic as hell. Maybe too aerobic for the first time out.*

He saw her suddenly veer to her right and then stop about two hundred yards ahead of him. She reached into the back of her sweatshirt and pulled a tiny pistol from a holster strapped to the small of her back She aimed under a sagebrush at the side of the road.

He started running again when he heard the pop-pop of the .22 caliber pistol, and pulled a nickel-plated .380 from the zippered pocket of his sweatshirt.

By the time he reached Larae's position, he was sucking for air. "What...?" he managed to pant.

"A rattler."

"And you killed it," he managed to squeeze out.

She watched him, a bit of concern in her eyes. "You okay?"

"No…I'm fat…"

"…dumb and ugly…" she finished for him.

He was propped with both arms on his knees, head hanging. He turned to look sideways and up at her. She wasn't even breathing hard. "I'm going to regret saying that, aren't I?"

"I won't tell if you don't."

He straightened slowly and took a deep breath. He was acutely aware that they were the same height; that the corners of her bright blue eyes were crinkled in amusement; that her ash blond curls were shiny and highlighted by the sun; that she was so close he could smell the fresh-from-the-shower scent of her; and that he was resisting an impulse to wrap her in his arms and kiss her.

"I didn't know police officers could blush," she offered.

"I'm not. I'm red from exertion."

"Are not!"

"Am, too! And you didn't answer my question. Did you kill the rattler?"

"No," she answered crossly. "I wasn't trying to. I just wanted to scare him off. He's not doing any harm out here. Just trying to make a living like the rest of us."

It was his turn to grin. "But he did scare the crap out of you, didn't he?"

"Yep. I wasn't expecting to see any snakes out here."

His breathing and heart rate were slowing to near normal. "Well, Officer Holcomb, why don't we walk a ways on down the road so you can catch me up on what you think is going on around here."

They walked another half mile before turning around and heading back to Christmas Valley. By then she had shared the basis for her suspicions of Cowboy, whose expensive lifestyle had no visible means of support.

But for some reason she didn't fully understand, but which caused a touch of guilt and a sense of disloyalty, she omitted telling Roger about the bottles-and-cans man. *There are two kinds of sin: sins of commission and sin of omission. Which is worse? Doesn't matter, I guess, because it's not going to change my mind. I really don't know anything except the guy really isn't what he appears to be.*

Roger shared in turn what the sheriff's department knew and what they didn't know about the John Doe in Ana Reservoir. In his good ol' boy style he told her about the feud that finally led to the shooting of Mrs. Pope. Grinning, he said, "The wild, wild West is still alive and kicking in the high desert of Lake County." And he shared some funny stories about the party Bud threw to celebrate Michelle's promotion.

When they were a half mile from the store, she jogged ahead of him and finished her run. He watched her make a right turn at the store and…once more…he resolved to get himself back in shape.

***

The next morning, in full uniform, with a Sunday *Oregonian* from the convenience store under his left elbow, Roger, leg muscles a little sore, walked the dusty block to the lodge and ordered breakfast. Larae was working the dining room, pinch-hitting for Billie. Wally was drinking his third cup of free coffee, "with cream, please," and Rocky in his white chef's hat was working the grill. Two elderly couples were discussing the seniors menu, trying to decide between the eggs Benedict or a healthy bowl of oatmeal and toast. Roger heard them choose the eggs Benedict as he settled behind a table next to the widows of the dining room and set his tan Stetson on the chair beside him.

Larae gave him a smile of genuine pleasure and walked to his table with a coffee cup, iced water, menu, and coffee pot in her hands.

"Good morning. Coffee?"

Roger nodded and grinned back. "Yes please, ma'am, with cream."

Larae poured his coffee and studied Roger. *Nice green eyes...five-ten maybe...although that wide body makes him look shorter...not fat, just husky...regular features...strong jaw...even teeth...mischief lurking behind those green eyes...light brown hair...receding hairline...gonna be bald someday...big hands.*

She flushed slightly as he studied her back and winked.

Slightly flustered, she said, "I hear we have a new cop...er...I mean a new neighbor."

Roger chuckled. "Yep, just moved in last night. Motelling it until the inside of my house is painted."

"Welcome. The special is eggs Benedict for $5.99 or country friend steak, two eggs, mashed potatoes and sausage gravy for $7.99."

Roger winced and patted his middle. "I better have the oatmeal, toast, and a large orange juice."

She grinned, thinking about their jog yesterday morning. "Are you sure? The eggs Benedict is awfully good."

"Unfortunately, I am. Dang it!"

"Okay, and I'll bring the cream right over."

Hips swaying slightly, she hurried to the little bar behind the counter. He wondered if she was deliberately teasing. Deliberate or not, it was seductive. Unconsciously, he sucked in a gut that was starting to get away from him.

I better keep working out. This sitting in a vehicle all day is not healthy.

Rocky called "order up." Four plates of steaming eggs Benedict slid from kitchen to service counter.

Amused at the banter of the older couples and their occasional "I know I shouldn't be eating this, but..." Roger slowly ate oatmeal and unbuttered toast, with each spoonful wanting the country-fried steak instead.

The seniors were ordering "some of that scrumptious apple pie, with ice cream, please" when Roger pushed the empty bowl to the side of the table, unfolded his paper and turned to the Living section for the crossword and jumbled word puzzles. He had decided long ago that he pretty well disliked the political slant of the *Oregonian*, but he was hooked on crossword puzzles.

He heard a diesel engine and watched a red Ford 4x4 extended-cab pickup, F350 roll to a stop in the graveled parking lot. The driver slid from the seat, slammed the door, hitched his britches, straightened his 49ers cap and strode up the walk.

Like the King himself. I wonder who this character is.

Cowboy slid onto a red vinyl stool at the counter and interrupted Wally's conversation with Larae. "Hey, honey. How 'bout some service here?"

Larae gave him a cool look and said, "I'll be with you in a minute, Cowboy."

Aha! The infamous Cowboy. Is that his nickname or just a general tag, like Buddy or Partner? Roger made a mental note to find out.

"Hey. I'm hungry here."

The older couples interrupted their pie eating to shoot disapproval in Cowboy's direction. Wally wondered if he could whip the big "son-of-a-bitch," and Roger started to get up. Larae shook her head at both Wally and Roger and slid a menu in front of him.

In a cool voice she asked, "Coffee?"

Cowboy muttered, "Bout time."

"The special is eggs Benedict for $5.99 or the country steak with two eggs, mashed potatoes and country gravy for $7.99."

"I'll have the country steak and a kiss."

Steely eyed, she answered, "Not on the menu. Not now or ever. Got it?"

Cowboy grabbed her left arm and tried to pull her over counter. Leering, he said, "Well, you get to know me, you'll change your mind."

Larae twisted free and threatened Cowboy with the steaming coffee pot. "Would you like this coffee in your lap or in your face?"

The restaurant was dead quiet. Rocky came out from the kitchen carrying a rolling pin, Wally slid off his stool, ready to wade into Cowboy, and Roger jumped up and moved behind Cowboy. He could smell the alcohol on Cowboy's breath.

Rocky yelled, "Cowboy, you get away from her and you get your ass out of here!"

***

Roger grabbed Cowboy, all two hundred and fifty pounds of him, slapped a cuff on his right wrist, and was reaching for the other when Cowboy spun and tried to pull away. Cowboy drew his left arm back to swing at Roger. And then Larae had him in a hammerlock. Cowboy growled as she pulled his arm back behind him. Roger snapped the other cuff, kicked Cowboy behind one knee and threw him on the floor. Cowboy tried to get back up, and Roger put a knee in his back.

"Don't move, asshole. I really don't want to shoot you."

"Thinks she's too good for old Cowboy. I'll fix her. You wait and see. I'll fix her good."

"The only things you are going to fix are license plates if you don't shut up."

"And I'll fix you, too, you hick cop."

Roger took a deep breath, got himself under control, the adrenaline burning in his system. He looked up at the wide-eyed group staring at him and at Cowboy. "Anybody know this joker's name?"

Cowboy bucked and Roger put more pressure in the small of Cowboy's back.

Wally answered. "That miserable puke is Bobby Clark, Robert I suppose, but he goes by Cowboy, although he couldn't wipe the shit off a real cowboy's boots."

Cowboy growled from the floor, "And I'll get you too, old man."

"Not in this lifetime. I'll spit you and roast you like a hog if you even try."

Roger glared at Wally. "Enough." He fished Cowboy's wallet out of a hip pocket, flipped it open and read the driver's license. "Okay then. Robert Clark, I'm arresting you for driving under the influence, for public drunkenness, for assault, for disturbing the peace, for resisting arrest, and for spitting on the floor. You have the right to remain silent. Anything you say may be used against you in a court…"

"Spitting? You're crazy!"

Roger gave Cowboy's back a grim smile. "…in a court of law. You have the right to an attorney. If you can't afford one, one will be appointed by the court. Do you understand the rights I just read you?"

Cowboy nodded.

Roger put a bit more pressure on Cowboy's spine. "I can't hear you."

Cowboy spluttered, "I hear you, you asshole."

Roger looked up and winked at Larae and said, "I wonder if there is a law against the use of foul language in front of ladies and seniors.

Larae suppressed a nervous giggle. "It might be worth a shot."

"Okay, Mr. Cowboy. These fine folks are going to keep an eye on you while I go get my pickup, and then we are going to take a ride to Lakeview. He winked at Rocky. "If he so much as tries to roll over, whack him with that rolling pin." Roger pulled a plastic quick tie from a belt pouch and snubbed it around Cowboy's ankles.

Roger released the pressure on Cowboy's back and stood up. He looked at Rocky. "And I didn't pay for breakfast."

Rocky shook his head. "Nope. It's on the house."

While Roger was jogging to his pickup, Cowboy managed to turn over and sit up, his face red and spittle dripping down his chin. He was trying to get to his knees. Rocky was shaking his head. "Don't make me do it Cowboy."

Wally kept saying, "Go ahead, Rocky. Whack him."

Larae finally got tired of Cowboy's silliness. She walked over, got Cowboy by his hair and flattened him on his back. "Stay, Cowboy, or I'll be the one to club you."

Cowboy rolled over on his stomach to take pressure off his handcuffed wrists.

***

It took less than two minutes for Roger to retrieve his county pickup and get back to the lodge. Roger hurried through the door, keenly aware of his mistake in leaving Cowboy in the care of civilians. *Last time I go anyplace without my vehicle, even if it's a hundred feet.*

Roger cut the quick tie, helped Cowboy up, marched him down the walk and stuffed him roughly into the back seat behind the cage. Cowboy asked Roger to take the cuffs off, but Roger just shook his head. As Roger was sliding into the driver's seat, Larae handed him a brown paper bag.

"Maple bars," she said.

He started to refuse, but a look at her raised eyebrows told him there was more than a maple bar in the bag. He sat the bag on the front seat and said, "Thanks."

The seniors, who had had a disgustingly good time, paid for breakfast, left a decent tip for Larae and, clucking joyous disapproval, shuffled out to their respective Buicks—one green and one white—eager to get home and call friends with this juicy bit of news.

Wally nodded at the retreating seniors. "That'll give them something to talk about for months. And the story will get better as it ages. I'll bet before it's all over the men will be claiming they helped the cop. Or, better yet, how the cop helped them take Cowboy down."

Rocky shook his head, went back to his kitchen, scraped burnt bacon off the grill and put some fresh bacon to cooking. The noon specials were a BLT and country-fried steak with mashed potatoes and sausage gravy. He tried to keep his mind on his cooking, but he kept glancing at Larae.

Wally and Larae perched on stools, elbows on the counter, sipping coffee, not saying much until Wally finally cleared his throat and asked, "Where'd you learn to handle yourself like that?"

Larae looked sideways at Wally. "Handle myself? What do you mean?"

"I mean you moved fast, you had a hammer-lock on Cowboy in nothing flat, and you never batted an eye. I don't even think you were breathing hard."

"Oh, that. My Old Man showed me that one. I guess I just went on instinct."

Shaking his head, Wally said, "Nope. You've had training. I can spot it every time."

"Let it go, Walter." Her tone reminded him of his mother who only called him Walter when he was in trouble.

"Okay. I'll let it go. But you can't fool a pro."

"You a pro, Wally?"

"Now you're the one who's pryin', Sweet Mama."

She got off the stool. "And so it's a draw. Enough. I have tables to bus."

Chapter 15

KAREN HIGHSMITH BOOKED Cowboy, grinning at the charge of "spitting on the floor."

Cowboy was surly but quiet as he sobered up. He finally asked to make a phone call. Karen dialed the number for him, handed him the receiver and quickly moved back to the booking counter. Bud and Roger stood guard until Cowboy finished his call. Roger pointed at the open door of a cell.

Cuffs back in his equipment belt, Roger hit the buzzer, peeked through the reinforced glass, and Karen hit the release button. Bud asked, "Did you get it?"

"Yes, I'm running a trace on it now. I can tell you this much. The area code is for Bremerton, Washington."

Roger and Bud retrieved their pistols from the lock box. Bud said, "Let's try it. Put it on the speaker."

Karen looked puzzled. "Won't they know where the call is coming from?"

"Well, I think Cowboy already told them that."

A pleasant female voice-recording answered on the second ring. "You have reached the law offices of Pettibone, Brown and Jones. We can't come to the phone right now, but your call is important to us. Please leave a message and we will return your call as quickly as possible."

Karen killed the speaker and hung up the phone.

Roger said, "Okay, so it was an attorney's office. But why would this high desert cowboy have an out-of-state attorney? Coincidence? We have two homicides, each a mirror of the other. One in Bremerton. One down here. And this guy calls a Bremerton lawyer. Coincidence?"

"No," Bud answered. "There are no coincidences in this business. Karen, why don't you get your Bremerton detective friends on the line. I'd like to see if they'll check out this attorney."

Karen was fairly bursting with excitement as she looked up Detective Maretti's number. "I think they'll be happy to help us."

"And I have one more request," Roger added. "I need to run the fingerprints on this bottle." Karen nodded, but her attention was on the really fun stuff, like being involved in a murder investigation.

Roger looked at Bud. "Talk to you for a minute?"

Roger closed the door to Bud's office and pulled up a visitor's chair. "Boss, I went for a jog yesterday morning with Larae. And, by the way, damned near worked up a heart attack trying keep up with her. Anyway, she is strongly suspicious of Cowboy. His ranch is too small to be very profitable, but he drives a pickup worth about forty grand. All of his farm equipment is new. He keeps a small airplane at the Christmas Valley strip. And all in all, lives way beyond his visible financial means. So…if there is a drug operation up there, he looks to be our number one suspect.

"But there's one other out-of-place guy up there. I've seen him riding the highway on his bicycle picking up bottles and cans. There's nothing wrong with that, but there aren't very many bottles or cans along the road. And the route he rides is from the Horse Ranch out on 30 to Christmas Valley. That's over thirty miles each way. And he does it every day."

Bud listened with interest. "How long, I wonder, has he been in Christmas Valley?"

"I asked Drinda, the gal who works the mini-mart. She said he's been bringing in bottles and cans for over a month. And she said he wouldn't give her a name when she asked. He calls himself Gar. When Drinda asked if that was short for Garfield, she said his eyes turned cold, and he said, "No, Gar as in garbage man.""

"We better be looking at this guy. His tenure in the county is awfully close to the timing of the murder of our John Doe."

"You know what bothers me, Bud? Larae knows practically everyone up there by first name, and she didn't even mention this guy. And she didn't mention having any fingerprints she wanted matched."

Bud stared hard at Roger for a long thirty seconds, thinking before answering. "The fingerprints wouldn't be Cowboy's. We have those, and we'll run a records check on him anyway. You want me to ask her, take a drive up there?"

"Not yet, but it bothers me to think we have an undercover cop who isn't being totally truthful with us. No," he said with a look that was inner focused, "let me chase this one."

An hour later, Howard Finch puffed into the office, slammed the door and plopped into Bud's wooden visitors chair. "You'll never believe this. Your guy is in jail less than an hour and I get a call from an attorney in Klamath Falls, says he represents Robert Clark and wants to schedule a bail hearing pronto…like tomorrow."

Bud sat on the edge his desk, folded his arms, leaned back slightly, pushed his Stetson back on his head, and then declared, "This doesn't make sense. If this Cowboy character is just a small time rancher, why call a Bremerton attorney? And why does an attorney in Klamath Falls wind up being his lawyer? Why not someone from Lakeview? Or LaPine? Or Bend?"

Howard snorted, "He's pulling some powerful strings for a Christmas Valley rancher. What else we got on this guy?"

Roger shook his head. "Nothing but suspicions. You don't suppose you could subpoena his bank records?"

"Done."

***

Two days later Cowboy was indicted for driving under the influence, drunk and disorderly conduct, resisting arrest, and for spitting on the floor. No one was clear about the legality of that, but Howard Finch roared about the menace to public health, and Judge Fay Harrington was in no mood to argue when Howard was on a roll. Judge Farrington set bail at $25,000, much to the disgust of Cowboy's attorney. The judge then lectured Mr. Clark on wisdom of cooperating with law enforcement, and the seriousness of resisting arrest "because it can only lead to injury."

Cowboy posted bail and was released.

CHAPTER 16

IN THE OFFICE of the *Lake County News*, Asa Connor leaned back in his old wooden captains chair and chewed on his unlit meerschaum, a hold-over from younger days when he still smoked. He said he could give up tobacco, but he couldn't give up his pipe. Said it helped focus his attention at the keyboard.

He looked past his pipe at Bud. "So you think a story about Robert Clark's arrest might shake some information loose?"

"We have a missing informant. It's kind of a long shot, but maybe, just maybe someone will come forward with some helpful information."

"Okay," Asa said past the stem of his pipe. "We'll run the story along with the awesome details, things like cussing in public and spitting on the floor." He chuckled, closed his notebook and stood up, but Bud just sat in the wooden visitors chair and looked up at Asa, one of his best friends. Bud admitted to himself that it was an unlikely friendship, given his deep antipathy of the press. But both men had that rare combination of deep-seated morality and ethical behavior, traits that were so often missing from people who practiced law enforcement or news reporting. Perhaps each recognized and responded to that basic decency in the other.

Asa sat back down. "Something else on your mind?"

"Yes." Bud gave Asa a copy of the Homeland Security alert and waited quietly while Asa read the bulletin.

Finished, Asa looked from the page to Bud. "You have a plan?"

Bud nodded. "We plan to leak this to a few people like Clyde Whittaker at Valley Falls, Jarred Warner at New Pine Creek, Amy in Adel, Buffalo…wherever travelers are likely to stop for gas or food."

"Uh-huh. But you don't want me to run this, do you? This is pretty juicy, Bud. Might increase circulation."

"All of the people we've contacted have promised to keep this quiet. But they won't. Some won't because they'll believe it's all nonsense so it won't matter if they talk about it. The rest will just have to tell a trusted friend who will tell another trusted friend."

"So how long do I sit on this?"

"I'm hoping you will wait until your reporter ears hear the story."

Asa shook his head. "And what story is that? You've got this uncanny knack of putting me on the spot." He pointed at Bud with the stem of his unlit pipe. "Okay, I'll give this some thought, but first rumor I hear we run a story."

Bud nodded. "Thanks."

Asa rose and started for the door but Bud continued to sit.

Asa sat back down. "Do you have more bad news, Bud?"

"Well, old friend, I don't mean to pry, but I've got ask. You feeling okay?"

Asa started laughing. "You've been hearing rumors from the Ol' Girl network, haven't you."

Bud nodded.

"Well, here she is, the straight and true. I'm not ill. I'm not giving up the newspaper, but I am going to turn the daily management of the paper over to Carol. And then I'm going to sit down and write the great American novel. I've put it off too long as it is." He put the unlit, unpacked pipe on the desk. "I do, however, have prostate cancer. It's no big deal. I go to Bend, check into St. Charles, and they take care of it."

He picked up the pipe. "Ironic, isn't it. I quit smoking out of fear of lung cancer and then something else pops up." And then Asa grinned, his blue eyes brightening. "I might just put some tobacco in this thing and light it up again. But I suppose it would just taste like shit." And then he laughed.

Bud rose. "Sorry to be nosy, Asa. You keeping this quiet?"

"Not really. Just not talking about it too much."

"When do you go to Bend?"

"Next week. And no, I don't need a ride. Agness has already claimed that privilege."

Bud looked surprised.

"Yep. Since all my secrets are coming out, you might as well know that Agness and I have been dating." He rubbed his right elbow with a long, slender left hand, looking a bit sheepish. "If this prostate business comes out all right, I think Agness and I might just scoot off to Reno and get married."

Bud grinned at the image of the diminutive Agness Lynch, all five foot three inches with the lanky Asa. "That'll give you an inside track on the Ol' Girl network."

"You know, Bud, her spies keep Agness pretty well informed. If she ever quits the post office, I think I'll run her for mayor."

Bud stood up and held out his hand. "Well, what to say? You get well, old friend. And congratulations to you and Agness."

Asa rose, shook Bud's hand and said, "Thank you."

"Can I talk about this romance?"

"Not yet. But Agness will let you know when. As long as we're on the subject of marriage, when are you going to let me run a story about the pending marriage of the sheriff of Lake County to that gorgeous woman I know you're already engaged to?"

Bud just shook his head and with a wry grin and said, "Asa, it's sorta like you and Agness. Nancy will let us all know when it's time. I think the date will depend partly on her mother's health."

He paused. "Did you ever hear the old joke about God granting a man one wish? The man wanted a highway to Hawaii, but God said that wasn't a good idea. So the man asked to understand women, and God replied that he could consider the highway after all."

Asa just shook his head and smiled.

Chapter 17

MARETTI SLAMMED THE phone back in the cradle, looked out of his office door at Grandfield who was pounding out a report and roared out, "Damn it, Grandfield, that pushy broad in Lakeview wants us, that is you and me, two of Bremerton's finest—make that one-and-a-half—to check out some lawyer's office, see if it's just a phone or not. Like we got nothin' to do but run her errands."

Grandfield grinned. "Gonna do it?"

Maretti shuffled his penny loafers out the door to Grandfield's desk in the bullpen and said with a bit less volume, "Yeah. She keeps hinting that she has some good stuff on the Bernard case. You know what I think? I think we should check this out, take the DNA tests down there and see what that hick town looks like. That's what I think."

Grandfield raised his eyebrows, a glint of humor in his blue eyes. "Maybe you just want to see what Deputy Highsmith looks like?"

Maretti sniffed. "Of course not."

Grandfield shook his head. "Yeah. Sure. But we don't have a budget for that anyway."

Maretti looked miffed. "Forget the budget. Let's go look for this attorney."

Grandfield grabbed his sport coat off the back of his chair and chased Gino Maretti's stubby receding figure down the hall.

He chuckled. *One thing about Gino: when he makes up his mind to do something, he gets moving.*

The car was already running when Grandfield slid into the passenger seat and grabbed his seat belt. "You always drive," he complained.

"Yeah, cause I don't trust your driving, Grandfield. You're too damned slow."

The car bounced over a curb as Maretti cut the corner getting out of the parking lot. He flipped a note card to Grandfield. "You know that address?"

"Yeah. It's up on the heights. Strange location for a law office."

Maretti was quiet again…or maybe for the first time that day. He turned up Fir Crest and started looking for Rhododendron.

Grandfield pointed. "There it is on the right."

"Hmmm. Doesn't that make you suspicious, Grandfield? Nothing up here but mansions."

"I don't get it."

"Damn it, Grandfield, it's a front."

Maretti drove slowly past the large home and then made a quick, tire squealing U-turn. "Let's go calling."

A young woman in a maid's dress and apron answered the door. She looked Hispanic. And pretty, Grandfield noted.

Maretti flashed his badge, flipped it shut and put it back into his inside jacket pocket. "I wanna see Mr. Pettibone."

"No habla Ingles."

"Don't give me that crap about not speaking English. You the maid for an attorney with a name like Pettibone, you speak English."

The girl flushed and repeated, *"No habla Ingles."*

"That so. Then why are you blushing? Look, you get Pettibone down here *muy pronto* or I'll get an arrest warrant and bust your pretty little ass. How do you say 'deportation' in Spanish?"

She glared at the detectives, but she left the door open and scurried across the entry and up the stairs.

"You are a crude man, Maretti."

"Yeah, I know, but once in a while you have to kick a little ass to stop the games. She speaks English well enough to know "arrest" and "deportation." Sometimes that's all you gotta know."

Basil Pettibone, a rather tall, slim young man with slicked back blond hair, an open-collar blue dress shirt and a gold chain came down the stairs. He crossed the landing, held the door with his left hand and said, "What the hell are you doing on my front porch scaring the hell out of the domestics?"

"Domestic," Maretti corrected.

"What?"

"Domestic. One."

"What do you want?"

"Mind if we come in?" Grandfield asked.

"Yes, I do mind. Now, why are you here?"

Grandfield countered with, "Are you an attorney?"

"I am."

Maretti shook his head. "Passed the bar and all that, I suppose. Where's your shingle?"

"Shingle?"

"Don't play dumb. Your domestic already did that. You know damned well what I mean."

Grandfield interrupted. "What he's saying is that it seems rather strange for an attorney with your obvious means to work from his home and not have some kind of sign advertising his practice. I mean, the universities turn out thousands of attorneys each and every year, and most simply starve." He looked pointedly at the expensive furnishing in the entry, pointed at the crystal chandelier, and swept his arm to include the expensive driveway and manicured lawns. "You aren't one of the starving."

"I do all right. I have private clients who want to stay private, so I don't advertise."

Maretti pushed it. "You mind giving us some names, references, cases you've handled in the past year?"

"Gentlemen, if you don't leave right now, I'll file suit for police harassment. Now get your dumb asses off my porch."

Maretti drew himself up to his full, stocky five-eight, and glared up at Pettibone. He resented Pettibone with his good looks, his height, his mansion, his pretty maid. Pettibone saw and didn't care.

Maretti thought, Rich son-of-a-bitch. Tall, rich, arrogant son-of-a-bitch. "I'll be back."

"I'll have your badge, you prick."

"Not from jail you won't."

Pettibone slammed the door. Maretti took a deep breath, turned and grinned at Grandfield. "Did we scare him?"

"Nope. Don't think so."

"We'll get him. Don't worry. The only attorneys who have private clients and no office work for the mob or very big, very crooked corporations."

"You Italians got mob in your brains. There is no mob any more. They've gone legit."

"That's what you think. But us Italians know better." He flipped the big house a single digit salute, and hurried down the walk leaving Grandfield to catch up. "Let's get out of here," Maretti growled over his shoulder.

Late in the afternoon Grandfield had run the records and done all the research needed to check out Basil Pettibone. Maretti always claimed he didn't know much about computers, but Grandfield figured he was just bored when he wasn't in motion… or lazy.

He hollered across three desks to Maretti who was sitting back in an old captain's chair, feet on the table, reading the sport section from the Seattle *Post Intelligencer*. "Gino, I got it."

"What you got, Grandfield, some kind of social disease?"

"Gino, there are times when you're not funny, not funny at all. And my name is Ron. We've been partners for a long time and you still don't use my first name."

Gino took his feet off the desk, put the paper down, and straightened up. "I know it, but I like Grandfield better. Grr-and-field. Grand name. Blue-blood name, that's what it is. I'll bet your ancestors came over on the Mayflower."

Ron turned red when another of the detectives in the room snickered. "I never bothered to look it up."

"Yeah, I'll bet. But I'm here to tell you that my ancestors came over on a boat, too."

"Okay, you want to hear this or not?"

Chapter 18

MID-WEEK AT THE lodge was always slow. Most of the people in Christmas Valley country worked, most at the hard, physical jobs of ranching, farming or logging. A few had jobs in LaPine or Bend. The rest worked in the store or the motel, taught school at the North Lake County High School, delivered the mail or worked in the farm equipment repair shop. A couple of the women worked at the Fort Rock Pizza Parlor. The rest were retired, worked odd jobs or were professionally indigent. Those few were the outcasts, the ones suspected of being into illegal activities.

And of course, there was the bottles-and-cans man.

Larae worked the bar alone on Wednesday. Rocky had the evening off. Billie closed the restaurant at nine and left for home, a short block down the gravel street toward the lake.

At ten Larae announced last call to the middle-aged California couple who were staying at the motel next door. They downed their drinks, thanked her, left a two-dollar tip, and arm-in-arm wove their way out the door muttering something about it must be the altitude and desert air that caused them to trip on the foot rug just inside the door. Larae smiled, shook her head, stuffed the tip in the tip jar and wiped the counter.

"Wally, I'm closing."

Wally answered without turning his head as Twin Win rolled through another cycle on the video poker machine. "Okay, Sweet

Mama. I'm about broke anyway." He doubled the bet, hit the spin three quick times and then printed a ticket for $4.35.

He set his empty beer glass and his ticket on the counter. Larae shook her head. "Wally, you have to stop gambling or start winning. And you know you can't beat the machines often enough to make it pay."

"Now, now, Sweet Mama, it's the only entertainment I have except for talking to you and Billie, so don't get on my case."

"You could read a book or watch TV."

"I do read books, lots of book, but TV is a waste, just rerun after rerun. The only unpredictable events on TV are the news and sports."

Distracted by the job of cleaning up, Larae acknowledged his discourse with a non-committal "hmmm."

Wally pocketed his miniscule winnings, said good night, and slipped out the door.

The till was counted, money, cash, and credit card receipts locked in the floor safe of the office. Larae looked out the window at the rising desert moon and decided to walk down to the lake before turning in. Actually only an oversized pond, it was still big enough for paddle boats and summer ducks.

She locked the door, pocketed the key and started down the walk. And then she was on the ground, stunned, and vaguely aware that she had been struck in back of the head. A knee ground into her back and big hands circled her neck, choking, shutting off her air. She was aware of a sour whiskey odor and the stink of an unwashed body.

A voice growled, "Okay, bitch, this time I'm gonna teach you some manners."

Her instincts took over and she tried to get up on one knee, scrabbled to get a grip on the fingers choking her, tried to roll out from under the heavy weight of the big man. He was simply too strong and too heavy. Her head was spinning and she was running out of air. She tried an elbow smash that bounced off a solid ribcage, and heard a snarl. "Why you..." The pressure on her neck increased and she began to black out.

As suddenly as it began, the pressure on her neck and the knee in her back were gone. She pushed up on her knees, sitting back on her heels, gagging and choking desperate for a breath of good clean desert air.

In the moonlight, a man stood over Cowboy. In a low voice he calmly said, "Don't ever touch her again. The smart thing to do is leave this part of the world...now...tonight. If I see you around here tomorrow, I'll hang you with you own guts."

Cowboy just lay there, propped on an elbow. "You? You think you're man enough, let's find out right now. He got one knee under him and started to get up. But that's all he did. The man in dark sweatshirt hit him square on the chin with powerful left, followed by a smashing right, and Cowboy loosely tumbled backwards and lay still, sprawled under the shrubbery by the walk.

The man grimaced and rubbed the knuckle of his right hand.

Larae, still sitting back on her heels, stared at the dark figure in amazement.

Finally she croaked, "Did you hurt your hand?"

A low chuckle answered, "Maybe I did. Big bastard, isn't he? You okay?"

She massaged her throat. "I think so. I couldn't get any purchase, couldn't get my knees under me. Damn. I think he meant to kill me."

"Not on purpose. He wanted you conscious when he raped you."

"That's Cowboy, isn't it?"

"I think it is, the miserable puke."

She digested what she had just seen. This medium-sized man, maybe five-eleven, roughly one seventy-five, had quickly and expertly knocked Cowboy unconscious, all two hundred and fifty pounds of him, with two short punches. She cleared her throat and asked, "Who are you? What's your name?"

"Just call me Gar."

"Just Gar, huh?"

"Just Gar."

He held out his hand helped her to her feet. "Get out of here. Go home."

"What are you going to do?"

"He'll live if that's your question, but I don't think he'll cause you any more trouble."

"No, I think I should call the police. He tried to mug me. I guess he actually did mug me. If you hadn't been here…" she let the thought trail off.

"Well Deputy Holcomb, if that's what you want, but you'll blow your cover."

She was clearly troubled. "What did you call me?"

He laughed. "You think you're the only one who can lift a fingerprint? That was a neat trick, by the way. Same way I got yours."

"So that's why you took that beer bottle. We just thought you were stealing a nickel deposit. Wally and I had a good laugh over that one. He was talking about stringing bottles along the road so you'd have something to pick up. But that doesn't tell me why you wanted my prints."

"Why did you want mine?"

"Hmm. Well, you don't fit the part you play. Your supposedly 'old' pickup has a huge hemi under the hood. I checked. And the tires are almost new. Not bad for a bottles-and-cans man."

"Looking for drugs, aren't you? Well, one beer on Saturday night is my style, not using or pushing drugs." He pointed at the still hulk on the ground. "I'd look closer at this piece of shit if I were you."

"That still doesn't answer my question."

"Deputy Holcomb, we have a little situation here. I think I just saved your ass, so what's it going to be?"

Cowboy woke the next morning in the cab of his pickup. He was some five miles east of Christmas Valley in a pullout along the main road. Except for his socks, he was naked, and the keys to his pickup were gone.

His head was throbbing and he had to pee. Looking in both directions on the straight section of road, he got out of the cab and opened the passenger side door. He gasped and stumbled back into the borrow pit. On the floorboard of the pickup, a big diamondback rattler was coiled, its forked tongue flickering, testing the air, sensing danger. And then it started its cold, blood-chilling rattle.

Grabbing a pitchfork from the bed of the pickup, Cowboy opened the driver's door and shooed the snake out the passenger door, watching as it slithered into the shade of a big sage bush beyond the borrow pit.

Cowboy was on the verge of tears from fright, frustration, and embarrassment.

"What the hell do I do now?"

His brain slowly turned over, and then he remembered his cell phone. It was still in the console. Now, if only he could pick up a cell signal.

Forty-five minutes later, an old, faded, blue International pickup came rattling down the road, Crazy behind the wheel. He held a boot out the window and laughed as he pulled up beside Cowboy's pickup.

"I gathered most of your clothes on the way out here, but I could only find one boot." He shook his head. "You must have been on the all-time champion bender, but at least you kept your socks on." He laughed again at his own wit.

"Shut up you moron. Give me my pants. Did you bring my extra set of keys?"

From a low hummock just east of Cowboy's pickup, bellied down under a big sage, Gar had watched with amusement through 10X binoculars when Cowboy found the snake. But his attention had become riveted on the other man. He couldn't make out the conversation, but he recognized the laughter.

Gotcha, you son-of-a-bitch. Gotcha.

When the blue International turned around, Gar could clearly see the license plate, and he used a small twig to scratch in the dirt the letters and numbers of the Oregon plate.

CHAPTER 19

IT WAS 3:30 a.m. when Gar turned off the highway into the Horse Ranch RV park. He killed the lights, switched off the engine, and coasted to the gravel parking spot in front of his 16-foot travel trailer, the gravelly crunch of the tires muted by a thick layer of pine needles. His RV spot, #18, was half-hidden at the back of the park by a thick stand of ponderosa pines.

Eastward, the land sloped gently to the "flats," the long-ago bed for a prehistoric lake that once covered this now-arid land. Wind and waves cut and shaped the prominent U-shaped spine of lava that later inhabitants called Fort Rock. The rolling landscape supported a scatter of sage, chaparral, rabbit brush and a few runty juniper where the pines gave up the struggle to grow in the arid climate. On the edge of the pine forest to the west, thickets of mountain mahogany snuggled under rims of lava and provided cover to a variety of animals, including mule deer, coyotes, badgers, and the ubiquitous sage rat—officially called Townsend's short-tailed ground squirrel, so named and identified by the botanist J. K. Townsend in his tour of the west in the 1830s.

Gar's closest semi-permanent neighbors, an older Montana couple RV-ing their way around the country in one-month stops, were parked in #2 near the front gate, so he lived in semi-seclusion, a condition he liked.

He was hungry, tired, and needed some unbroken sleep. The tension was easing, but it increased again at the sight of the black Harley parked near the back of the trailer. He flipped the headlights back on, illuminating a sleepy Larae Holcomb stretched out on an aluminum lounger, the hood of a dark blue sweatshirt pulled up over her head.

No one moved until Larae, turning her face from the headlights and holding both empty hands out to her sides, finally asked, "You want to kills the lights?"

Gar took his right hand away from his gun, killed the lights and waited until his eyes adjusted. He opened the door slowly and slid to the ground. With the door between him and Larae, he just stood and waited.

Larae noticed the dome light didn't come on when he opened the door. *I think this is one dangerous character. Cautious as hell for certain. Make no sudden moves, gal.*

Finally, in a semi-irritated voice, Larae said, "Bout time you got back."

He didn't say a word, but he stepped out from behind the pickup door and closed it as quietly as he could.

"I followed you, you know. Right up Highway 97, through the Paulina caldera and on out to the Fort Rock Road."

Still no answer.

"Want to know why?"

He just stood rock still, not answering.

"You see, I kept asking myself if you were just out on a sightseeing trip or if you had something else in mind. And then when you didn't stop at Paulina Lake, I knew you were up to something. No one, unless he was on a mission of some kind, would just drive by without stopping to take a gander at one of the world's most beautiful lakes. I thought about poaching as a motive, but somehow that doesn't seem like you."

Gar cleared his throat. "You here as my bartender or as Officer Holcomb?"

He could almost hear the smile in her voice when she said, "I'm not sure yet, but for now why don't we settle for friend, or at least friendly bartender. Mind if I stand up now?"

"You armed?"

"Actually, I've got my pea shooter in my boot, and it's staying with me."

He laughed. "Good for you."

She shivered. "Could we talk about this inside?" She heard a slow exhale as Gar relaxed.

"Come on in. I wasn't expecting company so the coffee pot's dry."

He unlocked the door, flipped on the interior lights and waved her in…ahead of him.

***

He pointed at the breakfast nook, and she slid onto one of the padded benches. Elbows on the table, chin in one hand, she looked with surprise. The interior of the small trailer belied the flaky scabrous exterior paint. Everything looked new—from the spotless paneling to the small refrigerator and stove, to the unblemished indoor/outdoor carpet. There wasn't even a spoon or a dirty dish in the sink.

Military trim. That's what it is.

She shivered, and Gar said, "These desert nights get pretty cool, even in summer. Want some heat?"

"Please. I got chilled."

He toggled a switch, waited until the furnace kicked on and then said, "You could have built a fire in the fire pit."

She looked up at him, struck by the thought that in spite of the frowzy beard and the traces of camo face paint, he was extremely good looking. "I thought about that. I even thought about picking the lock on the trailer and waiting inside. And then I thought, what if Gar decides to shoot me as an intruder? Besides, I didn't want anyone to know I was waiting. Here in the back, I figured either the other campers would forget I was ever here, or that I left without them seeing me."

He pulled a coffee pot out of the cupboard and started filling the pot. With his back to her he said, "Okay, friend Larae, how did you follow me? It sure wasn't on your bike."

She tilted her head slightly to the side, smiled smugly and shrugged. "I don't want to give away any trade secrets, but I will tell you Wally calls the Buick America's best kept secret."

He slammed the pot on the burner. "Shit. That damned green Buick. I should have known. But you didn't follow me out of the Caldera."

"Yes I did. I just laid back out of sight and followed your dust. I even found where you left your pickup and started out through the trees." She reached into the belly pocket of her sweatshirt. "Here, let me show you my map. Wally helped me mark all the ranches and homesteads in Christmas Valley and Fort Rock. I even know the names of most of the people who live here." *Except yours, and I'm working on that.* "According to Wally, the ranch you were sneaking onto belongs to Cowboy."

"Yes. But you didn't follow me on foot. *That* I would have known."

"Ah…I get it. You're pissed because I tailed you and you didn't spot me."

He shrugged. "I never get pissed when I screw up, but I like to know how to make sure it doesn't happen twice. So I want to know how you did it."

"I didn't set out to tail you. I was actually coming to talk to you. I didn't want anyone to know it, so I wore a frizzy grey wig and borrowed Wally's Buick. But just before I turned into the RV park, you pulled out on the highway. You're like a lot of people, normal people, who simply don't really see an older person in a Buick. That's all there is to it. And I'm not an amateur."

"God protect us from gifted amateurs. I'm not some innocent civilian without a clue about how to spot a tail."

"Ho! *Not* an innocent civilian. I like that. So you're not a civilian, not a bottles-and-cans man, and not a garbage man, just the man who laid Cowboy out with two quick punches." Her voice began to rise in volume. "You sneak around in middle of the night dressed in camo, keep your trailer military trim, sneak fingerprints from your bartender, carry a Glock, and wear combat boots."

"You don't want to go there, Officer Holcomb. Let it go."

She pointed as the coffee began to perk. "Fetch me a cup of that coffee, sit down and stop the bullshit."

He suddenly grinned at the peremptory tone of her voice. "Yes, ma'am. Right away, ma'am. Any further orders, ma'am?"

"Yes. Fetch the coffee now, please."

"It's not ready yet."

"It's close enough. I need something hot."

He took two mugs from the cupboard, poured steaming coffee and set the cups on the spotless table. "Cream and sugar?"

She shook her head. "You have a very nice face when you smile."

He slid his weary bones on the padded bench across from Larae and looked at her in skeptical silence.

"Look," she offered. "I'm a cop. To me that means I protect innocent citizens, enforce the law, and do my best to put the bad guys away. It also means I hate mysteries, especially mysteries in my jurisdiction. You know I have your fingerprints, and by tomorrow I'll know who you are anyway. So why not level with me? Who are you?"

He shook his head. "I already told you that. I'm the garbage man. I do other people's dirty work. Just like I said, I take out the garbage. And running my fingerprints through the FBI's Integrated Automated Fingerprint Identification System won't tell you anything. You won't find mine in IAFIS. In fact, you'll probably stir up a lot of trouble for yourself and your department. Officially, I don't exist."

"That sounds like romantic bullshit, to me. Everybody has a record someplace."

He just looked straight into her hazel eyes and then let his eyes wander to her tousled honey-colored hair. Without preamble, he reached slowly across the table and traced a hairline scar on her upper lip.

She was startled, but she didn't pull away either, stirred by his soft voice, his gentle hand, intense blue eyes, and the dusty khaki scent of this man.

Neither spoke for nearly a minute. He finally broke the silence. Almost in a whisper he said, "My sister had hair the color of yours."

She froze and didn't answer for a long minute, her eyes searching his face, looking for signs of meaning. Finally she asked, "Did something happen? You use the past tense."

His face contorted and then became impassive as he said, "I'd say rape and murder was something." A small tear formed at the corner of one eye but no others followed.

She touched the back of his left hand, a hand tanned, scarred, and calloused. "Is that why you're here?"

Harshly he said, "I keep trying to tell you I'm not here. I don't exist."

"And when you tell me that, you tell me more than you mean to. Just like saying you're not an innocent civilian." She paused, squeezed his hand and released it to pick up her coffee cup. She sipped and over the rim of the cup said, "You've never taken the time to mourn your sister, have you?"

He rose so abruptly he banged his head on the curved low ceiling over the breakfast nook. "Look, it's almost four. I've had a busy day, and this is getting too damned personal. So let's drop it. I like you, Officer Holcomb, and I can't afford the distraction right now."

Larae couldn't look directly at him. Almost in a whisper she answered, "I like you, too, And I'm afraid I can't afford that right now either. I'd better go. But when I get the fingerprint check, I'll be back." She tried and failed to stifle a yawn.

"Look at you. You're in no shape to ride your bike home. Besides, you'll wake the neighbors and give me a bad reputation."

"I'm in no shape to stay either. I'll just push my bike out to the highway and get on home."

She rose to leave and he stood aside to open the door. On a sudden impulse she hugged him and he responded so strongly she pushed him back. "Don't get any ideas. I'm just grateful that you saved my butt from Cowboy."

He held his hands up in mock surrender. "Yes, ma'am. All in a day's work."

He helped push her bike to the highway, waited while she fastened the chin strap of her helmet and started the bike. He watched her tail lights disappear over the first low hill in the road. "You are a lovely complication, Larae. I hope neither of us gets hurt."

Gar waited by the entrance to the RV park until the sound of the Harley's engine faded into the night. *Okay, back to work.*

At the trailer, he pulled a field pack from the storage under the gaucho. He knew what it held, but he did another careful inventory: radio, map, two-liter water bottle, power bars, camera, personal aid kit, cell phone in silent mode, 40X spotting scope with tripod, and a folded Armalite chambered for a .223 swift load, six twenty-round clips, two flash-bangs, handheld GPS and an ugly black knife. The garrote he left.

The door to the trailer closed quietly. He turned the lock, put the key under a rock by the pull-down steps, walked the path to the turnstile, and out into the desert.

Chapter 20

THE BUNKHOUSE WAS casting long shadows in the shallow morning sun when Crazy stepped out of the bunkhouse, coffee in hand, to have his morning smoke. The stone on the stoop stopped him cold. But Charlie was an old hand with surprises. He froze and scanned the perimeter. The tracks across the barnyard were plain, at least to Charlie's trained eyes.

There, right under that juniper, say a hundred meters. Came and went, he did. Laid right there under that juniper last night and watched me. How in the hell did he find me?

He felt a sudden chill, and it wasn't from the cool sage-scented morning air. In a defiant voice he shouted, "Stone Fly, you son-of-a-bitch! I'll find you and we'll settle this!"

He reached into his shirt pocket for a cigarette only to find he already had one between his lips. He broke a wooden match trying to light it, threw it angrily on the ground, pulled another wooden match from his shirt pocket, and struck it with his thumbnail without breaking it this time.

The cigarette steadied his nerves and eased the trembling of the cup. He wasn't afraid, exactly. In fact, he had always thought he was better than the legendary Stone Fly, but it was disgusting to get caught with his pants down. He remembered one of the instructors telling the team, "If you think you're among the friendlies and relax, you'll find you're still in Injun country."

***

A flood of poignant memories washed through his mind—and through his emotions. In spite of everything, he missed the life and the team. In a twisted sort of way, he even missed Stone Fly. And he was still killing angry at his old boss.

Give me the boot just because of a few steroids. Hell! That just made me better. All that bullshit about an anger problem. Bullshit, That's all it is. Just bullshit. Well, I'll show'em this time. When Stone Fly goes down, I'll make sure they know it was Crazy that got him.

He suddenly tossed the cigarette, threw the coffee mug at the bunkhouse. The cup smashed through a window. Crazy sprinted across the barn lot to Cowboy's low modular. He kicked the gate off its hinges, slapped the door with open palms, the sound like gunshots in the still morning air. Cowboy opened the front door just before Crazy kicked it in.

Crazy pushed past him into the living room, breathing hard and in a fine fettle.

"What the hell is going on?"

"He's out there, Cowboy, and this operation is blown."

"What are you talking about?"

"Stone Fly. That's what I'm talking about. He found me, and that means he found you and we are in some serious shit here. That's what I'm talking about."

"Crazy, you calm down. I have no idea what's going on so why don't you explain it to me. What the hell is a stone fly?"

"Not what, you big dumb bastard. Who! And the who is Stone Fly!"

***

From his spider hole on a low ridge some eight hundred meters northwest of the ranch house, a tired Gar watched the antics of his old teammate, a man who was once his best friend. Through the spotting scope he saw Charlie freeze.

Found the marker.

He couldn't make out the words, but he understood the defiant, challenging shout. And he almost grinned when Charlie kicked the gate off its hinges. And then he yawned, wondering what it was about sunrise that always made him drowsy after a sleepless night.

The jaunt across the flats had taken him nearly three hours. Where he could he used rocky ground, detouring to walk sheets of lava, walking on a few downed junipers, knowing all the while that hiding tracks in the desert was impossible. So he settled for leaving as few as possible and for building in as much misdirection as he could. He hurried, hoping Charlie was getting lazy in his old age and sleeping in. It was about five miles as the crow flies to the ranch, but Gar made a wide circle to the north, because he didn't want to make it too easy for Charlie to find him. Not yet at any rate.

At grey light he found the vantage point spotted the evening before. This time he was out in the open with only the shade of some short sage for cover. Charlie would be scoping the junipers, so he wouldn't be there.

He peeled the camo wrapper from a food bar and settled behind the scope. He knew he was as close to invisible as anyone could be. But he knew that unless the whole crew down there pulled out, including Crazy, he was there for the day—hot sun, rattle snakes, scorpions and all. He wondered if he dared to risk a short nap. He finished the food bar, took a sip of water, set the alarm on his cell phone for an hour downstream, stuffed it in his pocket where he would feel the vibration and, face on his field pack, fell almost instantly asleep.

Chapter 21

KAREN HIGHSMITH WAS on the phone when Bud opened the front door to the office. She didn't take the phone from her ear, but she waved Bud over and held the phone away from her head so Bud could listen. "...and she'll need a ride from the airport. ETA two hours." The man on the other end of the line paused. "Do you understand?"

Bud pulled the phone from Karen's hand. "This is Sheriff Blair. Maybe you had better tell me what's going on."

A man's voice. "This is Special Agent Thompson with NCIS. I'm sending an agent to see you today. She will arrive at ten hundred. We understand a Lear can land at your airport. She'll need a ride from the airport."

"Want to tell me what this is about?"

"It is a national security matter."

"Well, ain't that nice. As a matter of fact, I'm in the security business myself. I look after the security and welfare of the residents of Lake County. So unless you give me a better reason than you have so far, your agent is free to walk to town or thumb a ride."

"You started this, Sheriff, so don't go getting smartass on me. Do you have any idea what a hornets nest Officer Highsmith stirred up?"

"No idea. And where in the hell is 'up here'?"

"Silverdale, Washington. This is the Northwest Field Office for NCIS."

"I tell you what: a phone call out of the blue from some arrogant asshole who claims to work for the NCIS just won't cut it. You are going to have to do better than that."

Karen scribbled a quick note and shoved it in front of Bud. *The fingerprints!!*

Bud scratched a big *?* on the pad.

Karen wrote, *Larae's Person!*

He heard the man on the phone say, "Okay. Fair enough. Call this number back and I think you'll have the verification you need." Bud wrote a number that started with the area code 360.

Thompson broke the connection.

"Am I in trouble, Bud?"

He placed the handset in the cradle and grinned. "Nope, but I might be. Got any coffee?"

Karen hurried to the coffee pot, turned a clean cup over and poured a fresh cup for her boss. "What happened," she said as she returned to her desk by the booking counter, "is I came in early to see if we had a match from IAFIS. When I logged on, the screen was blinking, and this red flag jumps out of the screen at me, sort of pulsing in and out. When I tried to log on, my access to IAFIS had been terminated. And then the phone rang and that man was asking me all kinds of questions. And he wasn't very nice about it. And then you came in."

"Looks like I better call him back." Karen punched the phone number into the keypad and handed Bud the phone. On the first ring, a sweet young female voice answered, "Northwest Field Office, NCIS. Please identify yourself."

"Sheriff Bud Blair for Agent Thompson."

"Thank you, sir. He's expecting your call."

Thompson answered on the first ring. "Satisfied, Sheriff?"

"Some. Now what's going on? How can a fingerprint search cause this much ruckus?"

"We have certain personnel whose identities, including fingerprints, are highly classified."

"And we just happen to have the fingerprints from one of your 'personnel.' Is that it?"

"In a nutshell. What we want to know is how you came by them."

Bud laughed. "Well we have a policy of confidentiality ourselves. Officer Highsmith was acting on my request. It's part of an on-going homicide investigation."

"Damn it, Sheriff! You will tell me or I'll have your badge."

"Stuff it!" Bud slammed the phone down and stormed out to the front walk, reaching into his shirt pocket for the missing pack of cigarettes—even though he hadn't smoked in over seven years.

Calming down, he took a deep breath and waited for his heart rate to return to normal. Then he returned to the office. "Karen, if Thompson calls back, and I'm sure he will, send the call to Howard's office. And get Michelle over here pronto. Tell her to meet me there."

***

Howard's door was closed, but Bud could hear his big basso voice through the door. Short, portly, head covered by an unruly mop of blond curls that he generally forgot to comb, Howard was blessed with a commanding voice that would growl or soar with Churcillian splendor as he chose. In short, Howard was an accomplished orator and a first class prosecutor. Bud once asked why Howard chose to work as a small county prosecutor. His only answer was a quick, "Why are *you* here?"

Bud's knock was answered by, "It's open."

Bud shook his head and grinned as Howard looked up and over three tall stacks of case folders. Closing the door, he said, "Working hard, Howard?"

"No, no I'm not. This is my protective camouflage."

"Well, somehow I don't believe that. The judge has you working on something?"

"He's got a bee in his bonnet. Asked me to give him some feedback about our handling of child abuse cases. So..." He raised his hands in a blessing over stacks.

"What do you think?"

"I don't know yet. Did you just drop by to say good morning?"

"Actually, no. I suspect that in a few minutes your phone is going to ring, and an Agent Thompson from NCIS is going to ask for me. I just called him a pompous asshole, so I don't think this will be a friendly call."

"Really?"

"And he says we'll have an NCIS agent landing at our airport in about an hour. Let me start at the beginning. About three months ago, Roger had a tip about a meth lab in the Christmas Valley area, but the guy never showed for a meet. And the snitch hasn't been heard from since. So...and this has to be kept quiet... we hired a new officer to work undercover in Christmas Valley."

Howard interrupted, his tone accusatory. "You never said a word to me."

"That's the idea of being undercover, Howard. No one knows it's happening. And if it's any consolation, I didn't tell the Judge either. It's not a matter of trust, just a matter of prudence."

"You make me feel all warm and fuzzy, Bud."

His tone sharp, Bud said, "Howard, let's not get sidetracked. I'm bringing you in now. Anyway, my undercover officer sent us some fingerprints and asked us to run them. And when we did, we were red-flagged and our access to IAFIS was blocked. That's about the time this Thompson guy called."

"Judas priest, Bud! You do know how to stir things up. So what's the connection between the fingerprints and NCIS?"

"Guessing…there have been two men murdered…military people. One was killed in Bremerton, a sailor, and the other is the John Doe we found in Ana Reservoir. We don't have an ID, but judging from a chain and anchor tattoo, it seems logical to think our John Doe was also a sailor. I'm betting he was killed at the reservoir or someplace close by.

"It's logical to assume NCIS is investigating the Bremerton murder. And now NCIS gets very interested in the fingerprints our undercover officer up in Christmas Valley got off a beer bottle."

Howard shook his head, his mop of blond curls bouncing. "So…do you think their 'classified' person is in Christmas Valley?"

Bud nodded. "Likely. What I do know is that an agent from NCIS will be landing at our airport in about one hour. I want you to ride out to the airport with me. Sort of be part of the honor guard. Besides, you're good at asking questions."

He looked at the lint-covered blue blazer on the back of Howard's chair. "You might want to find a tie and dress the part of the consummate politician that you are."

Howard shot him a nasty look, but Bud didn't give him time to interrupt.

"In the meantime, I'm going to have Roger pull our undercover officer out and put her back in uniform. They can back each other up."

Bud pushed his chair back and stood up. "Let's head for the airport at about 9:45. I've got to get our people informed and organized." As he turned to the door, Michelle knocked, peeked in and said, "Am I interrupting?"

Bud grinned, "Aha, our esteemed undersheriff. No. Come on in."

Bud briefed Michelle. She pulled her notebook from her belly pack and started taking notes.

When Bud finished, Michelle said, "Okay. I'll have Roger get Larae back in uniform. And we need to talk to Larae. I'd like to know why she pulled this guy's fingerprints. And I'd like to know how long he's been in Christmas Valley. I also think we need to get Sonny back from the arson task force…at least for now."

Bud nodded. "Okay, take care of it. Howard and I will greet the NCIS agent at the airport."

The phone rang. Howard looked at the caller ID, picked it up and handed the receiver to Bud without answering. "Sheriff Blair." He listened, shot Howard a look and shook his head.

"Okay. We'll meet your agent at the airport. No. No need to apologize. Stress can do that to people. Bye."

Bud looked disgusted. "You know, since our NCIS friend is getting his way, he's just as nice as he can be. He even apologized. You know the nasty thing about apologizing? It means you can be an asshole, say exactly what you think, and then sort of make it okay by apologizing. I think it's like your attorney friends asking questions they want a jury to hear, and then withdrawing the question."

***

When Michelle and Bud unlocked the security door to the Sheriff's office off the interconnecting Court House hallway, they could hear Karen Highsmith giggling and a male voice in what could only be a story-telling cadence.

"…so when I asked the cabby to bring us over here, he nearly died laughing. I swear he could have been off the streets of Bremerton. It was, 'Hey, bro' this and 'Hey bro' that. But he did take us to a car rental place. You folks live in the sticks! Ninety-seven miles, it is. Nice country, but have you eaten in Bly lately? The burger was fine, but potato chips in a little bag? They had to be a hundred years old."

Michelle and Bud walked into the rear of the booking area. Two men were at the booking counter. Neither looked to be local. The shorter one wore a rumpled brown and red-checked pattern sports coat, the taller one a dark blue, expensive-looking blazer. Both were wearing white shirts and blue ties.

Bud walked up behind Karen, a scowl on his face. "Gentlemen?"

Karen started. She had been so intent on the storyteller she hadn't heard Bud and Michelle behind her. "Oh! Ah…Sheriff. Let me introduce detectives Gino Maretti and Ron Grandfield from Bremerton. This is Deputy Trivoli and Sheriff Bud Blair."

Bud looked at Michelle as if to ask if she knew anything about this unexpected visit. She just shrugged and shook her head.

Grandfield stepped to the booking counter. Stuck out his hand and said, "Ron Grandfield. It's nice to finally meet the legendary sheriff of Lake County. I take it you weren't expecting us."

Bud shook his head. "Nope. And your timing's shitty."

Maretti nudged Grandfield aside, put his hands on his wide hips and looked up at the taller sheriff. "We come five hundred miles to work a homicide, and this is the greeting we get?"

"I think you should have given us some warning."

"I did. I sent Karen, ah…I mean Deputy Highsmith…an e-mail."

Bud and Michelle looked at Karen. She blushed and stammered, "In all the excitement I just forgot to mention it."

Michelle frowned. "You forgot?"

Bud watched the quick, silent interchange between Gino Maretti and Karen Highsmith, and then began to smile. Finally he grinned and stuck his hand out to Maretti. "Well, hell, detectives, welcome to Lake County. We don't want it said that we lack hospitality. This may be better timing than you know. How about some coffee?"

Chapter 22

THE VIBRATION OF the silent cell phone brought a gritty-eyed Gar awake to the faint sound of a diesel truck in Cowboy's ranch yard, some eight hundred meters from Gar's spider hole. He heard the truck's door slam and raised his head slowly toward the ranch. He found a peek hole through the sagebrush, refocused the spotting scope and surveyed the action. The logo on the truck's door was obscured by dust, but he thought he could read something like "Fort Rock Ranches."

"More like Fort Rock Rustlers," he thought.

Then the load of rectangular hay bales caught his attention. The front half of the top layer was dark, almost black.

"You would never feed that to cattle. It would kill them. What the hell is going on?"

A man he guessed to be Charlie, judging from the way he walked, appeared from behind the truck, hurried to the green metal hay barn, and opened the big sliding door. He heard the airbrake release, and then the truck moved slowly into the barn. Cowboy followed the truck across the barn lot. When the truck was inside, Cowboy helped Charley pull the slider and both stepped inside just before the door closed.

Curiouser, and curiouser, said Alice. The thought reminded Gar of reading *Alice In Wonderland* to his little sister when they were kids. He'd had to explain parts of it to her...at least as his twelve-year-old mind saw it. Memory brought sorrow mixed with a bright, hot anger at her killers.

He shook the thought away, sipped some water, and slid a little further into his spider hole, thinking small, the way he trained and practiced. He peeled the wrapper from another food bar. The little patch of shade Gar borrowed from a small sage bush shortened imperceptibly as the sun continued its morning trek.

Chapter 23

THE COFFEE WAS poured, tea for Grandfield, and everyone was seated around Bud's small conference table. Bud glanced at Karen, who looked uncomfortable, and then stared at the Bremerton detectives, trying to decide if their trip had a purpose other than love.

Sensing his attitude, Grandfield cleared his throat, took a sip of some really bad tea, and said, "Sheriff, we have DNA from three men who raped and murdered a young woman, Sondra Bernard. One of her killers has also been killed. We know this from a DNA match. What we hope to find is that your John Doe is another of her killers." He gave Maretti a skeptical glance. "And we decided that trading information via e-mail or telephone calls wasn't as effective as a face-to-face."

Maretti was studying Bud's office, the map, the pins, the book titles, noting the lack of personal items. Apropos of nothing pertaining to Grandfield's briefing, Maretti said, "Damned big country you gotta cover. How do you do it?"

Bud's first thought was Maretti wasn't as dumb as he looked... or acted. The second thought was to wonder what the hell Maretti was doing in Lake County. He sipped his coffee, rocked back in his chair, smiled and said, "By horseback."

Maretti and Grandfield glanced at Karen to see if the sheriff was serious. She just grinned and shook her head. Then they all three laughed.

Bud grinned. *That broke the tension. Grandfield thinks this is a waste of time and money. Maretti wants to meet Karen and he's used to getting his own way. But they could be right. Maybe we can help each other.*

"Okay," Bud said, "to business. We have a DNA report on our John Doe. Let's see if it matches one of your killers. Karen?"

She slid a file across the table to Maretti who simply slid it on over to Grandfield. Detective Grandfield opened his briefcase—an expensive one, Bud noted—and pulled out a file folder. He opened both Karen's file and his own and started comparing DNA markers.

While Grandfield studied the files with Karen peering over his shoulder, Maretti said, apropos of nothing again, "I understand you were a detective in Portland?"

Bud rocked his head back and stared down his nose at Maretti, not liking him very much. He could understand now why Karen had called Maretti an asshole. What he couldn't understand was why she had changed her mind. She actually seemed to like the asshole.

"Where'd you hear that?"

Maretti grinned. "From a certain lady who wanted to impress me with her sheriff. Made me make a few phone calls to some pals of mine in Portland. Seems you were a pretty damned good detective…before you were shot."

Bud worked hard to keep his temper under control, liking this Maretti character less and less, and said nothing, unless a hard glance at Karen could count for a reply.

"Hell," Maretti shrugged, "I was shot once. Only the bastard missed my vest and clipped my hip bone. Hurt like hell it did, and I went on a big bender that lasted a couple of months. I think it rattled my confidence which both of my ex-wives say is totally unjustified in the first place." And then he laughed.

And Karen giggled.

Bud's anger died out. "I know what you mean. Even if your vest protects you, a bullet still hurts like hell."

Memory flooded, memory of a kid in a convenience store pointing a pistol at Bud and BB, Bud trying to talk the kid down, pistol still holstered, and then coming to in an ambulance, discovering he had a broken sternum. And he remembered drinking too much, the strain in his partner's attitude, and BB finally yelling that if Bud had drawn his own gun, then maybe the kid would have backed down and BB wouldn't have had to kill a fifteen-year-old.

Maretti said, "No offense. I'm not trying to get personal, Sheriff. Just getting acquainted. I like to know who I'm working with."

Bud decided to answer Maretti's first question. "The county is about eight thousand square miles, but a lot of it is National Forest or BLM lands, so that narrows our responsibility down a bit. We have six officers including me. Karen runs the jail with the help of three part time matrons, and I have a small cadre of three reserves. But I use those mainly in search-and-rescue and for crowd control during the county fair, and during twice-yearly rodeos. The leader of that bunch just finished the Monmouth Academy. I don't suppose I'll have him around much longer. And we do have a sheriff's posse, local people who like to ride horses and look for lost souls. My reserves tend to meetings, training and organization of those nice people.

"But basically we patrol alone, do some traffic control work, stop and talk with people in the stage stop stores, take calls, and follow up on leads." He walked over to the map. "Most of our 'towns' are just stage stops." He pointed at Plush. "We caught up with a couple of rustlers here not too long ago because the ranchers in the area kept us posted. Well, actually we didn't make the arrest, but we pointed the Malheur County police in the right direction. And we solved a murder case earlier in the year."

"You know," Maretti said almost wistfully, "that sounds like a hell of a lot more fun than what I've been having."

Michelle entered the room in time to hear the last of Bud's brief. She scolded her sheriff. "You left out the part about Casey shooting at you, killing your horse, and the horse breaking your ankle."

Maretti looked surprised. "Horses? I thought you were kidding."

"I was. This was an unusual situation."

Grandfield straightened up and smiled. "Beam me up, Scotty! We have a match!"

Before he turned to Grandfield, Maretti said, "I'd like to hear more of that story, Bud." And Bud noticed the switch from the formal "Sheriff" to a more informal and friendly form of address.

I'll be damned. I think I just passed some kind of Maretti test. But he hasn't passed mine yet.

Karen was patting Grandfield's shoulder. "Good job, Ron."

Ron grinned. "I didn't do anything but read. Besides, I had to. There is some doubt about Gino actually knowing how to read."

Bud smiled and Maretti just shook his head. "Who the hell gives you the scores on the ball games? Who the hell reads the speedometer and tells you hurry up before the bad guys get away? Who the hell showed you where Lakeview is on the map?"

He turned and winked at Michelle. "You know what Grandfield said when I showed him the map? He said—and I quote: 'It's only two inches from Klamath Falls.' And the guy claims he can read."

Michelle laughed. "I'd hate to walk those two inches."

Bud was beginning to revise his opinion about Maretti. The guy might be one of those interrogators who kept coming at people from odd angles, fishing for information, watching for telltale reactions, a left jab and a right cross technique.

He might just be good at it, and it takes brains to make it work.

Bud stood and picked up a marking pen, poised before a flip chart. "So what do we have here? Two homicides, both victims killed in identical ways, both castrated but both dead from broken necks."

The phone rang and Karen hurried from the room to take the call, hating to miss out on anything.

Grandfield suggested, "Why not start with the rape and murder of Sondra Bernard?"

Bud said, "That might be a good idea. Her murder hasn't been part of our puzzle...up until now."

"Three guys killed our lady," Maretti thought out loud, "and now two are dead. So what's the motivation? Revenge?"

Michelle asked, "What about a relative—a father or a brother?"

Grandfield tilted his head back, stared at the ceiling, expelled a deep breath and said, "That's a darned good question. When we found Pike's body, we queried the Navy about the brother. I mean it seems like a logical tie, but they said they had never heard of the guy. Didn't work for them. But they did want to know why we were asking."

"AWOL, maybe?" Bud asked Grandfield.

"Not a clue. Even Gino couldn't get a thing out of the Navy. Of course, that might be caused by his crummy attitude towards NCIS."

"Yeah, and I'm pretty good at that," Maretti said.

"Yeah, Gino. You are. They just love it when you butt in on military crimes and tell them what jerks you think they are."

Maretti ignored Grandfield and asked Bud, "Do you think the brother could own the fingerprints you tried to run?"

Bud didn't answer. In fact, he didn't really hear the question. His mind was busy filling in the blanks, running with a new theory, or actually with his first and only theory of the murder of his John Doe.

Bud looked at Michelle. "Okay. Fill 'em in."

Michelle walked to the map and pointed at the upper left corner. "Up here in the Fort Rock-Christmas Valley area we have had rumors of a meth operation, from a snitch who has disappeared, by the way. So we put an undercover cop in place. She works at the Christmas Valley Lodge as a bartender. She lifted some prints from a suspect, but," she nodded at Karen, "when Karen ran the prints through IAFIS, we were red flagged and our access to IAFIS has been blocked." She stopped and looked at Bud.

He shrugged and stated, "And in about forty-five minutes I'm going to pick up a special agent at the airport. They won't admit that the fingerprints are from one of theirs, but it's not too hard to figure it out if they're flying in an agent."

"Holy shit," exploded Maretti. "It's got to be the brother. We found pictures at the Bernard place of a Marine sergeant. Think about it…a Marine that doesn't exist according to NCIS and the Navy. So who doesn't exist except for very special people?"

Bud nodded. "It fits. If he is our guy, He's in the Christmas Valley area." He looked at Michelle. "You get Roger to pull Larae out?"

"Yep. Roger will have her here by the time you fetch NCIS from the airport."

Bud looked at the detectives. "Do you have a place to stay?"

Grandfield said, "We're staying at the Best Western. Haven't checked in yet."

"Why don't you get that done, and then come back here. I'll want Maretti to ride out to the airport with our D.A. and me."

Maretti looked surprised at the invitation. "Really?"

"Yeah. I think you only play the asshole to get people to open up."

Maretti winked at Grandfield. "Hey, Ron...I think he just complimented me. Not sure I can take so much praise. Maybe he ain't as dumb as he looks."

Grandfield winced. "Darn it, Gino, don't you ever let up?" He slid an extra copy of the DNA file, Pike's autopsy report, and his report across the table to Karen, and then snapped his briefcase shut. "These are for you, and we'd like anything you have as well."

Maretti laughed and winked at Bud and Michelle, "Damn. He's good, don't you think?"

Chapter 24

Deputy Hildebrand was in the Silver Lake Café having a morning cup of "sheepherders" coffee—fresh but strong enough to float a horseshoe. Pen and notebook in hand, he was filling in the blanks on an incident report. Darren Wilcox, the short, stocky sixty-something, grizzled, angry owner of the Silver Lake Café, banged a wadded bar towel on the counter as he described a late model, silver Chevy extended-cab pickup speeding through the little town.

The only other patron, Chuck Ritter, was sitting on a worn, red vinyl covered stool at the counter, sipping coffee, and reading a two-day-old edition of the *Bend Bulletin*. Chuck was wearing scuffed cowboy boots, blue jeans, a blue plaid flannel shirt, a worn fleece vest, a straw cowboy hat, and granny glasses. A tuft of gray hair sprouted through a hole in the side of the straw hat. If he hadn't known Chuck was a retired schoolteacher, Roger would have pegged him as a rancher or an old cowboy.

"He was doin' damn near sixty. Came close to rear-ending me when I was turning in to my place this morning. Wonder he didn't kill somebody! I know this isn't much of a town, but people passin' through should respect the lives of those that live here. He's abusing our hospitality."

Roger thought that was a new and interesting way of looking at the sin of speeding, but he didn't share that with Darren. "Did you get a license number or get a look at the driver?"

"Nope. Too dark for that."

"Which direction was he going?"

"He was headed east, towards Paisley. If we get lucky maybe he'll hit a deer and wind up in the ditch."

"Not mad at the deer, are we, Darren?" Chuck interjected.

Roger grinned. "What time was it?"

Darren glared at his old friend and said, "Smart ass."

"I open at six. Try to get here about fifteen minutes early. So I'd say about five forty-five, give or take a couple of minutes."

Roger mechanically filled in the appropriate blank. "Think he was local?"

"Nope. I didn't recognize the rig."

Roger finished the form, flipped his notebook shut and sighed. "Well, Darren, there isn't a heck of a lot I can do except file a report and keep an eye out for a silver Chevy pickup. If you see him again, try to get a license number."

Chuck looked up over the top of the editorial page. "I know that pickup. He rips through here every week or so in the wee hours of the morning. He's not local that I know of. Just somebody in a hurry."

Darren looked disgusted. "Why didn't you say so in the first place."

Chuck looked over the top of his granny glasses. "You didn't ask."

Roger became more interested. "Chuck, can you remember if it's the same day of the week each time?"

"Yeah, He comes through almost every Friday morning."

"All right. I'll be here next Friday morning for a 'come-to-Jesus' meeting."

The men both chuckled at the thought of some dude being confronted by wide-bodied Hildebrand. Mild mannered, quick to grin, he was also known by the citizens of Lake County as an intimidating son-of-a-bitch when he chose to be.

Roger pointed at a row of oil paintings hanging on the wall

between the restaurant and the bar. "Got some new paintings, I see. Who did the one of the old juniper? That's pretty good."

Chuck lowered his paper. "I did."

"And the rest?"

"Yep. Even sold one the other day to a young couple from New Mexico. They said they had a studio in New Mexico someplace, Taos maybe, where they sold western art."

"They're good, Chuck. Reminiscent of Ray Eyerly."

"Well, maybe. But if they get to be as valuable as Ray's, I won't be able to give any of 'em away when I want to."

***

In a county with a sparse population, Roger was still considered something of a local hero from his high school days—when the Lakeview Honkers won the State Football Championship. Sixteen years later you could still get up a good conversation in the county just by asking if anyone remembers when the Honkers beat Medford.

Roger closed his notebook, slipped it in his shirt pocket and then laid a dollar on the counter. "Thanks gentlemen. As my buddy Arnold would say, 'I'll be back.'"

Before the door of the café swung shut, Roger could hear Darren complaining to his old friend. "You never said anything to me about…"

As he settled in the seat of his white, extended cab 4x4 Dodge pickup and snapped the shoulder harness in place, his cell phone chimed "shave-and-a-haircut."

"Officer Hildebrand."

"Good morning, Roger. This is Michelle."

"You mean Trigger Trueshot, the Annie Oakley of Lake County?"

"Not funny, Deputy. And it's Sergeant Trivoli, the undersheriff of Lake County to you this morning. What's your location?"

"Why yes, ma'am. I stand corrected. I'm in Silver Lake. What can I do for you today?"

"Well, it's a little complicated. When Karen ran the fingerprints you brought back it got NCIS pretty excited."

"The Naval Criminal Investigative Service?" he interrupted.

"Yes. Bud had a pissing match over the phone with a special agent who claims he works for NCIS. I'm not sure what Bud is thinking. He didn't say, but I know it's another one of his theories or one of those hunches he gets. But I do know he wants Larae in uniform within the hour, and he wants us all to meet here by ten. Can you be here by then?"

"Wow! And I thought my excitement for the day was going to be filing a citizen's complaint about a speeder. No. I can't be there by ten...eleven, maybe."

"I'll tell Bud you can be here by eleven."

***

Michelle listened impatiently as Larae's voice said, "I can't come to phone right now. If you leave a message, I'll get back as soon as I can."

She hung up and searched her desk for the Lake County phone directory. She found a number for the Christmas Valley Lodge and dialed. Larae answered on the second ring. "Christmas Valley Lodge."

"Larae, this is Michelle. I have two things for you: The guy you lifted the prints from...how long has he been in the area?"

"Well, I'm guessing he's only been here about six weeks." And then she was finally admitting to herself that the timing fit the murder of the John Doe. "Don't believe it," she verbalized before realizing she had spoken aloud.

"Don't believe what?" Michelle asked.

"Ah...it's nothing. You said there were two things?"

"Yeah. In about thirty minutes Roger is bringing your gear and your uniform to the lodge. Bud wants you back in uniform."

"Why? I haven't finished this assignment yet!"

"He didn't say, but I know he has a good reason. Roger and you are to be here at eleven for a briefing."

"Okay."

Michelle waited for Larae to continue, and when she didn't, Michelle added, "And Bud is bringing Sonny back from the arson task force."

Larae finally asked, "What's going on? Must be something serious."

"I'm not sure, but we are the proud recipients of an NCIS visit this morning."

Larae muttered, "Oh, crap."

"Larae, do you know something? Something you need to share with us?"

"No. Not really. Some suspicions, maybe, but nothing concrete." She paused. "Look, Michelle, I'll tell you everything I know and everything I suspect when we get to Lakeview. Promise."

"Better, Larae...better. Okay...I'll wait. See you in Lakeview." And then Michelle hung up.

Chapter 25

OWEN MACDOUGAL WAS sitting at the coffee counter chatting with Larae and Wally, getting acquainted, wondering if she was the "friend" he had fictitiously bailed out of jail. Had to be. Other than the bottles-and-cans man, there hadn't been anybody new in Christmas Valley for quite a while...except tourists.

Larae was surprised at his age. Somehow she had imagined a grizzled, tough-looking older man. But this Owen MacDougal was all of thirty years old, about six feet tall, blond, bronzed by the sun to be sure, but handsome, wearing an immaculate white Western shirt, shined boots she guessed to Justins, blue jeans, and a tan Stetson. His smiling blue eyes were amused at her speculation.

And he was a good storyteller, even if he dropped into country slang when he was yarning.

He had a wry sense of humor, and was telling stories of Rueb Long and the wild horse roundups. "I missed all that fun," he said, almost wistfully. "It's hard to imagine it these days, but my grandfather told tales about thousands of wild horses running loose around here. It was a wild time. If you had the energy and the guts, you could make a good living by rounding up a herd of wild ones and then selling them to meat packers, or rodeos or dudes. The hard part was roughin' 'em out, getting 'em rider ready."

"Meat packers?" Wally asked.

"Yeah. Sold 'em to mink farms and the like. Even had a Chinese restaurant in Portland that bought a few horses. Ever eat horsemeat?" he asked with a twinkle in his blue eyes.

Wally rolled his eyes, and Larae looked skeptical. "You aren't funnin' us are you, Mr. MacDougals?" MacDougal looked out the window of the lodge as a white county pickup passed by the parking lot. "There goes that new county cop. Wonder what he's up to."

They all turned to look, and then MacDougal said, "I'd appreciate it if you called me Owen. And, nope, I tell tales strong and true. No Irish blarney for the wild Scottish MacDougals."

Wally smiled. "You sure there isn't an Irish ancestor hiding in the wood pile?"

Owen grinned. "As sure as I am that all the women in the family told the truth as to our fathers."

Wally laughed. "You know, that's the problem with this genealogy search stuff. I tried to track my ancestry a few years ago, and the more I got to looking at it, the less I trusted the information. There were records of husbands dying, wives dying, families moving in together, new babies...that kind of thing and it just got all mixed up. But when I tried to sort it out, I discovered one unfounded tale of a kind-hearted ancestor who married a pregnant girl just to give her a place to stay. Nope...just gave 'er all up."

Owen and Larae both chuckled, and Owen opined that all his family could find were outlaws or preachers. "And I never met a family with roots in the South who didn't claim to be related to Jesse James. Can't for the life of me figure that one."

Wally allowed that it was just because Jesse was famous, "...or infamous, if you choose."

Owen was flirting with Larae and trying to pry information from the young, nice-looking bartender and waitress when the sound of a diesel pickup drew their attention. Roger Hildebrand parked beside Owen's blue Ford pickup, hopped out, and unhooked a suit carrier from the hook behind his seat. As they watched through the windows of the lodge, he slammed the driver's door, hurried to the passenger's side, and took out a heavy dark blue traveler's tote, and a black shoulder pack. Arms full, he hipped the pickup door shut and started down the walk to the lodge. He was obviously in a hurry.

"Now what?" Wally wondered out loud.

When Roger pushed through the door, Larae looked with distaste at the suit carrier and the tote.

Without preamble, Roger held out the suit hanger and the heavy tote. "Bud's pulling you out and we need to be in Lakeview by eleven."

She just held her arms out for the gear.

Owen interrupted. "Bud? As in Sheriff Bud?"

Larae looked slightly chagrined and nodded.

Wally just shook his head. "Damn, I knew you were a pro. And there goes the fun."

Larae looked at Roger, almost pleading. "What about Billie? I can't leave Billie in the lurch. She's gone to Bend."

"Are you the cop?" Owen asked her. "The 'friend' I bailed out of jail?"

"Yes. Yes I am."

Roger pushed her gear into her chest. "Time's a wastin'. You better get geared up."

She took the tote, the day bag and the suit carrier and hurried to the rear of the restaurant and down the hallway leading to the living quarters.

Roger looked at Owen and stuck out his hand. "Owen, thanks for the help."

Owen shook hands and said, "My pleasure."

Roger grinned at Wally's disgruntled expression. "It's okay, Wally. She'll still be around"

"Yeah, but there goes my Sweet Mama. Damn. Damn, but it was fun when she was tending bar."

He looked at Roger. "What about leaving Billie in the lurch?"

Roger shrugged. "You're here, aren't you Wally? Can't you cover until Billie gets back?"

Wally looked disgusted, but answered, "Yeah, I can wait tables, but I can't cook for shit. Larae's the fry cook this morning."

"I don't have any choice, Wally. We need her in uniform now, right now."

Owen asked, "Anything we need to know about?"

Roger shook his head, walked behind the counter and poured himself a cup of coffee. "I don't know a lot yet. Just had a message that I was to get Larae in uniform and be in Lakeview by eleven." He added a little cream from the cream pitcher in front of Wally, and stirred the coffee.

Owen didn't say anything for a few minutes, just watched as Roger came around the end of the counter and sat on a stool between Owen and Wally. Finally Owen asked, "Did our scheme do you any good?"

Roger thought about that and then said, "Well...if there is a drug runner up here, we can't prove it. No evidence...yet. But what Larae found might help us solve the Ana Reservoir homicide. That's about all I can tell you." He looked at Wally. "And Mr. Pidgeon, I'm trusting you not to talk about this yet."

Wally shook his head. "No. No, I won't mention it, but you will allow me the courtesy of wee bit of mourning."

He sipped his coffee and looked up. "So...you two were in cahoots...set this undercover business up? Did Billie know?"

Owen shook his head. "No, Billie was just doing me a favor."

"You know, I had some suspicions, the way Ms. Holcomb handled Cowboy…both times."

Roger looked with interest. "Did she have trouble with Cowboy?"

"Yeah. One night he tried to pinch her butt, and she had his hand in some kind of grip that made him squirm. It happened so fast that no one noticed except me. She whispered something in his ear and he sorta minded his manners for a while. Called her some names under his breath, but kept his hands to himself. I thought I was going to have to whip him, but he left before it got to that. And he didn't pay his bar tab, that son-of-a-bitch."

Owen and Roger glanced at each other, both trying to imagine the gray-haired old man trying to whip Cowboy. They managed to suppress the smile that lurked behind their eyes. And they both gave him enough credit to believe he would have tried.

"Yep," Roger replied. "And I thought she had given herself away when she was wrestling with Cowboy."

"That bothered me also. Damn, but she was fast. Had that big arm of his in an arm lock so quick. And she wasn't even breathing hard. Didn't get excited or anything, just did the job."

Roger nodded. "But you didn't know?"

"Guessed. Asked her if she was a pro. She just fed me a line about her biker man teaching her some moves." He stopped, glanced out the window. "Tell me, was she ever in a gang?"

Roger looked hard at him and then relaxed. "Good question."

"And you aren't going to tell me, are you?"

Roger didn't answer, just took a sip of coffee and looked toward the doorway to the lodge living quarters. He glanced at his watch. "Wonder what's taking her so long."

Owen grinned, stood up, stretched and said, "Well…it's a woman's way to want to look nice…even in a uniform. I'll give her another minute and then I've got to get busy."

Wally stared glumly into his coffee cup.

The door to the living quarters opened and a uniformed Deputy Larae Holcomb pushed through. Dressed in brown khaki pants, dark brown field shirt and a tan cap, she was wearing her web belt complete with holstered pistol, personal portable and pouches filled with extra clips, handcuffs and the other paraphernalia of cop work. And she was almost beautiful.

"Damn," Wally said, "I was always a sucker for women in uniform."

She hurried to Wally, arms out. Before he could stand up, she gave him big hug and a kiss on the top of his balding head. "Wally," she said seriously, "You are my good friend, and you'll always be my favorite bouncer. Besides, I'm not going anyplace. I'll be working with Roger in this part of the county, so we'll see each other pretty often."

She released him, turned to Owen and said simply, "Thank you."

Owen gave her a smile and shook hands, and thought wistfully of what might have been. *Well, you never know. I've never dated a cop.*

After the deputies had left the room and were getting into Roger's county pickup, Wally looked at Owen. "So you knew about this?"

"Yeah, kind of. Roger asked me if I would put in a good word with Billie for a 'friend' who needed a job. And I was asked to post bail for this friend...but it didn't cost me anything."

"Why?"

"Because they wanted to run an undercover cop up here to sniff out a drug operation. I hate what drugs do to people. I especially hate it when it's in my part of the world. I figured their undercover cop was Larae, but I never knew it for sure. And you have to admit, she's a darned good bartender."

Wally sighed. "I think I liked her better as a bartender."

They were on the paved cutoff headed toward Silver Lake before either of them spoke. Finally Roger broke the silence. "You aren't asking any questions."

She took a deep breath, let it out and then paused a long thirty seconds before saying, "I think I already know, and I don't think I like the answer."

"Which is?"

"It has to be about Gar, or whatever his name is."

Roger suddenly found that he was pissed. "If we're going to work this end of the county together, we have to trust each other. You didn't even mention this guy. You talked about Cowboy, but you never mentioned our bottles- and-cans man."

"I didn't know anything about him, not enough anyway to include him in my report."

"The hell you didn't. You had enough suspicion to run his fingerprints."

She looked at Roger's red face, took another deep breath, and said, "You're right. But I owed him."

Roger took that in, frowned, swerved slightly to miss a jack rabbit that couldn't make up its mind to go left or right. It went left and Roger used the shoulder of the highway to clear on by.

"You know, my team had one guy, just one, who wanted to play lone ranger when we got to Kuwait. We didn't realize he wasn't a team player until we got there. And you know what happened?"

"No."

"He was the only one to get killed."

She was quiet for almost another mile, just watching the scenery, watching Antelope Butte slide by and the fringes of the forest and Hagar Mountain come into view.

She turned and stared at Roger and then asked. "Have you ever worked undercover?"

He shook his head, concentrating, not taking his eyes off the highway, glancing at his speedometer, keeping it under eighty.

"Then you can't know what it's like. You *are* the lone ranger, and you don't have a team to cover your butt. So you make choices, you make judgments and you live or die with those judgments. I pegged this to be a pretty safe assignment, so I relaxed. I let my guard down, and if it hadn't been for Gar, I'd probably be dead."

He glanced at her. "A bit melodramatic, don't you think?"

"No, damn it, it's not!"

"So what else didn't you tell me about?"

And so she related the whole episode about Cowboy knocking her down and choking her, about Gar taking Cowboy down with two short punches. About deciding not to report it.

"I had no idea," he said.

"Because if I had told you, you would have arrested Cowboy and my cover would have been blown."

"How would that have blown your cover?"

"I don't think that the court would let me just be a simple bartender. What I do would have come out."

Roger grudgingly nodded, and then said, "I don't like Cowboy, and now I have even more reason to dislike him."

"And there's one more thing," Larae added. "Gar knew who I was. He said he ran my fingerprints, and he called me Officer Holcomb. What bottles-and-cans man has those kinds of resources?"

"I'd say his resources could be NCIS...maybe."

She looked skeptical. "NCIS? Why would they be involved?

"I don't know, but we're going to meet an NCIS agent when we get to Lakeview. It seems your request to run this guy's fingerprints stirred up one hell of a fuss. Some high-muckamuk called Bud and told him an agent would be at the Lakeview Airport this morning."

"I hate this undercover shit!" she blurted out.

"You did okay."

"Yeah, but I like him and I owe him, and now it's looking like he's just a killer."

"Gar?"

"Yeah. I wasn't talking about Wally, that's for sure." She took another deep breath, trying to calm herself. "You do know he had a sister who was raped and murdered."

Roger looked surprised. "No, I didn't know that."

"Coincidence?"

"No. Bud says, and I believe him, that there is no such thing in this business as coincidence." He paused. "If your hero is tied to NCIS, it all fits. His time in our part of the country…training…motivation…resources. It all fits." He glanced at her. "Sorry, Larae. Even good guys do bad deeds sometimes."

She shook her head. "No I just can't see him running around killing people. There's more to him than that."

"Why did you run his fingerprints?"

"Well," she paused. "I guess because he doesn't fit the stereotype of a simple bottles-and-cans man. For one thing, even though the body of his pickup looks beat up, he has a monster hemi under the hood. And most of the scabrous looking paint is simply camouflage. And for another he's alert, wary, and observant. You should have seen his travel trailer. Small, dented looking, but new tires, and the inside is all new and military trim."

"You've been inside his trailer? Did you sneak in?"

And so she told him about following Gar, about waiting for him at his trailer, and wondering what he was doing wandering around on Cowboy's ranch in the middle of the night.

"You didn't tell me about that part either."

"As for that, I haven't had an opportunity, and I'm telling you now." But she couldn't tell Roger about the hug or the tears in Gar's eyes when he talked about his sister.

Conversation lagged until the pickup started up the grade to Picture Rock pass.

"I'm wondering," Roger finally said, "if it comes to covering my back or his, which you'll choose."

"Yours. Count on it."

Roger glanced in the rearview mirror and was surprised to see flashing lights and a white pickup gaining on him. His cell phone rang and he flipped it open. "Yeah?"

Sonny's voice said, "You speeding, boy. Better pull it over."

"What about you, Sonny?" he answered, "I might have to write you up." And then he laughed. The emergency lights in the grill of Sonny's pickup stopped flashing and Sonny dropped back to a safer distance behind Roger and Larae.

"Did you solve your arson case?" Roger said into the phone.

"Yeah, and you won't believe the story. The problem is we have more than one arsonist running around."

"So you're still stuck with the task force, right?"

"Not at the moment. Seems our esteemed sheriff can't do without me. What's going on?"

Roger briefed him, but the details were sketchy. "And we won't know for sure until we meet with Bud and this NCIS agent," he concluded.

"See you in town," Sonny answered and hung up.

Larae listened and thought it was a pretty good briefing. She moved Roger up a notch on her short list of smart cops. *Too bad he doesn't trust me, but I don't think I could have handle it differently. You make your decisions and live with them.*

Chapter 26

GAR WATCHED THROUGH his spotting scope as the hay truck backed out of the barn. The load was unchanged, moldy bales still in place. He spotted a dark face peeking through the curtain of the sleeper cab.

As the truck eased through the barnyard and out onto the gravel lane leading to the Bend-Fort Rock road, Crazy jumped into the same battered International pickup he had driven to rescue Cowboy. A second man ran to the old pickup holding what looked to Gar like an AK-47, jumped in and slammed the door. The old pickup followed the hay truck down the lane, and when the truck turned north onto the Fort Rock road, Charlie turned south towards the Christmas Valley highway.

"Not good," Gar said quietly to himself. "And damned odd. Why follow the gravel road out into the timber? No ranches that way unless you get way north. And the hay isn't any damned good anyway. If I was a cop, I'd want a look at that load. Maybe I need to slow it down a bit." He put the butt of the rifle against his shoulder, his cheek against the stock, sighted through the scope, found the left front tire in the crosshairs, held at the top of the tire, and silently prayed as he squeezed the trigger. He saw a puff of dust just behind the tire, adjusted his elevation and windage, and squeezed off another round. This time the round kicked dust slightly ahead of the truck tire. He adjusted his sight picture one more time and squeezed a third round. The truck veered to its left and then stopped, just like a tire had blown. He nodded in satisfaction. *Nine hundred meters. Nice weapon. Nice shot.* He slipped the cell phone from a shirt pocket.

***

The powder blue Lear taxied to the decrepit hanger, and Special Agent Amanda Spears watched three men, one in a khaki uniform and two wearing sports coats and ties, straighten from where they had been leaning against the side of a blue Dodge pickup. "The taller one has to be Sheriff Blair," she said to Toby Warren, her young partner. "I wonder who the other two are?"

"Local dignitaries," Toby offered in a mocking tone.

"Warren, it would be a mistake to underestimate these 'good ol' boys.'" The sheriff is a former detective from Portland with a degree in criminology. He has a damned good track record as a crime solver."

"I'll bet."

She turned and looked across the aisle at her young partner. "Toby, have you read any Robert Frost?"

"Yeah…some. Why?"

"Then you know he was one of our premier poets. And he didn't live in the city. There are people, smart people who prefer a rural lifestyle. The sheriff might just be one of those people."

The little jet came to a stop. They unbuckled and watched the steward open the cabin door and lower the steps. "We're here, ma'am." The steward, young Lieutenant Mackay, a graduate of the Air Force Academy, had taken a dislike to Mr. Warren, but nonetheless he offered requisite courtesy. "And sir."

Amanda glanced at Toby and said quietly, "You do know how to make friends, Toby."

She slid a briefcase from an overhead storage bin, and Toby hefted a laptop.

"Bags, ma'am?" Lieutenant Mackay asked.

"Let's leave them on board for now. I have a feeling this won't take long."

"Yes, ma'am."

The pilots opened the cabin door. Chief pilot Lieutenant Colonel Brownlee asked Amanda, "Can you give me an estimated time on the ground?"

She shook her head, straight black hair swirling slightly. "I wish I could say, Colonel, but I'll give you a call on my cell. I'm hoping this won't take too long."

Brownlee made a vague gesture at his co-pilot whose name Amanda couldn't remember. "We'll find some ground transportation and go get some breakfast...someplace."

Special Agent Spears just nodded.

Bud, Maretti, and Howard watched as a woman in a dark blue jacket and slacks took the four short steps down to the buckled tarmac. She was followed immediately by a tall, slender young man sporting a black suit, a white shirt, blue tie, and shiny black oxfords.

"Look at number two. FBI?" Bud speculated.

"Sure has the look, doesn't he?" Maretti answered.

Howard didn't say anything, just started across the pavement toward the plane. Bud and Maretti didn't really have any choice but to follow.

Bud was slightly irritated at Howard, and then caught himself. *Was I really going to make them come to me? Yep. I'll be damned if I'll toady to them simply because they're feds.*

As they walked the short distance toward the plane, three men in Air Force uniforms came down the steps, closed the cabin door, and hurried to the office of airport control, a large metal building left over from WWII, looking like it was still wearing the original paint…or what was left of it.

Lieutenant Mackay said, "Colonel, where do you suppose these long runways came from? You don't suppose they had commercial air in here at one time?"

The Colonel, a trim, tall man with a salt-and-pepper crew cut, just shook his head. "Nope. Just a left over from the Second World War. This was probably a bomber base for planes with enough range to reach the coast, but far enough away to be safe from carrier-based Japanese planes."

"I'll be damned. Makes sense when you think about it."

The three Air Force officers watched as a Forest Service contract air tanker, a refurbished C-130 with huge tail numbers made its approach to the airport from the north.

"You know, Sid," the Colonel said to his partner, "we should get ourselves one of those and go to fighting fire. It'd beat the hell out of playing taxi driver for VIPs."

Sid nodded. "I've almost got my twenty. How long for you, Al?"

"One and a half."

Sid stuck his hand out. "Well, Colonel Brownlee, I think you've got a deal."

Allen Brownlee, career airplane driver and light colonel of the U.S. Air Force, grinned. "Yes, Major Miner, I think we do."

Lieutenant Mackay looked uncomfortable.

"What's the matter, Lieutenant? Feeling left out?" Colonel Brownlee asked.

"Hell, no! Do you know how dangerous that kind of flying is?"

Both Miner and Brownlee laughed and then pushed open the door to airport control.

***

Nancy Sixkiller heard the 911 line ring and waited while Jack Henderson answered the call. "Emergency Services," he said. There was a long pause, and then Jack looked across the room to Nancy's dispatch cubby. "It's for you. Won't give his name."

Nancy shrugged her shoulders that she didn't know what that meant. She picked up the phone. "Emergency Services."

A man's voice asked, "Is this Nancy Sixkiller?"

"Yes. Who is this?"

The man chuckled. "Well, if you need a tag you can call me Gar."

"What's this about?"

"Ma'am, I know you and the sheriff are good friends, and I know that he is trying to run some fingerprints. So what I want you to do is get the sheriff on the line and give him a message. And I want you to write this down. I think it's important. Will you do that?"

She hesitated, and then said, "It depends on what you tell me."

"Fair enough. I spotted a truck loaded with moldy hay headed north up the Fort Rock Road. Now if it was an honest load, it should have turned south to Fort Rock-Christmas Valley. Here's a license number." Nancy jotted it down and read it back to confirm accuracy." Good," he said and then continued. "There is a sign on the door of the truck that said something like "Fort Rock Ranches." And here's the interesting part. I observed a passenger in the sleeper cab behind the driver. If I had to peg his race, I'd say he is Semitic."

She interrupted. "So what do you want from us?"

"I think it would be interesting for the local constabulary to stop the truck and search the cab and that bogus load of hay."

"On your say-so," she said flatly.

"Yes."

"Who are you?"

"Call your sheriff and ask him about the fingerprints. That's all he'll need to know. And you had better hurry if you plan on catching that truck."

"Give me a number I can call back."

He hesitated and then said. "Okay. I doubt my sanity some days, but here's the number. And maybe it would be better if the sheriff called me." And then he clicked off.

Jack Henderson who had been listening to Nancy's half of the conversation said, "That's weird."

Nancy nodded and hit the speed dial for Bud's cell phone.

Bud was a short ten feet from the approaching agents when his cell phone rang. He fished the phone from his shirt pocket, flipped it open and turned his back to the people converging on each other. "This had better be important," he growled.

"Stop being so damned grouchy on the phone."

"Nancy?"

"So...not in a good mood?"

"No. I'll explain it later. What's up?"

Nancy read her notes to Bud, heard him utter a not so mild expletive, and then waited.

Agent Spears who had edged up beside him, both curious and a bit miffed at the interruption, caught his attention and raised her eyebrows in a "what's up" look.

Bud raised held up his index finger to signal "one minute," but the effect on Agent Spears was the same as if he had raised his middle finger. She spun and walked back to where Maretti, Howard, and the "other guy" were introducing themselves. The only semi-friendly one of the bunch was Howard.

Bud noted the agent's abrupt behavior. *To hell with her, too.*

"Okay, I'm trying to decide if the info is credible. Hold one minute."

Bud walked up to the group and without preamble said to Agent Spears, "Okay. I've figured this much out. You NCIS folks are here because we pulled the fingerprints from one of your agents. So what's his name?"

She shook her head. "You have no need to know."

Bud exploded. "The hell I don't! He wants me to call him. What I want to know, and don't give me any of that 'need-to-know' crap, is can I trust him? Is he around the bend or sane? This is critical, so if you mess around, you can damned well get back on your plane and get the hell out of here."

Bud looked over at Howard and Maretti. Maretti was grinning and Howard looked like he was in pain. Agent Warren took a threatening step towards Bud and Maretti stepped quickly between them. "Now, now, Mr. Warren. You ever been mopped by a wop? You won't like it."

Bud raised both hands in a placating gesture. "Okay. Time for truth. I admit to feeling a bit unfriendly over the way your Special Agent Thompson treated my technical deputy. And I don't feel too friendly about this need to know crap. But I have a situation I need your help on. I think you need my help as well. So let's bury the hatchet and start fresh. Time is of the essence." And then he related the message he had gotten from Nancy. "So," he concluded, "I need to know whether to send my officers after this hay truck or not."

Amanda took a deep breath and said, "He is our best operative in terms of intelligence gathering. His call sign is Stone Fly, a sobriquet he earned for lying motionless next to a terrorist camp for over eighteen hours and eavesdropping...just like a fly on the wall. He has perfect recall, and related word-for-word everything he heard during those eighteen hours. So...if he says he saw an Arab in your hay truck, I'd bet my life on it."

"Does he have a name?"

"That you don't get."

Maretti interjected, "What's to hurt? I already know he's a Marine and his last name is Bernard. At least that's his sister's last name, and I don't think she ever married."

Agent Spears glared at Maretti and he just grinned back. And suddenly, the absurdity of the situation struck her. She walked up to Bud, grinned, and stuck out her hand. "Amanda Spears, your new partner."

Bud gave her a wry smile and took her hand—a hard, calloused one, he noted.

"Well, partner," he said, "where do we go from here?"

She stepped back and looked at him, really looked for the first time, and realized she liked what she saw. His hazel eyes were more in tune with smiles than frowns. A small scar perched on one eyebrow. His weathered, tanned face sported a slightly crooked nose and lots of laugh lines. *OK. Basically a nice guy, but tough enough to do the job.*

"I'd say that you need to stop the truck. And I'd say that I should talk to John Bernard. What's his number?"

Maretti growled, "At last, a first name."

Bud nodded, flipped open his cell phone and dialed 911. Jack Henderson answered. "Jack, I want you to turn Larae and Sonny around and have them check out that truck. You might get the state police or Deschutes County deputies to sweep the Fort Rock Road from the north."

He could hear the radio on his cell phone as Jack called Roger and Larae. And he could hear Roger's voice on the radio, give his location as Picture Rock Pass, and that Sonny was right behind him. *Damn, I'm not sure they'll catch them before they hit Highway 26. What if the bad guys go to Highway 97 through the Paulina Caldera, or to Bend on the Fort Rock Road?*

Jack's voice came back on the line. "Okay, they have a description of the truck and a license number. They're headed back to Fort Rock. All three officers are in pursuit."

"I heard. I think we also need Deschutes County to block the road through the caldera, the Fort Rock Road that comes into the southeast corner of Bend, as well as China Hat Road. Have Sheriff Redman call me if he needs more."

Amanda had walked away to make her call to Gar.

"John?"

"This sounds like a woman I know. Is that you, Amanda?"

"What are you doing out here, John?"

There was a long pause. She heard him sigh and then say, "You know damned well what I'm doing, Amanda."

"You're AWOL, John. You have to come in."

"No...you are wrong. I'm not AWOL. I'm on thirty days family leave, and thirty days furlough. I have two more weeks."

"I had your leave cancelled, and I have to ask: Did you kill Pike?"

"No. Someone beat me to it. I have a hunch Crazy killed him."

"Where are you now?"

"Doing a little sneak and peek on the bad guys."

"You all right?"

"I was until I got this figured out. I think these guys are smuggling Mid-East types into the country. Never thought Crazy Charlie would turn traitor."

She thought she detected a certain sorrow in his voice, even thought she understood, how she would feel if her best friend betrayed her county. "John..."

He interrupted, "Call me Gar. Saves on confusion."

"We need to talk...Gar."

"Good. Officer Holcomb can tell you where I'm staying. I should be there later tonight. And leave that dumb-shit partner of yours home. Don't like him. Amanda?"

"Yes?"

"What the hell are you doing down here?"

***

Bud turned to the small group who looked expectantly at him. "You heard my end. Three of my officers are going to chase the truck, and we'll try to block the exits. If they don't know they are being chased, they might take one of the three most obvious routes and we'll stop 'em. On the other hand, if they think they're being hunted, there are more roads out of that country than a rabbit warren. Let's think positive and get back to town."

Amanda started in as she reentered the circle. "I talked with John…or Gar, which is what I guess you know him as. Says he didn't kill anyone. No…he says someone beat him to it. Not quite the same thing. I'll hook up with him tonight. Alone. He's currently watching, as he put it, 'the bad guys.' Sheriff, any idea where that might be?"

"In a general sense, yes. Specifically, no."

"He said Officer Holcomb would know."

"Then we'll have to ask her."

Amanda nodded, knowing not to push any harder right now. She nodded at the three Air Force officers. "These gentlemen need a ride to town."

"We'll have to send someone back for them. I've only got room for five people in my rig…that is if the people in the back seat don't mind a squeeze."

Bud opened the rear doors and watched in amusement as Maretti and Howard made sure Toby Warren was sandwiched between them on the bench seat. Amanda settled in the front passenger seat, and Bud closed the doors. As he slid under the steering wheel and hit the starter, Amanda made a sweeping gesture at the stubble fields along the runways. "This is first time I've seen farming alongside airport runways. What do they grow?"

"Wheat mainly," Bud answered. "Yeah, it's a bit unusual, but except for private aircraft and Forest Service retardant planes, there isn't a lot of traffic. So the airport leases the in-between ground to a local farmer. It also makes for some pretty good pheasant hunting." As if to emphasize Bud's point, a rooster pheasant and two hens winged across the road to a line of willows and cattails that lined an irrigation ditch alongside the airport road.

"I wasn't sure what the country would look like, but I really didn't expect so much farming and ranching, or so many trees," she said pointing to distant tree blanketed ridges.

Bud slowed for a ninety-degree corner, a holdover from days when wagon roads simply followed fence lines and the square lines of surveyed sections of land. "It surprised me, too, when I first came into this country. Hooked me, it did."

She smiled at him, catching a glimpse of a man she suspected was more than a little complex.

From the back seat, Agent Warren asked, "How far is it to this place where the Stone Fly saw the hay truck?"

So you have been paying attention, Bud thought.

"Over a hundred miles," Howard offered before Bud could answer.

"A hundred miles? How are we going to get up there?"

Bud grinned. "Why by horseback, of course. If we ride hard, we could be there day after tomorrow."

Maretti guffawed. "He's doing it again. Pulled that same one on me."

Bud grinned and glanced at Amanda. Her eyebrows were raised in speculation, so he nodded and said, "Okay. This is how I figure it. We gear up, borrow or rent a helicopter from the Forest

Service. Should take us about forty-five minutes. We set up a command post at Fort Rock and go hunting for our hay truck."

"We have to let Homeland Security know about this," Agent Warren said.

Amanda sounded slightly irritated. "And tell them what? That we're looking for a truckload of hay?"

Stubbornly, Toby stuck to his point. "Yes, if that's all we have. It's regulation, Amanda. You know the standing order."

"Yeah," she shot back. "And I know that crying wolf isn't on the agenda. When we have something solid, we'll call it in. And if I'm wrong, we'll all swear that you told us so...and your skinny butt is covered. Right, guys?"

"Not me," Maretti laughed. "I'll swear it was Mr. Warren's idea."

Bud grinned. "What do you think, Howard? Is he in, or should we leave him home?"

"What do you mean, 'leave me home'!" Toby exclaimed.

"Good idea, Bud," Howard offered. "That way he can always say he had nothing to do with any of this. Of course, if you bag some big boys, he wouldn't get any credit either."

Amanda turned and gave Agent Warren a steely look. "I told you. Don't underestimate these guys. But they have a point. Either you wait until we have something solid to report, or go ahead and report in, and I leave you here. And what's more, I'll report that you didn't back the Agent-in-Charge."

It was quiet for a few long second, and then Howard's basso voice was heard. "Were you ever an attorney, Agent Spears?"

They all chuckled, and even Toby Warren had to smile.

Maretti laid his large thick hand on Warren's sleeve. "How long you been in law enforcement, my friend?"

"Three years."

"Masters degree?"

"Yes. I graduated from Columbia three years ago."

Maretti leaned forward and looked at Howard. "Kind of a priggish sort, don't you think?"

Howard just shook his head. "Maretti, I've known you for slightly over an hour, and it's been an hour of delightful surprises. Priggish?"

"What? You think I'm just an ignorant wop? I'll have you know I graduated from the University of Washington with a degree in criminology and minors in music and art. Even read a book or two. Besides, priggish also fits my partner, Grandfield."

Maretti, looked back at the really uncomfortable Toby Warren. "Well, my friend, experience teaches there are times when the book doesn't fit everything. Life's too complex to write it all down. So you learn to practice benign neglect and develop a selective memory. But most of all you learn that loyalty to your partner is paramount, rules be damned. Or careers for that matter."

Agent Warren just stared at him, uneasy at the thought that he had just failed some kind of test without even knowing he was being tested. He didn't like it much.

Amanda nodded without saying anything, and Bud moved Maretti up a notch on his approval scale.

As they pulled into the tree-lined streets of the little town, Amanda was charmed by a covey of quail skittering across a side street. "Look at that," she pointed.

Bud said, "Those are the neighborhood pets. Everybody puts seed out for them, so they just hang around."

The main street turned ninety degrees to the south past the emergency services building and through the downtown area with an array of full-service grocery stores—two of them—the tire center, a café, the *Lake County News* building and City Hall. Bud turned left at the county library and county courthouse sitting on a large city block surrounded by ancient cottonwoods.

He pulled the pickup into the back street parking reserved for the Lake County sheriff and sheriff's deputies.

"Well, here we are," he said.

Chapter 27

GAR SUDDENLY DIDN'T like the open country around him. His plan to take Crazy quietly in the night, either with a silenced .22 bullet in the ear, or bound and gagged—Crazy's choice—had turned into something else. If it had been a simple matter of running drugs, Gar figured that could be taken care of by local law enforcement later. He counted on Crazy to panic, to make his usual bull-headed frontal assault when he found the marker—to come hunting his old friend, Stone Fly.

What he hadn't counted on was an operation that appeared to be centered around smuggling people, Arab-looking people, into the country. That changed the game. That was treason. Crazy had to know there wouldn't be a trial for this betrayal.

So what would Crazy do now, he pondered. Run? Head for another country? Assume a new identity? Surely he had a backup plan.

He watched through the scope, studying the men changing the truck's tire. The big frame of Cowboy was easy to identify. He was clearly in a hurry, and he muscled the big, heavy wheel and tire around the front of the truck while a dark-faced man worked to get a big jack under the front axle. Gar wondered if they had more than one spare, and then decided to see. He had a still, unmoving target this time, and a better idea about bullet drop. His first shot at a rear tire clanged off the center hub, and he flipped the selector switch on the Armalite. He triggered a quick three-round burst that shredded a rear tire. Both Cowboy and the unidentified man disappeared around to the blind side of the truck.

The sound of an all-terrain vehicle, a four-wheeler commonly called a quad, refocused his attention. He looked through the spotting scope as three black quads, one carrying an extra passenger roared around the corner of a loafing shed and across Cowboy's barn lot. They idled at the fence between Gar and the barnyard while the passenger jumped down and opened the gate. The engines growled and roared back to life and the quads were through the gate and bouncing through the sagebrush and rocks, leaving columns of dust in the morning air.

While Gar watched, the driver of one black quad steered wide to Gar's right, the second one swung wide to his left, and the one carrying an extra passenger came straight up the middle, slowly, cautiously. He took one last look at the truck and could see Cowboy working to change the first flat.

He made no effort to hide any longer. He rose to his knees, put the spotting scope in his pack, slipped an arm through the sling on the Armalite and started walking across the broken, rocky, sage-covered ground. He had covered about fifty yards before one of the riders spotted him. He looked back at the center quad as the driver stopped and the passenger jumped off and knelt down, a rifle at his shoulder. Gar heard the zip of bullets through the sagebrush before he heard the pop-pop-pop of the rifle. He identified the sound of AK-47 fire, a sound he knew well from a tour in Afghanistan.

He began a steady jog, and when the ground dropped into a shallow ravine, he was temporarily out of sight. He turned left and ran hard toward the massive Fort Rock cliffs about a mile south, intending to close with the hunter on his left. *Better one than four.*

Chapter 28

KAREN HIGHSMITH LOOKED over the top of the booking counter as they all trooped into the reception area of the Lake Country Sheriff's office. She nodded at the closed conference room door and announced, "You have a visitor."

"What?"

"You have a visitor...from Portland."

"Judas! Not now! Who is it?"

At the sound of Bud's voice, the door to the conference room opened and BB stood there, a big grin on his face. "Hey, Honk... ah, Bud."

"BB, you old hound, this is bad timing, but I'm glad to see you anyway." Bud started to hold out his hand, but burly Dell BB brushed it aside and gave him a bear hug, pounding on his back.

"Looks like I got here in time to save your white ass from the bad guys...again."

Howard looked uncomfortable. Michelle, who had followed BB out of the conference room, just grinned, and Maretti and the two special agents hung back and waited to be introduced. Ron Grandfield poked his head around the corner. Michelle and Grandfield had stayed in the office to work up the details of their homicide cases for separate reports.

Bud motioned them all into the small conference room. "Okay, everybody. We don't have a lot of time. This is my old partner Dell BB from Portland. Introduce yourselves while I make a call."

He darted into his private office and hit the speed dial.

Nancy answered, "Emergency Services."

"I need a helicopter ASAP for a flight to Fort Rock, one big enough for three people and some gear."

"Slow down, Bud. I'll need each person's weight and the weight of the gear."

"I'd have to guess. I weigh one eighty-five, Agent Spears probably weighs one twenty-five, Maretti weighs one fifty-five or so, and the gear…to be safe say a hundred pounds."

He caught a hint of perfume and Amanda Spears whispered in his ear, "One twenty."

Startled, and a tad miffed, he said, "What?"

"I weigh one twenty."

Bud just shook his head and waited for Nancy to finish her call to the Interagency Dispatch Center, which handled dispatch services for the BLM, USDA Forest Service and Oregon Department of Forestry.

Nancy came back on the line. "They have a Bell available, but they are very, very reluctant to let us have it. There is a prediction for severe thunderstorms and lightning tonight."

Bud didn't react. "How about something from Kingsley Air Base?"

Nancy said, "I'll contact them."

Bud flipped the phone shut, stuffed it in his shirt pocket and stared at the big map on the back wall of his office. "Agent Spears, come look at this." He pointed to Lakeview on the map. "Air miles to Fort Rock…say 80…85….speed 120 knots…45 minutes or so… to here." He pointed to Fort Rock. "We need to get up there now."

Amanda nodded, took out her cell phone and hit the speed dial. When the call was answered all she said was, "Is he available?"

***

Roger and Larae, followed closely by Sonny, in both vehicles lit by pulsating emergency warning lights, turned off Highway 31 onto the Fort Rock-Christmas Valley Highway. Roger accelerated as quickly as he could, the diesel engine running hard against the red line. Off to the northeast, the tall U-shaped lava spine of Fort Rock dominated the rolling landscape.

Larae's cell phone vibrated and she answered, "Officer Holcomb."

Bud's voice growled, "Where are you guys?"

"About three miles from the Fort Rock Store, doing about ninety."

Roger glanced at her and then returned to driving. The heavy pickup felt a bit light as they topped a rolling rise in the road and then settled back on its suspension.

"Good! I'll be there in about forty-five minutes. I'm in a helicopter. Meet us at the little airstrip right by the Fort Rock store. Henry and some support people are driving up. ETA an hour and a half from now. We'll set up a command center."

Nancy Sixkiller's voice came on the radio. "All units, all units switching to TAC channel now. All units, switching to TAC channel now. Confirm."

Roger flipped a toggle switch on the dash in time to hear "County One." Sonny responded with "County Two," and Larae keyed the mike on their mobile unit. "County Three and County Four on TAC."

Roger braked hard and slowed to a crawl past the Fort Rock store. Sonny had to pull hard to his left to avoid rear-ending Roger's pickup. They both turned left onto the Fort Rock Road. A small Cessna airplane roared north overhead, not a hundred feet off the deck. Roger pointed back and said, "There's a small dirt runway just beyond the store. Parallels the little road. That's where we'll meet Bud."

A transmission cracked the speaker, and Trooper Prince was saying, "I have two troopers sweeping the China Hat Road from the north. And I'm gonna write two tickets when I catch you boys."

Sonny and Roger both looked back in time to see a dark brown state police patrol car, lights flashing, turn with them.

Deschutes County Sheriff Cal Redmond broke in. "Who's in charge of this ruckus?"

The roar and rattle of the helicopter nearly overrode Bud's voice, but they made out the name "Sixkiller."

Redmond said, "Affirmative. Sixkiller? You on the air?"

"Read you loud and clear," Sonny said.

"Okay. I've got the east summit of the Paulina caldera blocked. The old Fort Rock Road is blocked, and I have a deputy headed into that area from Cabin Pond. Maybe we can put a cork in this bottle."

"Good! What's your location?"

Redmond laughed and answered, "Why, I'm headed your way up 31. Don't want to miss the fun."

Bud's voice broke in, as hard to understand as before, but they could make out his plan to set up a command center at the airstrip behind the Fort Rock store.

"I'll be there," Redmond responded.

The TAC channel came to life again. "This is Control. All units, all units, we are being flooded by 911 calls about automatic gunfire in the vicinity just north of the Rock. Proceed with caution."

Sonny's vehicle accelerated and passed Roger. The turn signal came on, and Sonny slid his pickup to a stop.

Roger lowered his window as Sonny came loping back, and Trooper Charles K. Prince unfolded from behind the wheel of his patrol car and straightened all six-feet-six inches of his lean frame.

"Well, here we are again," he said as he approached Roger's vehicle.

"Charlie," Sonny said, and pointed at Larae, "That's Deputy Holcomb, Larae."

"You all hear the radio?"

They all nodded.

"Let's gear up. Get on your body armor. Roger, we'll need your .308. I've got my AR-15 and some flash bangs. What are you carrying, Trooper Prince?"

"I've got my shotgun with slugs up front and buckshot behind."

"That's not much firepower for open country. Larae?"

She shrugged. "My .40 Glock. Plus three clips, and my backup."

Sonny shook his head. "We'll have to make do. I have the lead. Roger will cover me, just like last time. Prince and Holcomb will back us up. Tune your portables to the TAC channel. Anything else?"

Roger said, "We need someone on the radio in case the proverbial substance hits the fan. How about Larae?"

"No," she said. "You don't even know what Gar looks like. I'm going."

Chapter 29

THE QUAD RIDER between Gar and the big ridge of Fort Rock made three mistakes: He was stopped, he was right at the end of the ravine where the sagebrush was the tallest, and he was looking the wrong way when Gar came boiling up out of the small wash. The rider barely had to time to look in Gar's direction before Gar knocked him out of the seat with a hard swing of the rifle butt. The man was out of the fight…unconscious…jaw dislocated…maybe broken. Gar really didn't care.

Gar rolled the unconscious man over on his stomach so he wouldn't drown in his own blood, took two plastic quick ties from a belt pouch, locked the man's hands behind his back, and bound the man's ankles.

He flipped his cell phone open, found the sheriff's number and hit Send. Bud answered on the second ring, the sound of a helicopter in the background, a sound very familiar to Gar.

"Sheriff, I'm in a little firefight about two clicks north of Fort Rock…not the store…the rock. You'll find one of the bad guys tied up and waiting for you."

"Firefight? We've had reports of automatic rifle fire. That you?"

"Gotta go, Sheriff, but don't forget to pick this guy up. There's plenty of room for a helicopter. I'm putting down a panel to help you locate this guy."

A female voice came on the line. "John? John? You stay right where you are. I'm ordering you to come in."

The sound of an aircraft penetrated the echo of the idling engine of the quad. Gar spotted a slow-flying aircraft barely fifty feet off the ground, headed right towards him. He said, "Buy me a drink when this is over. You know where."

He picked up the unconscious man's AK-47, checked the magazine and slammed the bolt on a live round.

***

On his first pass, Crazy came in just barely above the stall speed of the little airplane. Gar could see him grinning, and Charlie waved as the plane drifted by. The engine rpms picked up as Charlie made a gradual turn and then headed straight back at Gar. This time the passenger side was visible, only there was no door, just a man holding a rifle. Gar crouched behind what little cover the quad could give him and sighted on the nose of the plane, tracking it, waiting to see what Charlie intended. As the plane approached, the gunner in the door began popping off short bursts, but he wasn't shooting at Gar. He was trying to kill the man on the ground.

"You bastards," Gar shouted and held the trigger down, emptied a full clip as the plane simply flew into the string of slugs pouring from the rifle. The engine coughed and the shooter's rifle fell, turning slowly before hammering the ground a hundred yards beyond Gar.

He checked his prisoner, knowing without knowing why the man still lived. "They sure don't want you talking, my friend."

He took a short couple of minutes to search the man's pockets. *Nada.* No identification at all.

He glanced back across the sage and rabbit brush carpet at the other two quads. They had turned in his direction and were coming on as fast as the terrain would allow. He watched one quad bounce off a rock and nearly tip over. The violence was enough to dislodge the passenger who hit the ground running, stumbling, arms flailing for balance and smashing into an innocent rock the size of a small car. The driver was so focused on controlling the bouncing quad that for a full twenty seconds he failed to notice his passenger was missing. He finally stopped the quad and yelled back at the fallen man. When the man didn't stir, the driver shrugged, gunned the engine and continued racing toward Gar.

Gar glanced back toward the sound of the airplane's coughing engine and saw that Crazy was on a dead stick approach to Cowboy's alfalfa field where the big circle system was still running, slowly turning to irrigate the hopeful sprouts of young alfalfa.

He turned back toward the quads, tracking them by the dust clouds that floated behind each of them. With sudden inspiration, he stowed his pack in the rack behind the seat, and then picked up the dusty, battered cowboy hat worn by his prisoner. He slapped the hat on, hefted the AK-47, and shouted at the riders, pointing the rifle west. The pursuing quads slowed—the riders waving back at him—and turned to the west again. He straddled the seat, twisted the throttle and drove west towards the rim rocks and the pine forest.

As the police vehicles topped a rise in the road, they were about three hundred yards from a truck-tractor attached to a semi-trailer load of hay. The truck blocked the road.

Sonny pulled his pickup to a stop, picked up his 10X binoculars and stepped out of his rig. The binoculars brought three men into sharp focus. They were obviously changing a front tire. It was equally obvious they had robbed a rear tire from a set of duallys for a spare.

Larae's voice startled him. "The big guy looks like Cowboy." She studied the men for a few seconds without taking her binoculars from her eyes. "Wow! The other two look Mid-Eastern. What the hell is going on?"

Roger had sidled up beside the two. "Let's go find out."

"Affirmative," Trooper Prince stated.

Sonny dropped his binoculars and looked hard at each of them. "I don't like the looks of this. Roger, go left. I'll take flanking action from the right. Charlie, you've got the longest legs. Think you can circle around and get behind these guys?"

Charlie nodded. "Yep, I can do that."

The sound of a coughing, sputtering airplane engine caught their attention. They all turned to watch a small blue and white Cessna smack into Cowboy's hay field, the nose marking a groove in the ground as the tail rose in the air and then settled back down.

"Wow!" Sonny said. "He's lucky he didn't flip it. Larae, take Roger's pickup and check that out."

She ran back to Roger's pickup, fired up the diesel engine and executed a gravel throwing U-turn.

Sonny reached for his mike. "Control, County Two."

The response was instantaneous. "Control. Go ahead."

"We've located the hay truck on the old Fort Rock Road about two-and-a-half miles north of the Fort Rock Junction store. Proceeding to investigate. And we just saw a plane crash. Location is a hay field just south of a big hay barn. Officer Holcomb is headed to the site and will report in."

"Are there any injuries?"

"Unknown."

Trooper Prince had been watching the hay truck through binoculars. He nudged Sonny. "They spotted us."

"County Two, clear."

"Control, clear."

Sonny said, "Let's go get 'em."

"Use your binoculars, you guys," Trooper Prince said. "You see what I see?"

Roger exploded. "Shit! There's another guy. And he's handing out rifles."

Sonny's voice rose an octave. "Looks like they mean to fight! I'm calling this in!"

Roger continued to scope the men. They formed a loose skirmish line, one on each side of the road, and one under the truck behind a back set of duals.

"Hey, look at that, where the road rises beyond the truck." Roger said.

His partners raised their binoculars. "Yeah, I see him. Running like the hounds of hell were on his tail," Sonny said as he reached for his mike. "Control, County Two."

"Control. Go ahead."

"One of our suspects is headed north up the Fort Rock Road. I suggest we ask Deschutes County and State Highway to move their officers in to cut him off. He's on foot, and we think he's called Cowboy."

The sound of automatic rifle fire from the direction of the hay truck caused him to pause.

Roger and Charlie were still watching Cowboy running heavily up the road. Bullets kicked up dust in the road, around him, behind him and ahead of him. "Damn," Roger said. "They're trying to kill him."

"We need him alive, I think. Let's give him some help." Roger chambered a round in the semi-automatic .308, knelt down, and started firing in the direction of the hay truck as fast as he could pull the trigger. At three hundred yards there was only a slim chance of hitting the shooters, but the diversion seemed to work. The gunmen stopped firing at Cowboy and started shooting at the officers. Cowboy was still running when he crested the rise and dropped out of sight.

Trooper Prince ejected his empty clip and rammed a fresh one home. "I think he made it. And I scared the one on the left," he growled.

"Didn't even hear you shooting," Roger said breathing heavily as the adrenalin worked it way through his system.

"Focus, that's what it's called. Focus." Prince took a deep breath, his hands shaking slightly. "You know what? That's the first time I've ever fired my weapon at anyone. Scary shit is what it is."

"Know what you mean."

The radio squawked. "County Two. Control. You still there?"

A bullet punched a hole through Sonny's windshield and shattered the back window. Another slammed into the engine block.

"Cover!" Sonny shouted.

They ducked behind Sonny's pickup.

The radio came on again. Nancy's voice sounded urgent and concerned. "Control to Two."

Sonny keyed his lapel mike, praying he could pick up a tower to relay the weaker signal. "Control, this is Two. How do you read?"

All he got back was a whisper of static.

"Control, this is Two. I can't read you."

Larae's voice came over the radio. "County Two. This is Five. I can relay."

"Five, we are taking fire."

"I'll relay that. I'm at the crash site. There's the body of man in the airplane. He appears to have been shot. And there is a faint blood trail leading from the plane, but it disappears where the irrigation system has watered. Do you want me to investigate?"

"Negative. I want you back here. Be careful coming up the road. The bad guys are shooting at us. Hold your rig below the brow of the hill and sit tight. I need you for communication."

She didn't answer for a full ten seconds and then said, "Affirmative. Five out."

"Two, out."

A bullet kicked gravel between Roger's feet and he said, "We've got to find better cover. See that rock pile to our right? I'm going to lay down some cover fire, and when you get in place, return the favor." He dropped to the gravel behind the right rear tire, nodded at Sonny and said, "Go!" He fired a three-round burst, aiming at the shooter behind the rear tires.

In the time it took Roger to empty his clip, Sonny and Trooper Prince had scuttled through the low sage and flopped behind the rock pile. Roger popped the empty clip and rammed a fresh clip in place. He worked the bolt, rolled behind the wheel of the pickup and gave Sonny a thumbs up. Sonny and Prince began a slow steady fire, but instead of going to the rock pile Roger ran left and out into the sagebrush. "We need flanking!" he shouted as he ran.

***

Gar kept an eye on the two quads on his right. "Keep coming, boys. Keep coming."

He stopped, got off and walked away from the quad. He aimed at nothing in particular and fired two quick rounds at the desert in front him.

The driver on the first quad to Gar's right, stopped the quad, stood up on the floorboards, and let fly at the sagebrush with a full clip.

The landing wasn't Crazy's best. Even though he had enough sense not to stand on the brakes, the plane nearly flipped. And when the prop cut big divots in the alfalfa field and the nose ploughed a lone furrow, the sudden deceleration mashed his nose hard against the wheel—hard enough to crush most of the cartilage. It hurt like hell and bled worse than that.

He fished a handkerchief out of his hip pocket to staunch the flow, unbuckled, and walked around the plane to see about his passenger.

"Damn you," he said to the dead man. "You not only can't shoot for shit, you lost the rifle." And then he punched the hanging head with his fist.

"And now you broke my knuckle, you idiot." He settled for spitting on the dead man, and then headed across the field to Cowboy's ranch house. "I hope that son-of-a-bitch left me a rifle. I have some unfinished business with Stone Fly, that uppity shit."

He shook his head when he tried the handle on the front door. In spite of all the excitement, Cowboy had locked the door. Crazy kicked the door open and walked quickly across the living room. *What a mess*, he thought, as he strode to Cowboy's office. The filing cabinets were empty, but the computer was still running. His first impulse was to destroy it, but then he shrugged.

"The game's up, Crazy me boy. The game's up. Never knew what I was getting into, just that the pay was good." He sighed, turned around and headed for Cowboy's gun room. The only useful weapon was a scope mounted .30-06 semi-automatic hunting rifle with two empty four-round clips.

He was shoving rounds into the clips when he heard a helicopter. The sound got louder, and he looked out a south window. The Bell slowed and then turned west. He slipped out the door, ran across the barnyard to the cover of a loafing shed and watched as the helicopter hovered and then set down about three-quarters of a mile out in the sagebrush and runty junipers. Beyond the helicopter he thought he could see three dust plumes, but it was too far to be sure.

He muttered aloud as he shoved a final round in the second clip. "So the boys are still chasing the great Stone Fly? It doesn't seem likely. He could eat breakfast while he took those idiots and never put his fork down. He's not leaving until I get there. How you gonna mark it, John? How am I gonna find you?"

He shrugged it off. The trail bike in the loafing shed held a full tank of gas and a rifle scabbard. Crazy's field pack was strapped to the back rail, along with his night vision binoculars, water bottle, power bars, first aid kit, compass, GPS, radio, ground sheet, an ugly k-bar knife, a flask of opium-laced cognac, and a change of civilian clothing. In the back of his mind, he had always known Cowboy was too arrogant and too careless to operate for long without causing suspicion. His backup plan was simple: ride across the desert to the first Forest Service road, work his way north back to the Fort Rock Road, and follow it until he got within a few miles of Bend. Don his new clothes and hitch or walk to town. Nothing to it.

He checked a side pocket to make sure the papers for his new identity were still there. Satisfied, he put them back and zipped the pocket shut. Then he pulled a wad of bills from the other side pocket, nearly $20,000 in twenties, fifties, and hundreds. With the gold coins in his money belt, he figured he could make a clean start…maybe go to Canada, put his medical corpsman skills to work as an EMT or something.

The helicopter's motor took on a deeper growl, and the wop-wop-wop of the rotary blades grew louder.

The helicopter flew almost directly over the ranch house and then headed south towards Fort Rock. Crazy peeked around the end of the loafing shed. He couldn't see the ship.

He pushed the bike directly away from the shed, straight west, making hard going of it through the sand, sagebrush and rocks. It wasn't until he was more than a half mile from the ranch that he started the engine of the trail bike and mounted the seat. His route took him past the landing site of the helicopter, and he took enough time to piece the story together even though the silk panel anchored to the ground told him all he needed to know. It was easy enough to see how his old friend, John, aka Stone Fly, overpowered someone, marked the spot with a white panel, and then mounted up and drove the quad west through the desert.

He had to admire his old friend's work, and he shook his head and said, "Got yourself another prisoner, didn't you, John. You always were big on prisoners. Kept telling the team that dead men told no tales, but live ones had lots of stories to tell.

"Damn, I miss that life, and you took it from me, John. You took it from me." Bitterness gave him a selective memory, one that dismissed the fact that Sergeant John Bernard had covered for him, had excused him and counseled him, and then had finally reported him as "a danger to the team, a reckless loner prone to anger."

Crazy shook his head, snugged his cap down and followed the quad's tire tracks across the desert and toward the waiting rim rock and pine forest.

***

Bud could clearly hear Larae's report about the plane, the body and the blood trail. He keyed his mike and called Emergency Services. Nancy's voice came over the radio." Control. Go ahead."

"Control, we have a report of a body in an airplane about a mile or so north of the Fort Rock store. We need to get Doc Loeffler up here."

"Confirming…County Coroner Doc Loeffler to Fort Rock."

"Affirmative. County One, clear.

Bud lost the argument that he should support his officers first, and then pick up Gar's prisoner. Agent Spears hammered at him through the intercom earphones that his officers were more than holding their own. The bad guys were staying put, and the prisoner might give them information that would save lives. Maretti stayed quiet. Experience had taught him that there was more than one right answer…as long as no one got hurt.

When Bud saw from the air the short distance between his officers and the white panel marking the prisoner, he relented. "But it has to be fast."

Maretti was out of the helicopter before it had truly settled on its skids. He rolled the man over, felt for a pulse and nodded to Bud that the man was still alive. Bud got a grip under the man's armpits while Maretti lifted his legs. Bud helped place the man on the floorboard behind the pilot's seat. It was cramped for Maretti and Spears, but they managed to buckle up without stepping on their new passenger.

Amanda thought she might throw up when she looked at the bloody face. But then, she decided, she had felt like throwing up ever since the helicopter had lifted off in Lakeview. It surprised her. She was a seasoned air traveler, but she had never had a bumpy ride like that one. Thermals had buffeted the ship every mile of the way, and the pilot, a veteran of Desert Storm, had turned to send a look of apology at her.

***

Roger ran, slid and crawled through the low scrub as searching fire tumbled tufts of sage and shattered rocks behind him. He borrowed shelter from an old, twisted juniper and planned his next move.

He heard slow, aimed fire from Sonny's rifle, and keyed his mike. "Sonny, I need you to keep the bandit on the left side of the truck busy for about five or six seconds."

"Can't see 'em from here. I'm moving."

Roger looked back and saw Sonny scoot from the rock pile to get back behind the County's pickup. A burst of automatic rifle fire chased Sonny across the open ground and slammed into the pickup. Sonny flopped behind the rear tire and began shooting left-handed, the selector switch on the AR-15 on full automatic.

Roger rolled from behind the tree and crabbed towards the low ridge, counting...one one-thousand...two one-thousand... three one-thousand...four...and then dove to drop behind the protection of the ridge as bullets peppered him with sand and rock from strikes on the ground above him.

"I'm good," he said into his mike.

He heard pistol fire, assumed Charlie Prince was covering Sonny, and crawled north along the back side of the little ridge.

His earpiece crackled and he heard Sonny saying, "You got a shooter headed your way."

Roger crawled to the top of the ridge in time to see one of the men from the truck running directly toward him. He triggered two quick rounds and saw the man drop.

"Sonny," he said into his mike. "Can you see him?"

"No. You either hit him or he went to ground. I can't spot him. How you fixed for ammunition?"

"Runnin' low. Never planned for an extended fire fight."

"Let's just sit tight and see what they do."

"Okay, but keep your eye on the spot where he went down."

"I see a boot," Trooper Prince said, looking through binoculars. "Need a better angle." As he rose from behind the rock pile to get a better sight angle, the gunner under the trailer fired a short burst, and Prince sat back down heavily. "Damn, I think I'm shot."

"Where you hit?"

Prince touched his stomach. "Right here," and rolled over and vomited.

Sonny patted his back. "Got lucky, Trooper. Hit you right in the breadbasket."

Charlie rolled over. "Lucky??"

"Yeah. Right in your body armor. Here's the slug." Sonny dug a flattened bullet out of Charlie's vest.

"Wow! Really hit me hard."

"Just sit still for a minute."

Sonny turned back to the shooters. "I think I see what you were looking at." He keyed his mike. "Roger, we see a boot about seventy-five yards ahead between you and the truck. I'm going to dust that spot. When I do, you raise up and see what he does."

Roger clicked the mike twice to acknowledge.

Prince heard Sonny talking quietly to himself. "Range say two fifty, nine-inch drop…right there…and squeeze…" The round zipped through the sage concealing the man's body. The boot twitched, but never moved again.

"He's done, Roger."

With a double click on the mike, Roger was up and running behind the final fifty yards of the little ridge.

As the Bell rose into the air, Bud's radio came alive. "Redmond on TAC. County One, can you read me?"

"This is County One. Go ahead."

"I'm five minutes from the Fort Rock store."

"Hold there. We're en route. Rendezvous at the airstrip behind the store. We have a prisoner for you. Can you get some medical help rolling this way?"

"Copy. We'll roll an ambulance ASAP."

"Thanks, Cal. County One clear."

Bud heard a *"de nada,"* but that was all.

Bud fingered the call button on the intercom. "Take us back to the Fort Rock store. We'll land in the airstrip behind the store."

The pilot nodded and turned the helicopter south. As the ship turned, Bud spotted what looked like the body of a man in the sagebrush. He keyed the call button again and pointed north. "I spotted something just north of where we set down. I want a look."

Amanda swallowed hard to keep from upchucking, wanting to be on the ground again, for good. "What are we looking for?"

"I think I spotted a body. Won't take long."

A quick circle took them over the fallen man. The pilot said. "There he is. Do you want to set down?"

Bud shook his head and pointed south. "We'll come back. He looks dead. If he is, he won't be going anywhere."

Redmond's Deschutes County Sheriff's vehicle, a 4x4 Chevy Suburban, was stopped at the gate to the airstrip behind the little Fort Rock store. Cal Redmond was pulling the barbed wire gate back.

The Bell settled and the pilot shut the engine down. They waited for the spinning rotors to slow and then hopped out. Cal pulled his rig through the gate and then trotted over to the ship, ducking the still slowly turning blades—even though he knew they were several feet above his head.

Two people from the house behind the store came out back and watched, fascinated by the hubbub. The only time helicopters landed at the little strip was when they had a grass fire or a forest fire going.

The man nudged his wife. "Wonder what's going on. Suppose we'll get some business out of this?"

The pilot, Bud, Maretti, and Sheriff Redmond eased the wounded prisoner out of the helicopter and onto a stretcher.

Only then did Bud stretch out his hand. "Cal, my thanks. What do you have coming our way?"

"I've got Air Life inbound. ETA twenty minutes. I've got two deputies headed down the Fort Rock Road…looking for a big man allegedly named Cowboy? And I've got a deputy I pulled back from that country around Hole in Ground. He'll be here in the next fifteen or twenty minutes."

"I need to get some help to my deputies. Can you put a guard with this guy? Someone who can stay with him at the hospital."

Amanda spoke up. "I'll do that. He's mine."

Bud looked pensive and irritated all at the same time. "Agent Spears," he said tiredly, "we don't know yet that he's done anything criminal. No…he's mine until you can tie him to a Federal crime. But I'm alright with you keeping an eye on him."

Maretti grinned at Bud, and pointed at the ship. "Let's go join the party."

Larae startled Sonny as she slid behind the rock pile, breathing hard. "What are you doing here," he asked.

"Thought you could use some help." She pointed at Charlie Prince. "You look like shit. Are you hit? I saw you go down."

He shook his head, face pale and shiny with sweat. "Took a round in my vest."

"Where?"

"Stomach."

"We need to get him out of here, Sonny. He may have internal injuries."

Another burst of gunfire stung the protecting rocks. "How do you propose to do that?" Sonny asked.

"We shoot the bad guys and drive away." With that she took off at a dead run out through the sagebrush on a diagonal line northeast, away from the rock pile. Not a shot was fired in her direction.

"Shit. She's gonna get hurt," Sonny said.

The shooting had stopped, and Roger could hear what sounded like an argument. He cautiously got to his knees and looked out over the sagebrush. His sneak-and-peek had shortened the three hundred yards to less than one hundred, enough to give him a partial view of the front of the truck. He could see one man bent over and shouting back under the truck. The rear shooter had abandoned his place behind the tires and was crawling under the truck toward his partner.

He keyed his mike. "Can you guys hear that?"

Larae answered first. "They're arguing. But I can't figure out what they're saying."

"Larae, where are you? I thought you were back with the rigs."

"I'm about a hundred and fifty yards east of the truck. I can see somebody in front and another man crawling back under the truck." She paused and then added, "Prince is hurt, so I thought you could use some help. Use a little 'divide-and-conquer' on those assholes. So…what language are they speaking?"

Roger listened for a minute and shook his head. "I don't know. My Farsi is pretty much limited to "yes," "no," and "surrender," but I'd swear that's what they're speaking."

Sonny broke in. "You sure, Roger?"

"Pretty sure."

The arguing stopped, and a man's voice called out. "American! American! We surrender. Don't shoot. We surrender."

Roger hollered, "Come on out where I can see you. Put your hands in the air."

"Okay. No guns."

The two men, both dressed in blue jeans, cowboy boots and denim shirts came slowly around from in front of the truck, hands in the air.

"Move to the rear of the truck," Roger ordered. He stood upright and started walking towards the truck. Sonny watched through his binoculars, and then keyed his mike. "Roger, stop. Don't go any closer. Look around and find some cover…quietly… now. You too, Larae. I don't want to scare you, but the bigger one has a detonator in his hand."

Roger started easing back towards the little ridge, saying to the two men, "That's it. Just keep walking. I want you at the back of the truck." Larae found a shallow wash and looked back at Sonny. "Good, Larae. Get down…flat…now!"

The men on the west side of the truck didn't see her take cover, so they just kept walking slowly back alongside the truck, the bigger one saying, "Don't shoot. We surrender. No guns." They stopped walking, and the little one, tears streaming down his cheeks dropped to the ground and put his arms over his head.

"Now, Roger, now!" Sonny screamed into the mike.

Roger took three quick steps and dove over the little ridge to ground as the world erupted in a towering sheet of flame and a thunderous concussion heard for miles.

The group at the little airstrip just gaped at the sound of the bomb and watched in disbelief as a huge column of dust and steam rose higher and higher, forming a chilling mushroom cloud.

Bud was the first to react. "Get me up there," he shouted at the pilot and jumped in the passenger seat. Maretti climbed in the back, and Redmond headed for his Suburban, yelling at Amanda to "take care of things here."

Amanda was too shocked to even reply. She just stood still and watched as the Suburban, lights flashing and siren howling, spun through the gate and out of sight beyond the store.

The helicopter took a little more time to get airborne, but as soon as the rotor speed built up, the pilot started a take-off taxi down the little dirt strip, and when all systems were in the green he lifted off and headed directly for the boiling cloud two miles north.

Chapter 30

GAR STOPPED THE quad when he reached the fringes of the pine timber. He stayed deliberately in sight, and dismounted to squat on his heels like he was studying the ground. Then he raised up and waved the two riders his way. They waved back, and started toward him. He watched until he was sure they would come on, then stepped behind a big yellow pine, listening as the engine noise grew louder.

The quads finally stopped and both men killed the switches on the quad. One of them called out, "Sammy? Whatcha got?"

Gar slipped quietly from behind the big tree, the AK-47 held level. They jerked around when he said, "What Sammy's got is a terrible headache right now."

One of the men, a dirty bewhiskered brute of a man with a flattened nose, a scarred cheekbone and cauliflower ears, started to pull his rifle from the boot on the quad.

"Uh-uh. You don't want to do that."

The smaller man put his hand up. "Give it up, Chase. I don't even know what we're doing out here. Sure as shit Cowboy has sold out. We don't even have a boss anymore. Don't have anybody to pay us."

The big man slowly raised his hands, and shook his head. "You might be right, Harley. Ain't nothing here to get killed over." He looked Gar over and said, "Okay, we give…but I'd sure like a crack at you with my fists. Fooled us with that damned hat.

Shit." He spat a wad of tobacco in Gar's direction, and wiped at a fresh cut on his swollen upper lip.

Gar raised his eyebrows. "Another time, maybe. Now you boys climb off those quads...on this side...slowly. And keep your hands in the air."

They complied, Harley complaining to Chase, "I told you we shouldna hooked up with Cowboy. Didn't I tell you? I knew it the minute I saw that Crazy fella."

Gar interrupted. "Now I want you to sit on the ground. Not there. Away from the quads."

"Ah, hell," Harley said. "You gonna shoot us?"

Gar gave them a ghost of a smile. "I'm studying on it, but I think I'd like to hear your story first." He nodded at Chase. "You first, big guy. Did Crazy give you that fat lip?"

"Sucker punched me is all. I'll take him next time. Say... how'd you know his name was Crazy?"

"Old friend of mine. I'd say you were lucky he just gave you a fat lip, you stupid shit. Wonder he didn't kill you. You know what? He did try to kill your old buddy Sammy. Tried to shoot him to keep his mouth shut."

Chase didn't say anything, just glared.

"Now here's my dilemma. If I leave you, Crazy is going to find you, and when he does, he's going to kill you...to keep your mouths shut. You don't want that, do you?"

Harley shook his head.

"That's right, Harley. You want to stay alive, but I need a reason to keep you healthy. So you had better start talking. You got a good story for me? Something I can write down? Something to swear to?"

"Don't say a damned thing, Harley," the big man growled.

"Yeah, but one or the other is gonna kill us." Harley whined. "I'll take my chances with this guy."

"What makes you think he can protect us, Harley? Little runt like that."

"No, no, Chase. Look at 'em. Look at the gear. He's a pro... just like Crazy."

"You didn't buy that Special Forces shit Crazy talked about, did you?"

The smaller man nodded. "Look at what he did to you. Didn't even breathe hard. Just slipped your punches and gave you a six-inch jab, and...boom...you was on your butt. Don't that tell you nuthin'?"

Chase glared at the younger man, but didn't argue.

Harley asked, "What do you want to know?"

**

Gar left them hugging a tree with two quick ties snugged each to a right and left wrist. On his cell phone he had a video recording of them detailing what they knew of Cowboy's operation. And once they started talking, he wasn't sure they were ever going to quit. From what they said, it was obvious that Cowboy had a boss. They didn't have a name, but they were sure it was some slimy lawyer in Bremerton. They both swore they didn't have anything to do with smuggling arms, didn't know nothing about any terrorists, but they were pretty certain Cowboy had a pipeline to smuggle in wetbacks, and sure, they knew he was into drugs, but all they did was provide a little muscle.

Gar asked them why Cowboy needed muscle out in the desert. They admitted things had gotten too warm for them in Tacoma, so Cowboy was giving them a place to stay while things cooled down.

They balked at telling him why they needed to leave Tacoma, but a little prodding with the AK got them to admit they had busted up a cop who was trying to milk a little cream out of the drug cow they had going.

Harley glared at Chase at that point. "Shoulda just paid him, Chase, you dumb bastard."

***

Gar ran Chase and Harley's quads out into the open where they could be easily spotted. With his cell, he keyed in an e-mail address and sent the video into cyber space. Then he dialed Agent Spear's cell number. When she answered he said, "Don't talk. Pull up your e-mail. I think you'll find something very interesting."

He decided the only thing left to do was take Crazy head on. If Crazy survived the plane crash, Gar knew he would follow the quad tracks across the desert. There were two places that offered good ambush sites…if Crazy got careless, of course. "I wonder if he'll think I'm waiting in the timber?" he speculated out loud.

***

He had traveled less than half a mile when he saw the flash and then heard the thunder of an explosion. The mushroom cloud was clearly visible. He couldn't help but wonder who Crazy had killed this time.

Chapter 31

BUD POINTED AND the pilot set the chopper down in the middle of the road, the blades kicking up a cloud of dust and rocks and bits of shredded sagebrush. Bud and Maretti ducked under the still-turning blades and started running up the road towards the blast site. After about fifty yards they were both breathing heavily, and Bud touched Maretti's arm. "We can't help if we're both winded when we get there," Bud panted. Maretti nodded and slowed to a fast walk.

Roger's pickup was untouched, sheltered from the worst of the blast by the rise in the ground. Bud grabbed a first-aid kit from behind the seat and hurried after Maretti who hadn't stopped. Scratches marred the top of Prince's cruiser, and cracks starred the windshield where rocks had pelted the glass. Sonny's pickup had taken the most damage. Hundreds of small glass shards covered the interior. A fist of rock had imbedded itself in the wire cage behind the seat.

Bud spotted Sonny and Prince, both prone, both partially covered with rocks. "My God! Sonny! Sonny!" He and Maretti worked frantically with bare hands to move rocks and scrape the dirt away from the downed officers. Sonny was flat on his back. He groaned and scrubbed at his eyes with a knuckle to get the grit out. Bud grabbed his hand. "Sonny, don't do that. We'll have to wash them. Understand?"

Sonny nodded, put his hand down while Bud frantically searched the first aid kit for a sterile wash. He glanced at Maretti, who was helping Prince sit up.

Maretti said, "Where you hurt?"

Without looking at Maretti, Prince croaked, "What happened?"

Maretti chuckled, "Well at least you can talk. Some assholes tried to blow you up."

Prince's glazed eyes looked past Maretti and out across the desert. "Oh."

Bud found the eyewash and squirted the sterile fluid into Sonny's eyes. Sonny flinched, and Bud said, "Sorry," as he used a compress to gently wipe the dirt away. "That better?"

Sonny nodded, blinked and tried to sit up. Bud pushed him back down.

"That you, Bud?"

"Yeah. Can you see me?"

"It's a little blurry, Bud, but I can see."

Eyes tearing, Bud took Sonny's face in his big hands. "I'm so sorry, Sonny. I should have been here."

"Wouldn't have made any difference, Bud."

"The others? Roger...Larae?"

Sonny made a vague gesture back toward the big crater in the ground. "Out there."

Maretti tapped Bud's shoulder, and pointed to Prince. "That one's in shock, and he may have internal injuries. I can see where he took a slug in the stomach. His vest stopped it, but he took a hell of a punch. And," he pointed to Bud's fingers, "your man is bleeding. Hold the back of his head up."

Sheriff Redmond's Suburban pulled up beside the rock pile. Redmond had put the rig in four-wheel drive and by-passed the line of police vehicles blocking the road. He ran over with a big first-aid kit, took one look at Sonny and opened the kit. Seconds later he had a compression bandage on the wound. Maretti's big hands tore a long strip of tape off a dispenser and gently wrapped it around Sonny's head to hold the compress in place.

Sonny looked at Bud, tears running down his cheeks, but Bud couldn't tell if it was crying or if his eyes were tearing up from the dust and dirt in them. "They were on each side of the truck. Maybe a hundred and fifty yards out. That's where you should look."

Redmond ran to his vehicle. They couldn't hear the words, but they could hear the urgency.

Bud rose, took a deep breath and started walking toward the crater, his heart aching at the thought of what he would find.

Maretti stopped him. "Bud...look over there. To the right." A dirty, blood covered Larae was on hands and knees trying to crawl through the sage brush.

Bud was running, his heart pounding. "Larae! We're coming. Stay where you are."

Marretti started to follow him, and then—his brain working again—went back for the first-aid kit.

When he got to her, Larae was still on her knees, staring at nothing in particular, just staring.

Bud dropped to his knees beside her and wrapped his big arms around her shoulders. "I've got you, darlin', I've got you."

She refocused for a time and croaked, "That you, Bud?"

"Yeah. It's me."

He felt her go slack as Maretti came sliding in beside him. "Oh...hell of a mess. She pass out?"

Bud just shook his head. "I don't know."

Maretti swatted him on the back of the head. "Pull it together, Bud. She don't need no weepies. She needs your help. You can be heart-broken later."

Bud pushed hard on his emotions and gathered himself.

"Lay her down, Bud. Keep her head turned so she can breathe. Check her pulse."

Bud gently lowered her stomach down on the ground, her face sideways, and then grabbed a wrist. It took several agonizing tries, but he found her pulse. "She's alive! Damn, she's alive."

"Knew that. She's still bleeding. Let's get the bleeding stopped."

Bud placed a big hand over the worst wound, a long gash in her right calf, and applied pressure while Maretti tore open a sterile compress. "That's right. Keep the pressure on."

"Looks like she had her head down, pointed in the direction of the blast. The vest protected her right down to her butt. Can't figure out how she got so cut up. Ankle's broken...no doubt about that." He pulled Bud's hand away and slapped a compress on the wound. "Hold that while I get some tape. We'll just bandage the rest. Gotta knife?"

"Yeah."

Maretti wound tape around Larae's leg, sat back on his heels. "Let's have that knife."

Bud fished his Leatherman out of its sheath, opened it up, pulled the knife blade out and snapped the handle back together. "Here."

Maretti slit the back of her trousers, exposing smaller wounds on each leg. "I'll take care of this little gal. Go find your other guy."

They turned at the sound of Redmond's Suburban crawling its way to them.

Bud rose as the vehicle stopped. Redmond pointed at Larae and Bud said, "Looks like she'll live, but we need some medical help...soon."

"Got Air Life from Bend and Klamath Falls on the way. ETA ten minutes for the Bend chopper. ETA for the Klamath ship is twenty-five minutes. Central Oregon Air Life says they can take our prisoner and one more, but no one else, not even a deputy. Bend police will meet them at St. Charles and keep custody of the bad guy. So…who goes to Bend first? Your call."

Bud pointed at Larae. "Her."

"Tough call, isn't it?"

"You have no idea." Bud took a deep breath, looked at his bloody hands and then stared across the crater. "One more to find," he said and started walking across the blast area.

"Stop," Redmond said. "That's a crime scene. The forensic boys will want a clean site when they get here." He pointed at his Suburban. "Why walk when you can ride, right?"

The Suburban growled a wide swing out through the sagebrush, crossed the road beyond the blast site and bounced and jounced to a stop on the far side. Bud heard a shout and looked back to see Sonny standing in front of his shattered pickup.

"What?" Bud shouted, and then remembered the radio. He keyed the mike. "Sonny, what are you saying?"

Bud gave the Almighty his deepest thanks when he heard Sonny come back with, "Walk straight ahead toward that little ridge. He was behind that when the blast went off…I think."

Bud started walking slowly ahead.

Sonny said, "Stop. Come back toward me about thirty yards. He should be right…" Sonny's voice choked.

Bud waved, fighting back his own tears. "Now's not the time, Bud," he said softly to himself.

He spotted a pant leg behind a small sage bush and nearly cried for joy as Roger slowly and painfully rose from a pile of loose, sandy soil, staggering a bit, the barrel of his rifle still clutched in one hand, the butt dragging on the ground. Roger spat dirt and blinked his eyes clean.

He looked bewildered, but when he saw Bud, he took a few staggering steps and then sank to his knees. "Boss, he croaked, "sure good to see you."

Bud ran to him, dropped to his knees and wrapped his arms around his dazed friend. "Thank God, Roger," he whispered as he let the tears go.

Roger pushed him back a bit, looked in Bud's eyes, his own tears still under control. "The others?" he asked softly.

Bud nodded, swallowed hard and finally managed to get his voice to work. "Alive, hurt but alive, although only the good Lord can tell us why."

Roger sagged, and Bud had to prop him up. "I got behind this little hump before the blast when off. It knocked me out, but the shrapnel went over the top of me. I don't think I got a scratch." He took a deep breath. "And I thought I had it rough in Iraq."

Redmond walked down the shallow draw and stopped, pretending not to notice the tears on Bud's cheeks.

"You two okay now?"

Roger pushed himself back to his feet. "Where did you come from, Cal?"

Sonny was hollering and limping as fast as he could in their direction. Roger turned and started a foot-dragging, weary walk to meet his best friend.

For a split second Bud started to say no, to stop them both, and then just hurried to put an arm around Roger to keep him upright, to protect him. *Like I should have before.*

Cal hollered at him. "Not a good idea, Bud. We've got another problem."

Arm in arm, they turned and looked. Cal was pointing out in the sagebrush beyond Larae and Maretti. Smoke was creeping through the low sage, wisps of smoke like writhing snakes puffing up and then floating away to disappear in the air.

Suddenly Bud was angry. "Damn those bastards! Call it in. We've got to get Larae and Maretti out of there. Come on, Roger. Get in the rig." He keyed his mike. "Sonny, there's a fire out beyond Larae. We're going to get her. You get back to the rigs. Roger's shaken up but okay for now," he added.

Redmond and Bud helped Roger to the Suburban and up into the back seat. Bud snapped Roger's seatbelt in place and then took the rifle out of his hand. He popped the clip loose, ejected a live round, and slid the empty rifle across the floorboards under Roger's leg. He jumped into the vehicle. "Go!"

"To hell with it," Cal growled and headed the Suburban directly across the blast site.

He picked up his mike. "Control, this is Redmond on TAC. All personnel alive and accounted for. Medical support en route. The bandits blew themselves into paradise, but the blast started a fire in the sagebrush about two miles north of Fort Rock. There's a bit of southeast wind, and the fire's picking up. We better get some resources on it pronto."

Larae started to make some sense of what was going on. She was propped in the back seat between Roger, who had his arm around her, holding her up, and a grinning Italian with a mop of unruly hair, blood on his hands. "Hey, sleeping beauty. Looks like you're gonna make it."

Groggy, she looked at him. "Who you?"

Chapter 32

GAR SPOTTED THE smoke from the brush fire and thought, "Yep. Just what they need...a fire. Bet the blast started that."

He pulled in behind a low crown of red rock, just waiting for Crazy to show up. He knew Crazy would want to talk. He always wanted to talk—before, during, and after each mission.

Eating a power bar and sipping water, he sat on the seat of the quad, dog tired, and acutely aware of how much the long hike, the short sleep, and the adrenaline-pushed action was eroding his senses. If he could, he would just curl up in the sagebrush and take a nap. *One to go, Dena. One to go. I can't bring you back, but I will have justice.*

His ears picked up the sound of a trail bike as a rider gunned it up a small rise. And then he heard the engine pop-pop-popping, telling him the rider had stopped the bike. He slid off the quad and circled the backside of the rock, belly crawling to the crest of the outcrop for a quick look.

Crazy's trail bike was tilted on its kickstand, idling, with no rider in sight. He caught a glimpse of Crazy circling to his right. *Trying to get a peek behind the rock, he is.*

He triggered a three-round burst, knew he had missed, wondered if he really could kill his old partner. "Dangerous thinking," he said under his breath.

He rolled back below the crest. A split second later a bullet clipped the ground he had just vacated, sending a small, dry-smelling puff of dust drifting in the slight breeze, the heavy report of the .30-06 rolling across the desert. Unbidden, the memory of the fresh, pungent smell of the sage after a rainstorm came to mind…and then was gone in the urgency of the moment.

Crazy yelled out, "John…that you? Talk to me. I don't wanna fight you, boy. I just wanna talk."

Gar didn't answer.

"Did I clip you, boy? Listen…we need to talk. I didn't kill Dena. Pike did that. I took care of him for you. Didn't want to see my old pal Stone Fly goin' to jail for murder. Took care of Scully, too."

Gar kept silent, just waiting and watching the low hillside beyond the quad.

"John? You owe me, boy."

Crazy's voice told Gar that Crazy was still working his way around to get a look behind the rock.

"I know I didn't clip you. I know where my shots go. Saving you, John. Want you man-to-man."

Gar saw a flicker of movement. Not Crazy, he decided, just a small dusty desert sparrow flitting from the top of one sagebrush to another. The sparrow suddenly left, flitting, dodging through the sage. He wondered if Charley had startled the bird.

"You remember that mission in Afghanistan? The one you screwed up? They made you out as some kind of hero…layin' there with all those ragheads hoppin' round. Yeah, you were like stone all right, layin' there crappin' your britches. You remember who came to get you? Your old pal Crazy Charlie. Nobody remembers that. You get a medal, and I get nothing…not even a thank you. All that intel you had was just piss in the wind until I showed up."

Gar shook his head. "Yeah, Crazy," he said to himself. "If you hadn't shot your way into the camp, they would never have known we knew their plans. I had to break cover to help your ass. And MacGregor. Instead of a live MacGregor, we filled a body bag."

He was angry all over again, killing angry. "All right, Crazy," he shouted. "You want me, come on out. No weapons, just fang and claw!"

Crazy laughed, that crazy high pitched cackle that fit his nickname, his "handle."

"That's better! No weapons. Just *mano-a-mano*. You and me."

Crazy rose up out of the sagebrush about fifty yards from Gar, the barrel of his rifle in one hand, butt on the ground. "Put your weapon, down, John. And I'll drop mine."

"This is your party, Crazy. You first."

"Okay." Crazy bent to lower the rifle to the ground. Gar's finger tightened slightly on the trigger of the Armalite until Crazy straightened and held out both hands...empty of weapons.

Gar walked slowly to the quad, his eyes never leaving Crazy, and leaned the rifle against the handlebars. Arms spread, he started walking to meet Crazy.

They met in a small sandy clearing not more than twenty feet in diameter. Crazy stopped at the edge, eyeballing his old friend for the first time in over a year. "You're looking tired, John. Been up late?" And he giggled.

"I saw you find the marker."

"I figured you were there. Why didn't you pop me right then?"

"I have other plans for you."

Crazy snorted. "Won't go that way, boy. But before we open the ball, tell me...how did you find me? I mean, I've been clean. No phone calls, no e-mail...haven't even been to town for a month-and-a-half."

Gar shrugged. "Luck."

"Your bad luck, you mean."

"Crazy, you've always talked too much. I remembered you saying one time when you were drunk that if you ever had to run, you'd go home to Christmas. And it hit me. You didn't say go home *for* Christmas. You said go *to* Christmas. The Internet gave me several places called Christmas, but this was the only place that looked likely. So I spent the last five weeks on recon."

Crazy let his hands fall, sighed and shook his head. "I still don't get it."

"You mush-brained idiot. The only real asshole in the whole area is Cowboy. Where else would you be? I was watching when you rescued Cowboy in all his nudity."

"So you set that whole thing up? Even the rattlesnake?"

"Just got lucky…why'd you kill Dena?"

"Didn't. Pike did that. She got to screaming, so Pike choked her to keep her quiet."

"Won't wash. They found your DNA."

"Ah, hell. I had me some fun with your uppity, snot-nosed sister, but I didn't kill her."

"You're lying. I think you killed Pike and his buddy Cully to cover your ass."

With a snarl, Crazy reached reach behind his back and pulled out a big, black, ugly K-bar knife. "Gonna cut you, John. Slice your traitorous ass in tiny pieces." And he launched himself across the sandy opening. He took two lunging steps before Gar shattered his right knee with one round from a big, black, uglier .45.

The heavy slug knocked Crazy's feet out of from under him. Gar moved in quickly and kicked Charlie in the jaw. *Fight over, Crazy. You still talk too much.*

By the time Crazy started coming to, Gar had him tidied up…shattered knee wrapped tight to stanch the bleeding, a crude splint made from pieces of an old fence post Gar found next to a fence line. Crazy's wrists were snugged tight in a quick tie, and another was looped through that, keeping his hands tight against his belt.

He groaned and blinked his eyes, trying to focus through the pain. Through gritted teeth he muttered, "I thought you said no weapons."

Gar down at him and shook his head. "I lied."

Charlie asked. "What now?"

"Well, I'm going to tie you in that little square rack on the back of the quad and drive you out of here. I called Amanda. She and Special Agent Warren are going to take you in. You'll get appropriate medical attention, and depending on how cooperative you are, maybe life instead of a firing squad." He stopped, and then added, "Or I suppose you could get lucky and bleed to death."

Crazy groaned. "Damn, but I hurt. You got anything for pain?"

Gar shook his head. "Nope...not even any Tylenol."

"How about some water."

The rumble of distant thunder caught Gar's attention and he glanced up at the gathering clouds as they built into anvil shaped storm cells.

"Oh, hell." Gar unzipped a side pocket of his pack and pulled a bottle of water free. He held the bottle to Crazy's lips and watched him drink almost a half-liter before stopping to catch his breath. Crazy nodded thanks.

The rack on the back of quad was built for hauling tools, big game or camping gear, about three feet square with metal sides and a plywood floor. Gar lifted Crazy and sat him facing backwards, his feet sticking out over the back. Crazy gritted his teeth and groaned but didn't say anything until Gar looped a piece of nylon line around his neck and tied it to the back rail of the box. "Wait a minute. You'll strangle me!"

Gar didn't say anything, just ran another loop around Crazy's neck and snubbed it to the back of the seat.

He stepped away and looked at his handiwork. "Now…you can't head butt me, and if you fall off, you'll hang. So you be a good boy."

"John, in my pack is more than twenty grand. I'll give you that and another five thousand in gold coins. All you gotta do is turn me loose and look the other way. I swear I'm telling the truth. It's there."

Gar looked disgusted. "We'll take it with us, but you can't buy your way out. Not this time."

He mounted the quad, said, "Comfy?" and drove the short distance to the still idling trail bike.

He shut down its engine and retrieved Crazy's pack. He shoved the pack behind Crazy's back, straddled the seat, and started across country toward a fence line hoping that the fence builders had also done some road building—or at least cleared the big rocks away.

As they bounced across the desert, Crazy groaned and cussed, begged and pleaded, offered bribes, taunted and damned Gar until Gar finally stopped the quad and taped his mouth shut. All Crazy could do was groan and mumble.

Chapter 33

REDMOND DROVE AS carefully as he could across the rough ground and almost sighed in relief as the Suburban finally crawled up on the smooth surface of the road. He pulled up behind the helicopter. The pilot trotted up as Bud opened the passenger door.

"I'm being called to work this fire," the pilot said.

Bud shook his head and said, "No. You still belong to me... at least for now. I want you to wait until we get medical help for my people."

Sonny came limping up. The big white bandage around his head made him look like an actor from a war movie. Bud took him by the elbow and sat him in the seat of the Suburban. "Quit wandering around. Stay put."

Redmond leaned over and looked out at Sonny. "We have two Air Life flights inbound and one ambulance. He'll go on one of them."

Redmond's radio came to life. "Deschutes One, this is Deputy Hampton. I'm at the Fort Rock airstrip. Do you need assistance?"

"This is Redmond. You got any medical people there yet?"

"Almost. I hear an ambulance screaming up the road. And I see a chopper. Looks like Air Life."

"Do we have radio contact?"

"Affirmative on the chopper. Negative on the ambulance."

"Okay, when the chopper picks up the bad guy, see if they can take one more. At least have them land here and give these guys some medical help. And send the ambulance up here."

Maretti hopped out, hands bloody, dirt on his face, penny loafers half full of dirt, and announced he was going to check out Trooper Prince. He grabbed a water bottle out of Redmond's cooler and half shuffled, half trotted toward the rock pile.

Bud looked at Larae, who was slumped and barely conscious. "We need to lay her down, Roger. I think the seat will do. And let's get an inflatable cast on that ankle."

They eased her down on the seat and straightened her out. Roger fished a space blanket from the kit, covered her, rolled his shirt for a pad. Meanwhile, Bud slipped the inflatable cast on her ankle. She moaned a little when he lifted her leg to slip her boot through the cast.

He shot a questioning look at Roger. "I don't know, boss. She took a more direct hit from the blast, enough to break her eardrums." He pointed to the blood coming from her ears. "I had better cover."

Bud nodded absently, and then heard a siren and saw an ambulance coming up the Fort Rock Road.

Redmond's radio spoke again. "Deschutes One, this Deputy Hardman." A siren could be heard in the background. "We found a big guy just sitting along side the road…bleeding from a gunshot. The wound is awfully near a kidney, and he's lost a lot of blood. We've administered first aid and are hauling ass for Bend. Before he passed out, he said his name was Cowboy."

"Hardman, when he gets to the hospital, put a guard on him. He's wanted for some serious crimes. So, no slip-ups. Acknowledge."

"Read you loud and clear. Hardman out."

"Deschutes One, out."

He turned and looked at Bud, shaking his head. "Damn, but I hate that Deschutes One, County One shit. Causes more confusion than it stops. When this is over, we're gonna overhaul our radio procedures. I don't give a…care if anybody's listening in or not."

Bud almost smiled. "Sure hope that ambulance has more than one EMT aboard."

Roger was sitting on the floorboards of the Suburban, his feet on the ground, a shoulder touching Larae's.

Bud pilfered another bottle of water from Redmond's cooler and handed it to Roger.

"We've got a mess, Roger. All that's left in the crater is some twisted metal, and not much of that. Had to be a lot of explosives in that thing. I'm guessing they intended to set it off in a city, port docks, courthouse—someplace to cause a lot of damage and kill a lot of people. But there's nothing left to help us identify the bad guys."

Roger shook his head. "Wrong, Bud. There's a dead bandit about a hundred yards west, southwest of the blast center. Might be enough of him left to identify. I swear he's Arab…Arab-looking at any rate. And I heard the other two speaking what sounded like Farsi."

"How do you know there's a body out there?"

"I shot him. At least I think I shot him. He was charging me, firing an AK-47, so I took a shot at him. I thought he might be playing possum. Then Prince spotted the guy's boot. So Sonny took a shot, and the guy never got up. That's when his buddies set off the explosion."

The siren of an ambulance caught Bud's attention. He waved Redmond over. "Let's clear the road."

Sheriff Redmond nodded and headed for Prince's cruiser. He started the engine and then simply drove it off the road into the ditch, bumper digging into the berm beyond the borrow pit, tires spinning until he was convinced it would go no further.

Bud waved and shouted at the pilot. "I'm thinking we need to clear the road. Can you move your ship to the alfalfa field?"

The pilot gave him thumbs up and trotted back to the Bell.

While the chopper warmed up, Bud put Roger's pickup in four-wheel drive and moved it across the ditch and into the sage.

The driver of the ambulance killed the siren, turned into Cowboy's lane and then backed around. The Bell lifted off as the ambulance backed up the road towards Redmond's Suburban.

Two EMTs got out, hurrying to the rear door to grab a kit. They paused briefly at the sight of the huge crater where the road had once been, but refocused when Bud walked up. "There are three injured officers in the Suburban and another over by the rock pile. And we have one injured person at the airstrip by the store."

The senior EMT checked on Prince while Maretti hovered like a mother hen. Maretti said, "He took a slug in the stomach," and pointed at the tear in the vest.

A few minutes later, the senior EMT caught up to Bud who, door open, sitting under the wheel, was talking on the radio in Roger's pickup. He heard enough to know that the sheriff of Lake County was giving his dispatcher an update on the injuries. When Bud said, "County One, clear," and put the mike down, the EMT said, "Here's what we're going to do. The state trooper, the big guy, and the lady go with Air Life to Bend. The injured man at the airport goes by Air Life to Klamath Falls. The tall guy with the head injury goes with us. And the burly one…Roger? He needs to be examined by a doctor, but I don't see any life-threatening injuries."

"What's wrong with Prince? The state trooper?"

The EMT shook his head. "I don't diagnose, but we're going to treat him as though he has a bruised, maybe ruptured spleen. The diagnosis is up to the MDs."

Bud's shoulders sagged a bit, and then he stepped out on the ground and held out his hand. "Thank you."

The EMT trotted to the ambulance, hauled a stretcher out of the back, and jogged the short distance to the rock pile.

The buzz of a small twin-engine plane making a pass over the fire caught Bud's attention. He watched a big C-130 follow the smaller lead-plane, motors deafening as it made a low-level drop on the head of the growing sagebrush fire. The retardant turned into a long bright, pink cloud before settling to the ground. Bud watched and thought he could see a hesitation in the intensity of the fire, and then he turned back to the job at hand.

Fifteen minutes later, Bud watched as an EMT closed the back doors of the ambulance taking Sonny—gurney bound, an EMT beside him, an IV drip in the back of his hand—on a sixty-mile ride to Bend. Sonny had protested some until Bud told him to shut the hell up and get on the gurney.

The engine of the Air Life helicopter took on a deeper growl, the noise increasing as the blades spun faster and faster. And then the ship lifted from the road carrying Trooper Prince and Officer Larae Holcomb on a fast ride to St. Charles Hospital in Bend.

The helicopter was out of sight by the time the big C-130 made another pass at the head of the now fast-moving fire. The retardant plane had been held out of the area by a Forest Service Air Attack boss who had rightly considered the area dangerously congested by aircraft. Only when the Air Life helicopter had cleared the area did he give the green light to resume the aerial bombardment of the fire.

And then it was silent. Maretti, Bud, Cal Redmond and Roger found themselves in front of Sonny's shattered pickup, staring at the crater, trying to make some sense of what had happened here.

Bud finally spoke. "Glad you and Cal were here, Gino. You did good. You both did good."

A disheveled Gino Maretti, nodded. "Don't go getting weepy on me again, Bud. And don't try to make sense out of this 'cause there ain't any."

"Yes, there is," Roger finally said, "But only if you see it as war. Those departed souls were waging war on us. Pure, simple war."

They could hear the distant sound of a helicopter taking off south of them, but they couldn't see the ship. "Now what?" Bud asked.

Bud's cell phone rang, and he glanced at the incoming number. It wasn't one he recognized. "Sheriff Blair," he answered. The voice of Special Agent Amanda Spears said, "Bud, my…I mean, our captive is en route to a Klamath Falls Hospital. They had room for a passenger, so I sent Agent Warren to keep an eye on him."

"Warren? How did he get up here?"

"Your ground support just got here. He hitched a ride. Want to talk to them?"

"Uh…yeah. Put 'em on."

Michelle spoke. "We're here. Do you still need us?"

He thought for a minute. "Yes. But don't set up there. Come on up the Fort Rock Road. We'll stage in an alfalfa field up here. Who's with you?"

"I have Henry, your friend BB, and Detective Grandfield. Henry drove his pickup camper so it took us a little longer than we thought it would."

"Camper?"

"Yeah. You should see it. He has it wired to take our base set, complete with antennas. He even has a generator and a computer and a printer/copier."

"Sounds good. Bring 'em up." He tried to match her enthusiasm, but just couldn't make it sound like he cared.

"You all right?" she asked.

"Sure. See you in a few minutes. Can't be more than a couple of miles up here."

Michelle said, "Amanda wants to talk to you."

Amanda? We're on a first name basis? That was quick.

"One more thing," he added. "Who's minding the store?"

"I swore in Lonny Beltram. He and the City will answer any calls until we get back."

"Long as we have coverage, I'm okay. Put Agent Spears back on.

He heard Special Agent Spears say, "There are two things I need to share. One, John is bringing in another prisoner. He wouldn't tell me much except to ask you not to shoot at the quad he's riding. Said he would put the white flag up, whatever that means. He wants to meet you at Cowboy's ranch house…ETA about five minutes. He specifically asked for you. And he wants an ambulance to meet him there."

"Did he say why he wanted to meet with me?"

"Negative."

"What about the ambulance?"

"Officer Trivoli tells me that one is en route from someplace called Pine. ETA twenty-five minutes."

"LaPine," he corrected.

"Right. LaPine. Where do you guys come up with these classy names?"

He ignored her question. "You said two things?"

Without missing a beat, she said. "Homeland Security has an FBI forensics team on the way. Special Agent Thompson told me to tell you to leave the blast scene alone."

"It's still *my* county, Amanda. I'm still dealing with other things right now, but the FBI *will* coordinate through me or get their asses kicked back to where ever they came from. Understood?"

"I assure you that won't be a problem. We can talk when I get up there."

Bud didn't answer. Just shut the phone and slipped it in his pocket. When he turned, Maretti was grinning. He looked at Roger and said, "That's my kinda sheriff."

Roger tried to stifle a laugh and then couldn't hold it. "A might touchy, are we?"

Bud finally grinned and shrugged. Nothing more needed saying.

"Looks like we aren't quite finished. Amanda's guy…Gar…is bringing in another prisoner."

"Roger, let's go shut that irrigation system down and see what Gar has to say."

"John Bernard," Maretti corrected.

"Sure. John Bernard, my number one suspect in the murder of my John Doe."

Maretti nodded. "And in mine."

Roger looked unconvinced, but didn't say anything, just headed for his pickup.

Chapter 34

As he drove the quad around the corner of the loafing shed, Gar could see two police cars, a Suburban, and a white pickup parked at the edge of the barnyard, and four men out of the vehicles, waiting. He identified the three in uniform as county cops. *But who's the other one?*

He stopped the quad about fifty feet from the four men, shut the engine off and—hands still on the handlebars—just waited.

Bud studied the man for a moment and then, satisfied in some inner recess of his mind that Gar wouldn't fight them, walked to the quad. "Stone Fly, I presume. Or is it Gar? Or maybe John Bernard?"

Gar sighed. "Amanda talks too much." He motioned behind him. "Brought you a little present. You can close the case on your John Doe. His name was Scully Brockman. I don't know his real first name, but Brockman was his last name. Crazy killed both him and Leroy Pike."

Crazy growled at Gar, mumbling and groaning and cursing through the gag, his face turning deep purple as he thrashed against the neck ropes.

Gar didn't even look at Crazy, just fished his cell phone from his pocket, punched a button and turned the volume as high as he could. He held the phone out towards Bud. "Listen."

As the other three men edged up, flanking Gar and his prisoner, Bud could plainly hear the recording of Gar and another man in conversation, Crazy Charlie bragging about how he helped his old buddy out by killing Cully and Pike.

Crazy jerked at his ropes and groaned and succeeded in banging his shattered knee on the low tailgate.

Gar shut the phone down. "Satisfied, Sheriff?"

"Some. I don't know if it'll convict him in court, but I'm satisfied you didn't kill Brockman."

Maretti added, "Or Pike."

Gar looked at him. "You some kind of cop? From Bremerton, maybe?"

"Detective Maretti, Bremerton City Police."

Gar nodded. He looked at Bud. "Can I get off this thing now?"

Roger and Gar carried Crazy to the porch of the bunkhouse while Maretti, Cal, and Bud looked for the irrigation system's control panel.

Roger broke into the bunkhouse and took two pillows and a blanket from a bed. He placed a pillow under Crazy's head, and another under his knee before covering him with a blanket. When he started to undo the gag, Gar shook his head and said. "At your own peril. He's got a terrible mouth on him."

Roger nodded. "We can take it. He's gotta breathe."

Crazy took several deep breaths and then started in on what can only be described as creative cursing.

Maretti laughed. "Sounds like the ghetto incarnate, doesn't he."

Roger was tempted to stuff another gag in Crazy's mouth and then just shook his head.

Redmond's radio blared and he hurried back to his Suburban to take the call.

Maretti and Bud sat down on the low porch of the bunkhouse, and Bud patted his pocket, fishing for the cigarettes that hadn't been there for several years. Gar sat beside them, a weary sigh his only comment.

Cal came back over. "The ambulance is about five minutes out. I have a two-man patrol right behind them. One of my guys will ride the ambulance as guard."

Bud nodded. He was quiet for a long sixty seconds. "Well, we're getting there. I almost forgot. There's a dead man out in the sagebrush west of here. We'll have to bring the body in."

Gar gave Bud a wry smile at the thought of Harley and Chase, tied to the big pine...probably still arguing about what a dumb shit Harley was. "And...I've got two more of Cowboy's idiots tied to a tree about three miles west. I parked their quads in the clear so we can find them again."

Special Agent Spears rode the passenger seat as Officer Trivoli wheeled the Ford Expedition into the ranch yard. They stepped out and came trotting over to the bunkhouse.

Amanda looked from Gar to the still cursing, moaning Crazy. "That who I think it is?"

Gar nodded. "Yep. Our old friend, Charles Augustine Flock, aka Crazy Charlie."

Crazy groaned and spat at her and called her a bitch.

Roger looked at Gar, shook his head and said, "Put a sock in it," and slapped a piece of tape over Crazy's mouth.

Gar nodded. "I warned you."

"So you did." He waited a few seconds and added, "We arrest people in Lake County for spitting, you know."

Gar stifled a yawn and rose wearily to his feet. "Sheriff, we have some unfinished business." He started across the yard to Cowboy's house. Bud got to his feet and followed, but when Agent Spears started to follow, Gar shook his head and said, "Not yet, Amanda. This is between me and the sheriff. You stay out here."

She gave him a hard stare and then simply nodded.

Bud noted the splintered door jam as he followed Gar into the low-ceilinged living room. "In there," Gar pointed to Cowboy's office.

The file drawers were open, empty, but the computer was still running. Bud gave Gar a questioning look. "I think we should see what Cowboy left us before the feds get here," Gar answered.

"Why?"

Gar sighed, "Because I don't trust our domestic spies to be honest. Cowboy left any evidence, I thought you could be my ace-in-the-hole, my 'Deep Throat.'"

He opened the documents file, slipped a disk into the DVD drive and burned copies of all the files he could find. The hard drive hummed and blinked for a few minutes before stopping. Gar removed the disk, and handed it to Bud.

Bud slipped it into his shirt pocket, shook his head, and asked. "Why me?"

Gar shrugged his shoulders. "You gotta trust somebody."

"Any idea what's on this?"

"Nope. I'm gonna leave that to you."

Chapter 35

WHEN THEY WALKED out of the house, Amanda insisted that Bud and Cal take John Bernard into protective custody. When they challenged her and refused, she raged about John being Absent Without Leave, cursed him as a lone wolf, and finally gave up and gave him a wry smile. "You dumb ass." She put her arms around him and whispered in his ear, "John, why didn't you trust me enough to tell me what was going on?"

He shrugged, patted her back and murmured, "I was just following a hunch, Amanda. Nothing to go on really until a few days ago."

She released him and stepped back. "Not coming in, are you?"

"Not true. As I figure it, you can't change a man's leave without first notifying him. Since you didn't notify me, I still have five days to get back. So I'm going to pack up my gear, hitch my pickup to my trailer, and I'm going on R&R for five days."

"You know the rules about checking in. You haven't checked in for the past five weeks. We figured you'd gone off the reservation."

He didn't say anything.

The wail of an ambulance broke the tension. The ambulance followed by a Deschutes County 4x4 with a "Sheriff" decal drove past the lane to Cowboy's place.

"Missed the turn," Bud said. "Michelle, go fetch those guys."

Michelle was gone a full minute before Bud finally spoke up. He looked hard at Amanda and Gar. "I had my friendly dispatcher look you guys up on your website. Two activities caught my interest: mainly that there are two groups within NCIS, a counter-terrorist group and an anti-terrorist group. I'm guessing that you two work with the counter-terrorist group. Just say nothing if I'm right."

They both gave him a cold look.

"Oh, I know, I know. You can't say because it's a matter of national security. But," his voice rose, warming to his subject, "if you knew enough to send out a bulletin suggesting that maybe the main north-south highway through our county might be—or possibly is, or there is a chance that, or may be—used to smuggle terrorists into the country, why didn't you bother to tell us?" He was still in control of his temper, but just barely. "I have four officers hurt, one critically, and I'm thinking you should have shared a bit more information, forewarned us. Because, as it happens, it *is* being used as a pipeline. So...tell me, how much did you know?"

Amanda looked uncomfortable, and then John Gar Stone Fly Bernard answered. "These guys have so much money, they can make an instant millionaire out of anyone, so they look around and they buy police captains, judges, county sheriffs—anyone they can turn. And I'm here to tell you it doesn't take all that much money. Some people sell out for a lot less than you can imagine. The upshot is we don't know who to trust. So we sit on the information, and just leak enough for the right people to stay alert."

Bud raised an eyebrow. *But you trusted me. I wonder why?*

Amanda picked it up. "I'll bet you went to the same tortured thinking when you got the Homeland Security bulletin...who to tell, who to trust, how to sift the guilty from the innocent, how to protect U.S.-Arab citizens...all of that. Didn't you?"

Bud nodded. "Tell 'em, Roger."

Roger nodded, dragged a line in the dirt with a boot toe, and then added what looked like four branches. "The difference is we went after intel we can trust." He marked a square in the dirt. "Think of that as Lakeview. Here," and he marked an "x" to the east of Lakeview, "we have a long-time resident we know well and trust. That's Adel on our main east-west route to Winnemucca. Here at the bottom we have New Pine Creek and another store owner we trust. Here at Valley Falls is Clyde Whittaker." He drew another branch from Valley Falls that represented the shape of the highway to Paisley. "We've got Buffalo Boggs here. And in Summer Lake," he continued dragging his toe to mark the shape of the highway to Summer Lake, "another stage stop store, restaurant, and motel, we have another person we trust. And so on…right on up to Silver Lake and Christmas Valley." And then he grinned. "And of course we figured that it was too juicy for Clyde to keep quiet, so informally the word got out."

Amanda nodded. "Exactly what we try to do, except we don't have your intimate knowledge of people to set up a good watcher system. So we rely on you. And you done good."

"Yeah, you bet," Bud said with a touch of venom.

The ambulance, followed closely by the Deschutes County police vehicle, trailed Michelle's vehicle up the lane, pulled around in a tight circle and backed up to the porch of the bunkhouse. The doors flew open and two EMTs got out, one a long, tall woman in a black jumpsuit, and the other a short, stocky man in a rumpled black jumpsuit two sizes too big. The woman opened the back door and grabbed a big kit while her partner examined Crazy Charlie. The man pulled the tape off Crazy's mouth, "a-hummed," nodded, and said, "We need to start an IV. The splint stays on… for now. Not a bad job for field work."

Crazy started his cussing and crazy talk, and the EMT said, "Let's give this dirty-mouthed s.o.b. a sedative." He then filled a syringe from a small metal capped bottle marked "Vicodin," and injected Crazy with the clear liquid.

The two Deschutes County deputies walked over to Cal. "What's happening, Cal?"

"What to say? Basically, a couple of crazies blew themselves up and tried to take some police officers with them. This guy," Cal said, pointing to Crazy, "is connected to some kind of drug and people smuggling operation. We don't know exactly what he did here. Any word on Cowboy?"

The older deputy said, "In surgery, last we heard. No word on his condition."

Cal nodded. "Okay. Well, we have to put a guard on this one from here to the hospital, and then full time until someone decides who gets him." He pointed at the younger deputy. "Greg, you ride shotgun."

Roger and Gar helped them load Crazy on the gurney and into the ambulance, and Deputy Greg Moffit got in and sat on a bench beside the gurney.

And then Bud said, "Roger, I want you to go with the ambulance, and I want a doctor to look you over. You had a concussion. That calls for at least a medical look-see."

When Roger protested that he was all right, Bud just said, "Humor me," in a tone that brooked no nonsense. Bud looked at the EMTs and asked, "You got room for one more?"

The tall woman looked at her partner and then nodded. "As long as he sits up front. There's not enough room for four back here."

Roger shrugged. "I can ride. I'll check on the others when we get up there and give you a call, Bud."

"Appreciated, Roger."

Chapter 36

MARETTI SAT ON the bunkhouse porch and said nothing, just watching as the ambulance pulled away followed closely by the Deschutes County Sheriff's vehicle.

Michelle took Bud by the arm and guided him to her vehicle. "You doing okay, Bud?"

"Yeah. Well, at least I'm going to be. How about you?"

"I'm worried about the others. Think we should go to Bend?"

"In a bit." He pointed to a thermos on the floorboards. "Is that what I think it is?"

"Yep. Hot coffee." She opened the passenger door and said, "Sit. I'll pour you some."

He gave her a wry smile. "You're getting better."

While he sipped the coffee, Michelle got on the radio and talked with the command center. Bud heard the Colonel say they were set up in the alfalfa field and open for business. And to ask Bud if the Forest Service can have their helicopter back for the fire. He also said he had blocked the road because curious locals were showing up.

Bud thought about the two guys Gar had stashed in the timber and shook his head. "Tell the Colonel to keep the road blocked, and let the Forest Service know I need the ship for another thirty minutes. Got just a little more business to take care of."

He looked at Michelle and finally said. "Thanks for the coffee. And now I think you better get over to the command center. I'll bet an hour will see the start of a media feeding frenzy. The Colonel has lots of experience in the liaison business, so I expect you to lean on him when you need it. You have the lead. I've got two more prisoners to bring in, and then I'm going to Bend to see how our people are doing."

While Bud talked to Michelle, Cal Redmond sat down beside Maretti, fished a pack of cigarettes out of his shirt pocket, lit up and took a deep drag. "Bremerton, huh? Kinda off the reservation aren't you?"

Gino pointed at the pack. "Got an extra?"

Redmond handed him the pack and a lighter.

Gino lit up, took a puff and then extended his arm, inspecting the cigarette. "Nasty tasting thing, ain't it."

He looked up at Redmond. "We gotta homicide investigation going. So up comes this bulletin from Sheriff Blair describing a John Doe homicide…same injuries, same cause of death… castration followed by—and hear what I say—followed by a broken neck. Got it? Castration *before* death.

"My partner Grandfield spots the bulletin, and we think to ourselves there's got to be a connection between the two. I mean…what are the odds of two people being killed that way? Anyway, we know from DNA that our victim was one of three guys that raped and killed a woman in Bremerton. So Bud gets DNA from his dead guy and we decide to bring our DNA report down here and see if we have a match…see if we're after the same killer. And then all hell breaks loose."

Cal nodded. "Did for a fact. Never had a day like this in my life, and I thought I'd seen it all."

Bud came from around behind the loafing shed where he had gone to answer a call of nature.

"Where's Amanda and John Gar Stone Fly Bernard?"

Cal pointed at the house. "She announced she is the Agent in Charge with the authority to investigate alleged incidents of terrorism, that this is her crime scene, so we could just butt the hell out."

Bud thought about the disk in his shirt pocket and then sat down on the stoop, looked at the cigarette in Cal's hand, and asked, "You want to bum me one of those?"

Cal shook his head, but handed Bud the pack. "You are going to get hooked again."

"Maybe, but right now I don't care." He took a deep drag and coughed as the acrid smoke hit his lungs. "You know," he said, "there was something wrong with that whole scene with the EMTs. I haven't put it together yet, but something was wrong."

Maretti nodded. "Local amateurs maybe?"

"No," Cal said. "EMTs all go through the same training and have to pass the same certification. Doesn't matter where they work."

Amanda was hollering as she came running out the front door, waving a computer disk and a page of printer paper. "We hit the jackpot! Cowboy kept computer records of everything he did. He tried to hide it in some homemade code, but John cracked it in about six seconds."

They all stood up as she hurried across the yard. "See here," she said holding the page out to them. "He simply used the keyboard and just changed the position of his hands. Like 's' is really 'a' and 'd' is really an 's' and so on. He moved his hand position to the right on the next line and 'f' becomes 'g.' Simple really."

Gar walked up to the tight circle. "When it comes to brains, Cowboy doesn't have a full barn. He proved that when he hired Crazy."

Bud asked Amanda, "So…do you have enough to know who he worked for?"

"Not yet. I think Cowboy also used some kind of personal shorthand. But I'm sure our cryptologists won't find it much harder than the *NY Times* crossword puzzle."

Bud stood up, dusted the seat of his khaki pants and looked at Gar. "You up to taking a little helicopter ride…bring in those other two?"

Gar nodded and grabbed his pack off the quad. Bud didn't say anything when Gar also hefted Crazy's pack and started toward the pickup.

Chapter 37

CHASE AND HARLEY were still tied to the big ponderosa pine when the helicopter set down. Their wrists were bleeding from their efforts to break the quick ties, and both had pissed in their pants.

Bud pulled his pistol and covered the men while Gar cut them loose. Harley started in on Chase again, "Ain't this a fix, Chase. I told yuh we shoulda cut and run. Now look what you got us into."

Chase growled, "Shut your mouth, Harley. I ain't the one been runnin' his mouth."

Gar looked at Bud and smiled. "They've been like that since I captured them...just like an old married couple...pick, pick, pick."

"We ain't queer," Chase said.

"Never said you were. Now stand real close to each other. Ever been in a three-legged race?" He took the last of his quick ties, bound Harley's left leg to Chase's right leg and stepped back to admire his handiwork.

"Well, there you go, Sheriff. They're all yours. Take 'em away."

Bud nodded. "Not coming back with me?"

"Can't do it. I've got five days R&R coming."

"You want to give me a statement before you go?"

"I don't think I can do that either. In fact, I was never here at all."

Bud shifted his pistol to his left hand and extended his right to John Gar Stone Fly Bernard. "Good luck."

"I think I might just be back one of these days...sorta check on Officer Holcomb...see how she's doing. Have another beer or something."

Gar used the bungee cords on the back of one of the quads to tie down his pack and Crazy's, slipped the Armalite into a saddle scabbard on the quad, hit the starter, revved the engine, and then drove west into the timber.

***

Bud read them their rights, stated he was arresting them for assault on a federal officer, other charges pending, and herded them to the helicopter. Harley and Chase only fell once getting to the helicopter, but they managed to pull themselves into the back. Bud made them buckle up, but he didn't shut the back door. As the ship lifted off, the pilot asked Bud through the intercom headphone, "Why'd you leave the door open?"

Bud shrugged and asked, "Where can they go?"

Ten minutes later, Bud's helicopter had lifted off to go fight fire, and Cal Redmond had the smelly pair behind the cage in the Suburban. "Bud? You got room for these two in your jail? We're about full up. You want me to run them down there?"

"Let me check. We had one bed when I left."

He hit a speed dial number, listened to one ring, and then heard Karen's voice say, "Lake County Sheriff's Office."

"Karen, it's Bud. You got any jail beds open? I've got two customers up here."

"Oh, Bud, thank the Lord. We are just sick to death with worry. How are Sonny and Roger...and Larae, of course. Are they all right?"

"Karen, I'm sorry I didn't call sooner. I did fill Nancy in, but it's been kinda busy. Ah, let's see. Larae was hurt the worst. She's alive and was talking when Air Life took her to Bend. Roger and

Sonny were knocked out by the blast. And Charlie Prince may have a ruptured spleen. That's all I know."

"Terrible, just terrible. What's happening to our county, Bud? How can this happen?"

"We'll have to talk later. Right now I need to know if you have two jail beds open."

"Sorry. Yes, but I don't know for how long."

"Good for now. I'm sending you two guests: a man named Harley...that's all I know...and a big guy named Chase. They are to be charged with assault on a federal peace officer. Sheriff Cal Redmond will bring them to you in a couple of hours." He paused and then remembered to ask, "How's Lonnie Beltram doing?"

She laughed. "He's driving that old pickup we plan to surplus, and staying close to town. No business so far...thank goodness."

"Good. I'll give him a call later."

He flipped the phone shut, and nodded at Cal. "Yes, Karen has two beds open, so if you were to run them down there, I would be more than grateful. Can't tell you how much I appreciate you being here, Cal. You and your guys have done a great job. We needed all the help we could get on this one."

Cal held out his hand. "The brotherhood sticks together, Bud. By the way, I've moved Cowboy to a medical room at the jail. Easier to protect him that way. We have a guy at the jail who was a Navy corpsman, and we have a contract doctor who stops in twice a day. Now, before I go, I have one more question. Where's our boy...this John Gar Stone Fly Bernard?"

Bud looked down, shook his head and then looked back up at Cal. "Took one of the quads and, as he put it, went on R&R."

"Get a statement?"

"Nope. Says he can't give statements. Also said he had never been here."

"Damned feds. It's always the same story."

Chapter 38

THE AMBULANCE RIDE was uneventful except for Crazy's rage, but as the sedative took hold, he quieted down. It was a sixty-mile ride, but the driver kept the siren and red lights on all the way to Bend at about seventy-five. When the ambulance wheeled into the ER ambulance parking at St. Charles, the driver smiled at Roger and asked politely if he minded waiting a minute. "We'll be right back," he said.

Three or four minutes passed before Roger decided that the EMTs should have taken Crazy inside by now. He opened the door and got out just as Deputy Moffit opened the back of the ambulance. "Where did the EMTs go?" Roger asked.

The deputy shrugged. "They just told me to sit tight and they'd be right back."

The older deputy, Barney something, got out of the sheriff's vehicle and walked up. "What's going on?"

"Oh, shit." Roger said.

He stepped into the ambulance. Charlie looked like he was asleep, but when Roger nudged him and said, "Hey, Crazy, we're here," Crazy didn't stir, and Roger couldn't see any sign that he was breathing. In fact, his face had the waxy pallor of the dead.

Roger unlocked the gurney and started pulling it to the rear of the ambulance. "We need to get this guy into the ER right now. I think those two killed him. And we need to get out an

APB right now. You know what they looked like, so we have that much at least.

Deputy Moffit, helped Roger set the gurney on the pavement and push it into the ER while Deputy Barney something called his dispatcher with the latest news of what Roger was coming to think of as the mother of all snafus.

A doctor and two nurses worked on Crazy for twenty minutes before calling him DOA.

Roger was on the phone to Bud, telling him about Crazy, wondering who in the hell was so well informed and organized that they could intercept an ambulance, kill Crazy, and then simply walk away. Then his vision blurred, he got lightheaded and dropped to his knees. He managed to say, "Gotta go," before he passed out.

Chapter 39

BUD WAS SEATED on a canvas camp chair under the picnic awning behind the Colonel's pickup camper eating a bowl of Dinty Moore stew the Colonel heated up on the camper's stove. He watched another air tanker make a drop on the fire. "His" Bell helicopter, a bucket swinging on a long line under the ship, followed a few minutes later, hovered, and let fall a shower of water.

An early afternoon thunderstorm pounded the Fort Rock area, and heavy rain was rattling on the camper roof and the awning. Bud took a long sniff of the fresh sage scented air, picked up his cell from the table under the awning, looked at it, and then set it back down. *Too many players to keep track of.*

A lightning down-strike lit the top of a pine tree north of the fire, and a few seconds later thunder rolled across the sky.

Thirty minutes earlier a four-person FBI forensics team had swept into the command site in a big, black, unmarked helicopter, disembarked before the rotors stopped spinning, ignored Bud, commandeered Michelle's Ford Explorer and directed Agent Spears to take them to the blast site.

BB sipped a cup of coffee and watched his old partner. "Only two people coulda ratted you out in time, Honky. That one," he pointed in the general direction of the blast site, "or…the other one. That prissy guy, Agent Warren. No other way to see it."

Bud nodded, took a sip of the Colonel's strong coffee, and said nothing, just waiting for BB to continue.

"Now, as I see it, our young missy is the most likely. She's a gamer, that one."

Bud had a flash recall of perfume and a soft voice saying *one-twenty*.

"I know," Bud said.

"You got a plan?"

Bud shook his head. "Not unless we shoot them both. No...I think I'll talk to Special Agent Thompson. Either he'll believe me or he won't, but I think it's worth a try."

The noise of another helicopter, not quite as big as the FBI's, but bigger than his Bell, and wearing a big "Fox News" on each side, settled in the field. A cameraman, a sound man, a director, and a vaguely familiar-looking woman exited, and started across the alfalfa field toward the command center.

"Here comes the fun," BB said. "Don't you have someplace you need to go?"

Chapter 40

It was two days before the Lake County Sheriff's Office could shut down the command center. In the first twenty-four hours news photographers, reporters, and wannabees from all over the world flew in, drove in, walked in and, for all that Bud could tell, crawled in to take pictures of the blast site, Cowboy's ranch, the command post, the still-smoldering sage and forest fire, Fort Rock, and just about anything else they could pounce on.

Several helicopters ignored the no-fly zone imposed by the Forest Service to keep the air clear for air-tankers and helicopters fighting the fire. They risked mid-air collisions to get an aerial view of the bomb crater.

Michelle had the good sense to have Sonny's pickup hauled away before most of the news media types showed up. And the Oregon state police rescued Prince's cruiser.

Bud typed up a press release on the Colonel's computer, printed copies to give to the media, and refused all interviews. He pointed out to BB, Maretti, and Cal that Michele could handle the press, was better looking than he was, and knew to stay with the script.

On the morning of the second day, an FBI public relations specialist—a tall, good-looking blonde—showed up, told Bud not to make any statements unless she approved them first—a matter of national security. Bud gave her a grim, tight-lipped stare and

"State Police Trooper Charles Prince was hit by a bullet. His vest protected him, but the impact ruptured his spleen.

"As my officers approached, the assailants detonated explosives hidden in the truck. They were killed, and my officers were injured by the blast.

"The officers were taken by Air Life and then by ambulance to a hospital in Bend. I visited them yesterday afternoon. Two are in satisfactory condition and will be released this afternoon. One was in surgery for a shattered ankle, and Trooper Prince was in surgery to remove his spleen.

"An FBI forensics team examined the site, collected samples of the debris, took the body of the man killed by my officers, and left by helicopter late yesterday afternoon. That, in a nutshell, is what happened here yesterday." *Took Amanda Spears, too. And another body you don't know about.*

The familiar-looking blonde reporter asked, "Sheriff, wasn't there a running gun battle west of the ranch house yesterday?"

Reporter heads swiveled to stare in her direction. This was new news, something fresh to feast on.

Bud stopped for a second, nodded, and said, "Yes. An NCIS agent was making an arrest of a man suspected of killing two Navy personnel. The suspect resisted and there was a firefight between the NCIS agent and four armed men. All four men were apprehended and have been taken into custody by NCIS."

She pushed forward and asked. "Wasn't one of the armed men killed?"

Where is she getting this stuff?

"Yes, but he was killed in an ATV accident, not in the fight."

Reporters began shouting questions, but Bud held up his hands and refused to answer. The furor finally died back a bit and Bud shouted over the din, "Until the evidence is evaluated, That's all I have to tell you."

He stepped off the stool and turned back toward the picnic awning. A reporter trotted alongside asking, "Can you give us the names of the officers that were injured?"

"That's in the press release I gave out yesterday. See that officer over there," and pointed to Michelle.

Other reporters tried to follow Bud, but Sheriff Redmond, detectives Maretti and Grandfield, and the Colonel formed a protective shield around him, not too gently discouraging the most persistent. Most just went back to their sound trucks or helicopters, cell phones to their ears, hurrying to file a story.

Bud walked over to the FBI spokesperson and held out his wrists. "Okay. Arrest me."

There was a sly grin on her face as she reached for her handcuffs, but she didn't take them out. "Would you believe I was bluffing?"

Bud gave her a weary smile in return. "Didn't know for sure, but I just had this other business to take care of first. So…how did I do?"

"Well…I imagine that in spite of your bald recitation of the facts, the talking heads will make the terrorist connection, some will speculate about a lone NCIS agent taking down four armed men, and some will speculate about why you left that part out. You can be damned for omission as well as commission." She stopped. "Why did you leave that out?"

"Well…I guess I left it out because it really didn't happen, not officially. If NCIS wants to talk about, then they will."

"A national security matter?"

"Not for me to say. You want some coffee?"

***

The blonde reporter from K-Falls collared Michelle and gave her a business card. "He's one of the most interesting police officers I've ever met. Sure doesn't like the press, though. Please tell him after this has all died down, I still want to do a story about him."

Michelle took the card, glanced at it, and asked, "How did you know about the fight out in the sagebrush?"

The blonde shook her head. "Trade secret. But if you ask, I think the guy that runs the store might tell you that someone watched the whole thing through binoculars from the top of Fort Rock."

Michelle nodded. "It's hard to hide anything in the desert, isn't it?"

"Michelle Trivoli. Interesting name. How's the Sheriff to work for?"

"The best."

"Maybe there's a story in here about a woman undersheriff."

Michelle stared at her and then said, "Don't even think it."

Chapter 41

WHEN SHE AWOKE in the recovery room, her mouth was dry and her head was pounding. The first person she saw was a small strawberry blonde dressed in blue scrubs.

"Larae?" the nurse asked, "How are you feeling? Awake now?"

Larae nodded, or at least thought she did, and then asked for water. She sipped at a straw, laid her had back down and fell asleep again.

Later she had the sensation of being wheeled down a hallway, the ceiling lights making her wince.

When she awoke the second time, Sonny and Roger, both in hospital robes, were asking her the same dumb question. "How you doing, Larae?" She managed a tired "Okay," and then asked, "What happened?"

They looked at each other. Roger thought for a few seconds and then said, "You were injured in a bomb blast. Do you remember the hay truck?"

She shook her head. "No. I can't remember anything. Where am I?"

Sonny said, "You're in St. Charles Hospital in Bend." Sonny patted her arm. "That's okay. You go back to sleep now."

She felt more alert by evening, and she was trying to sit up when a familiar voice said from the doorway, "Hey, Sweet Mama."

"Wally! What are you doing here?"

He handed her a bouquet of roses. "Had to come and see you for myself, lay eyes on you. Make sure you were alive."

"I think I'll live, but I feel pretty bunged up."

"Yeah. Bomb blasts will do that to you. So what happened?"

"Wally, I can't remember. The doctor said that was normal and I'd probably start remembering in a few days. Did you see Roger and Sonny? I think they got hurt, too."

"Yep. They're going to be all right. And they're going home in the morning."

There was a knock on the door, and then Bud and Michelle walked in with another bouquet of roses. Michelle gave Larae a hug, blinking her tears away. Bud fiddled with the flowers and then finally laid them across the meal tray.

Wally stood up and extended his hand. "We haven't met, but I know who you are, Sheriff. I'm Wally Pidgeon."

Bud shook Wally's hand. "Christmas Valley, right?"

Wally nodded. "Who's this beautiful officer?"

Bud introduced Michelle.

And then Larae said to Michelle, "I remember you now. You were on the interview panel." Larae looked embarrassed. "I can't remember what happened and it scares me."

***

Wally was still sitting in a visitor chair at Larae's beside when Bud and Michelle left some fifteen minutes later, murmuring the traditional bedside litanies of "You get well," "We'll be back to see you," "You're looking better." Wally grinned in spite of himself at the "You're looking better" one. He always wanted to say, "Better than what?" But he didn't figure this was an appropriate occasion.

Larae looked at Wally and asked, "Do you think I can keep my old job at the lodge?"

Chapter 42

Larae was released from the hospital two days later equipped with a walking cast, pain pills and a bottle of antibiotics. When Roger had phoned and said he was coming to take her home, she said, "I don't have a home."

He laughed. "Not true. Billie says you'll stay with her until you get back on your feet. See you in about ten minutes. Wally and I just passed Lava Butte."

"Wally's with you?"

"Yeah. We're driving his Buick. He insisted."

"How are you feeling, Roger?"

"Just had my bell rung is all. I'm fine now."

"And Sonny? How's he doing?"

Roger laughed. "He's too hard-headed to stay down. We do have a small problem, though. We're both on administrative leave pending a review of our "use of deadly force.""

"Suspended?" Larae sounded incredulous.

"Yep. Bud says it shouldn't take too long."

"Who's doing the review?"

"Oregon State Police. The state Attorney General gave them that task."

"That's bullshit, Roger. You were defending yourselves!"

"Now, now. Don't worry about it. One thing though. How's your memory? I think they'll be asking you some questions."

She was emphatic. "My memory is just fine."

He said, "Good. Is Trooper Prince still there?"

She nodded her head, and then realized he couldn't see that. "Yes. His mother and father will take him home tomorrow to recuperate."

"Well, I see the city limits sign. See you in a few minutes."

"Roger, how did you get home?"

"Sonny's sister, Nancy, came and picked us up."

Chapter 43

LATE IN THE afternoon of the second day following what Bud thought of as the mad bomber caper, Maretti and Grandfield had said their goodbyes and driven to Klamath Falls to return their rental car and catch the Seattle flight. Before they left, Maretti stuck out his hand, grinned, and said, "Well, Bud, Grandfield and I are going to head back to the peace and quiet of our little city. This country life is just too rough for us city boys."

Bud shook Maretti's hand, and then held out his hand to Grandfield. "We didn't have much time to get acquainted, Ron, but thanks for the work on our John Doe. By the way, here's a little something to take back with you." And he handed him a small cassette from a tape recording. "I know Gino hates paper work, so you keep this safe."

Grandfield looked puzzled. "What's on it?"

"Good question. When I last listened to it, it sounded like a confession by Crazy Charlie, now deceased, to the murder of some guy named Pike, and another man named Scully. Might need that for your report to close that case."

"You have a copy, Sheriff?"

"Yes, a paper copy. The Colonel transcribed it for me this morning. And one nice thing about being the sheriff: I can decide when a case is closed."

***

The Lake County Sheriff's Department—what was left of it—took down the picnic awning, loaded the tables and folding chairs in the back of Roger's pickup, which Bud was still driving, and broke camp. Bud and BB shook hands, and then BB folded his big frame into the seat of his aging dark blue Corvette. "Honky, I got this suspension to take care of, and then I'm coming back. If you need a deputy, I might be in the market for a job."

Bud nodded, but said, "BB, I couldn't even come close to matching what you're making now."

BB closed the door and lowered the window. "I'll be in touch." The 'Vette roared into life and BB spun out of the alfalfa field and down the Fort Rock Road.

***

The Colonel lifted up the jacks for the camper and pinned them in place. He made a circle around the vehicle and camper, inspecting, making sure all the hatches and windows were closed before setting out on the hundred and twenty-plus-mile trip home. Bud caught him as he was locking the door to the camper.

"Henry, Colonel sir, I am deeply grateful for your help. This vehicle of yours is a gem. And I'm really proud of the way you and Michelle handled the press. I think we did okay."

"Actually, I enjoyed it, Bud...except for the injuries. Hell, I even had another fire to watch. So you call me anytime you need to set up a base camp for a command center."

"You are on the top of my list."

"Well, my woman is anxious to see me, so I'll skedaddle."

***

Michelle and Bud watched as the Colonel made the turn onto the Fort Rock Road. Michelle turned to Bud. "Was he really a colonel?"

Bud laughed. "No. He was something much better…a Marine Sergeant. The "colonel" tag came from his fire fighting days as a military liaison for the Forest Service. His habit was to find out the rank of the officer in charge of any troops, and then pin the same insignia of that officer on his FS uniform. Said it made dealing with the officer's subordinates a whole lot easier. One such officer was a lieutenant colonel who was something of a strutting rooster. When the lieutenant colonel wouldn't cooperate, Henry pinned on his eagles and told the guy he was a full bull colonel and he would damned well do as he was told. And of course, the lieutenant colonel did just that. When he turned around from giving the guy his orders, Henry's incident commander was standing there, holding a salute and saying, "Yes, sir, Colonel, sir, right away, sir." He became the Colonel after that."

"I hadn't heard that story."

"Well, ask him sometime. He tells it a lot better than I do. By the way, in all the excitement I just forgot about the dead man in the airplane. I never did see Doc Loeffler. Did he haul the body away?"

Michelle nodded. "While you were meeting with Gar, the Colonel helped Doc put the cadaver in a body bag and put in the back of Doc's Suburban. And then Doc left for Lakeview."

She paused. "How are you going to deal with that?"

"You mean, do we have another homicide? I suppose. But I think we'll write his death up as killed while assaulting a federal officer, rule the officer's action as self-defense, and close the book. Any ID on the guy?"

"Yes. His name was Juan Sanchez. I asked Karen to run him. There were two outstanding warrants, one for the sale of a controlled substance, and an assault charge. He has...or had...a rap sheet a mile long."

"Figures. Well, before we head for home, I want to look at the crater one more time. You can go ahead and head for town if you want."

"No. If you don't mind, I'll go with you. Then we can caravan for home."

***

Two hours later the tires in the gravel driveway brought Nancy hurrying through Bud's back gate. He was scarcely out of the pickup before she had her arms wrapped around his waist, her head against his chest. She blinked hard to keep the tears back. He held her and simply rocked back and forth, his chin resting on the top of her head.

"Welcome home, Bud."

"Glad to be back. And awfully glad you're here."

Molly jumped up and tried to lick his face.

Nancy released Bud and said, "Molly, you behave yourself."

He locked the door to Roger's pickup and followed her through the back gate. The smell of Mexican food caused him to remember how little he'd had to eat in the past seventy-two hours. "Oh, man. That smells good."

Nancy grinned, her green eyes full of mischief. "You don't. Why don't you take a quick shower while I finish up."

***

Nancy was taking a tamale pie from the oven when Bud, showered, shaved, in clean blue jeans, white socks, and blue sweatshirt, sneaked up behind her and wrapped her in his arms. "Bud," she scolded, "you'll make me drop your dinner."

"Can't have that."

"Let me go and go sit down."

"Yes, ma'am."

Bud thought the food was wonderful and said so. Nancy said, "Hunger is the best spice."

"No. It's really good."

Not until the table was cleared, the dishes rinsed, and in the dishwasher did Nancy say, "Okay. Now…tell me what happened."

He sat down at the kitchen table, an old Formica-topped bachelor special with metal legs, poured them each a small glass of wine, took a deep breath, and said, "What I know is this."

It took him the better part of an hour, and the bottle of wine was almost gone before he was done. He talked about Larae's undercover assignment…about how he and Gino found her all bloody and banged up out in the sagebrush…about the anonymous phone tip, and speculated that it came from John Gar Stone Fly Bernard…told her about the murder of Crazy Charlie and speculated about a possible mole in NCIS…about the great help he got from Cal Redmond…about the crazy Italian, Gino Maretti…about how well Michelle had handled the press…the Colonel's camper command center…about Chase and Harley… and how glad he was that Nancy was here.

"I saw you on TV giving the press what for," Nancy said. "You looked pretty rough, but you spoke well. I imagine that the major networks will be looking for an interview. And I saw Michelle and the Colonel twice. She did a good job, by the way."

He covered a yawn with his hand and managed to mumble, "Yes she did."

"I think you should go sit in your recliner for a while."

"I'll just go to sleep."

"Might not hurt. I'll stick around for a while."

"Thanks for the dinner...and for listening. I think I needed to decompress a bit. Nancy, did you get up to see your mother?"

"Too much going on, but I need to and soon. Will you take me?"

He nodded. "I have to go into the office in the morning, file my report, which should be easier now that I laid it out for you, and then in the afternoon let's see if we can get Bruno to fly us. I can't be gone for long...a few hours up there and I have to get back. Not enough people to cover the county."

"I had hoped to stay a couple of days with Mother."

"I can't do that right now."

"I know. Bud, do you think it will always be this way?"

"I sure hope not. I'm praying that this is a one-time aberration and I can go back to writing a few speeding tickets and locking up drunks."

"Bud, I would prefer a wedding, but since I already had that once, I'm thinking we should just run down to Reno when we get back."

His eyes brightened, and suddenly he wasn't so sleepy anymore. "Tomorrow. I'll work fast, we'll fly to Yakima and you can introduce me to your mother. Then we come back here, pack up and head for Reno. Right?"

She came around the table and plopped in his lap. "Deal."

"One more thing," Bud said. "Will you start wearing your ring?"

She laughed and then kissed him with all the passion of her soul.

Bud whispered, "I love you so much," and then picked up and carried her to his bedroom.

She giggled and asked, "What will the neighbors think?"

"Hush, woman. We've waited long enough."

Chapter 44

ASA WAS WAITING in front of the sheriff's office, a newspaper in his hand when Bud wheeled the county's pickup around and backed into the "Reserved - Sheriff" parking spot.

As Bud stepped out, looking fresh and ready for the day, boots shined and starch in his khaki shirt, Asa said, "Morning, Bud. Brought the latest edition for your approval."

"Hell, Asa, you don't need my approval."

"I'd like it anyway. Scooped the big boys on this one. Had your story out on the AP before they ever knew what had happened."

"Come on, Asa. They were all over it before I called you."

"Yeah, but they couldn't quote the sheriff of Lake County."

"How have they treated me since?"

Asa grinned. "Why, you are the fair-haired boy, the type of law enforcement officer this country needs. You broke up a big terrorist operation and saved hundreds, maybe thousands of lives. Nothing but praise for you and your injured officers. Trouble is, it'll probably go to your head, because it actually happens to be true."

"Come on in, Asa. I need a cup of coffee. Want one?" He pushed open the door.

Karen came running around from behind the booking counter, smelling of lilac and gave him a big hug. "Oh, it's so great to have you back!"

He gave Asa a wry smile over the top of her head, took her shoulders and pushed her back to arm's length. "Karen, I am glad to be back. Got any coffee for me?"

She fussed over to the coffee pot, put two cinnamon rolls on a small paper plate and carried them into his office, and finally remembered the coffee.

Asa chuckled. "See what I mean? The kind of law enforcement officer this country needs, wants, and loves."

Bud turned a bit red and waited for Karen to go back to her booking counter before he said to Asa. "We had a lot of help from an NCIS agent I'll just call Stone Fly. He was hunting his sister's killers and just sort of stumbled onto this terrorist ring…if that's what it was."

"You know it's true, Bud. It all fits. Mid-East types, explosives, AK-47s, suicide bombers. What else could it be?"

Bud looked sternly at Asa. "Where did you hear they were Mid-Eastern?"

"Well, from a friend who watched the whole thing from the top of Fort Rock."

"Won't wash, Asa. The distance is too great to make out that kind of detail through the best of binoculars."

"Seems your watcher plan worked. My friend got suspicious of Cowboy and stayed up late one night. Sort of sneaked in and took a peek. Said he saw two or three people that looked like Arabs."

"And he gave you a phone call."

"That's the size of it. Wouldn't give me a name."

"I'll give you one: Stone Fly."

"Now the question is, Bud, why do that?"

Bud nodded. "Maybe because he doesn't trust his own organization to share that information. And maybe because he wants the citizens of this country to wake up to the fact and realize that those boys are waging war on us. Maybe. Or maybe he believes that a small town editor hasn't been corrupted by political influence."

Asa rose, plopped the paper on Bud's desk, and said. "Elliptical thinking is what we have here. We'll be doubling back on ourselves before you know it." He pointed to the paper. "Enjoy the article about Lake County's heroes. Sit still, I'll let myself out."

Bud said to Asa's back, "Thanks, my friend."

Michelle marched into his office. "Here's your copy of my report. And here's a copy of the press release."

He looked surprised.

"I wrote most of it on the Colonel's computer yesterday."

"Oh…well, good thinking. I still have to write mine."

Bud sipped coffee and munched on a cinnamon roll while he read the report he had spent the last two hours writing. "Too many players, but I think I've covered the basic action."

He took the report to Karen and asked her to make the requisite number of copies. Suddenly he was bored with the whole thing. He pulled the phone directory from his top drawer and looked up the number for Bruno's Air Service.

Bruno's wife Julia answered on the second ring. "Bruno's Air Service."

"Mrs. Kowalski, this is Bud Blair. I was wondering if Bruno could fly me and Nancy Sixkiller to Yakima this afternoon."

"Well, let get him on the radio. He had a charter to Reno this morning. I'll get an ETA Lakeview."

Bud's Call Waiting beeped, but he ignored it while he listened to Mrs. Kowalski radio Bruno's aircraft. He could hear enough to know that Bruno would be back about eleven.

She came back on the line. "Bruno said he could give you a ride to Yakima by noon. Will you want him on standby in Yakima?"

"Wonderful. Yes, we'll be on the ground a couple of hours, and then we need to get back here."

"Okay, Bud. You're booked. Ah...how're our boys doing?"

"You mean the injured officers?"

"Yes...how are they doing?"

"Fine, Mrs. Kowalski. Just fine. We'll be back to normal in just a few days."

Michelle was standing in his doorway when he hung up. "Just had a call from Amanda. She'll be here in about an hour. Wants us to bring Harley Spencer and Donald Brice, aka Chase, to the airport. NCIS is assuming custody."

"Hmmm...because they assaulted an NCIS agent, I'll bet. Okay, you and Lonnie load 'em up when they get here. I hope they've had a shower."

Michelle grinned. "Of course. First thing Karen made them do."

"Where is Lonnie, by the way?"

She smiled. "On patrol. I sent him up Highway 395 just to fly the flag. Don't want the bad boys to think we're understaffed."

"Good idea. Now for the bad news. I'm leaving at noon, and I won't be back for about three days."

"Where you going?"

He grinned like a school boy. "Yakima, back here, and then on to Reno."

"Going alone?" she teased.

"Not on your life."

EPILOGUE

MARETTI WAS SITTING at his desk in one of the few private offices in the Bremerton police station, rocked back in his old captain's chair, feet on his desk, reading the sports page from the Seattle *Post Intelligencer*.

"Hey, Grandfield," he shouted out the open door, "Listen to this. The Seattle Mariners are looking for a new manager. Won't do 'em any good until they find some pitchers."

In the silence he asked again. "You listening?"

Grandfield looked up from his computer monitor and muttered, "No."

"You need to broaden your world, Grandfield. Expands the mind."

The phone on Gino's desk rang and he put his feet down, holding the paper in one hand while he picked the receiver out of the cradle.

"Detective Maretti," he answered. He listened for a couple of minutes, and then said, "Hold on...let me get something to write on. Okay...give it to me again."

He was chuckling when he came out of his office. "Grandfield, you're never going to believe this, but NCIS and the FBI are inviting Bremerton's finest—that's you and me—to join them in a take-down of that snooty lawyer up on the heights...what's his name?"

"Pettibone."

"Yeah…that's the one." Gino snorted. "Said he was gonna have my badge."

"Who we going with, Gino?"

"Why, with that good lookin' lady, Agent Spears, of course. We be buddies now, the Bremerton Police and the NCIS. We rendezvous with the good guys right here in an hour. And Grandfield, you get to drive."

Bloodstone
by Rod Collins

Legend has it that when Christ was crucified, the blood from his wounds dripped onto the green jasper ground, spotting it red and forming the bloodstone. And it was believed that if one covered the stone with the herb heliotrope, the owner became invisible.

The shaggy, gray haired, unkempt figure of Bobcat Larson stopped behind a lean six-foot juniper that somehow grew out of a crack in a low basalt bluff. He pulled his greasy flat-brimmed leather hat lower and squinted against the rays of a setting sun. Without looking back, he motioned Bud and Roger up beside him.

Bobcat pointed at a boot print and some scuff marks where the man they hunted had skirted the low bluff and slid down the dusty, pine-needle covered bank. He studied the tracks and then eyeballed the far edge of a scab-rock flat decorated with cheat grass and struggling sagebrush. "There's your varmint," he whispered.

"Where?" Bud whispered back.

"At the base of that little cliff over there... across the clearing...in the shadow just to the right of that leaning pine tree."

"I see him," Roger said quietly.

Bud took the small ten-power binoculars from his pocket and glassed the hiding place of Bobcat's "varmint." The man they hunted was sitting behind a fallen pine about thirty inches in diameter, his back up against a small ledge, a rifle across the dead tree. He appeared to be staring at the ground...like he was trying to figure out what to do next.

"Yeah, there he is. He's not looking too good."

"I wonder," Bobcat speculated in a whisper, "if he knows a cougar is about to have him for supper. Look right above him... about ten feet...on that little ledge."

"Damn," Bud whispered back, "I want that guy alive."

Roger peeled his jacket off, wadded it up in a ball and dropped to the ground in a prone shooter's position. He pushed the bundled jacket out in front him a little and then nestled the barrel of his rifle on the makeshift rest.

"You gonna shoot the varmint or the cat?" Bobcat whispered.

Roger didn't say anything. He just adjusted the scope for eight-power magnification, found his target, and then concentrated his attention on the head of the big yellow cougar.

"How far is it, Bobcat?" he asked.

The old hunter squinted and stared, estimating the distance.

"I'd say about 240 yards...maybe 250. Hard to tell in this light."

Roger's big frame seemed to settle into the ground. He took his time, setting his site picture to allow for bullet drop, took a deep breath and exhaled slowly.

The binoculars gave Bud a clear view. He watched the cougar twitch its tail and then bunch its legs up under its body, like a housecat getting set to pounce on a mouse.

The muzzle of the .308 belched fire, the heavy report rolling through the pine timber, and then the cat twisted and fell sideways off the bluff. The cougar's hundred and twenty pounds of dead weight smashed into the wounded legs of a medium-sized man who started screaming like a rock concert fanatic. Bud couldn't tell if the man's scream was pain or terror, but it sounded like terror had trumped pain.

Bobcat grinned. "Where'd you hit him?"

Roger stood up, brushed the dust off his knees, and picked up his brown khaki jacket, a "Lake County Sheriff" logo on the back, and then grinned at Bobcat. "I was aiming for his right eye."

"Did you hit it?"

"No. I think I shot him between the eyes."

Bobcat slapped Roger's meaty shoulder and said, "Well, son, if you practice enough you might just make a shooter yet." And then he let out a whoop and a laugh and danced an old man's jig, thin arms and legs pumping in time to some tune that only Bobcat could hear.

Bud watched the exchange between the lean seventy-something retired government trapper and Deputy Roger Hildebrand, shook his head and said, "Roger, what the hell did you do for the military? Between the eyes? At 250 yards?"

Roger just shrugged and said, "Anybody in my unit could make that shot. No big deal."

Bud stared at Roger for a long thirty seconds, then just shook his head and pointed across the clearing at their quarry. "Let's go get the bad guy and see if we can get out of here before dark."

Bobcat nodded, and without looking at Roger, he asked, "You want the tail or the scalp?"

• •

You can get more info about Bloodstone and my other books by visiting the BrightWorksPress.com website. I've a blog there too, so stop on by and let's talk. I'm thankful for every one of my readers. You're the reason I write these stories. They must be told. ~R.C.

• •

ROD COLLINS has done a little of everything: teacher, newspaper editor, logger, truck driver, soda jerk, construction worker, wildland firefighter, fire lookout, aerial observer, and business consultant.

More important, he is a devoted husband, father, and grandfather. And, like Louis L'Amour, he has walked the land his characters walk.

In addition to *Stone Fly*, Rod includes *Spider Silk, Bloodstone, Mariah's Song* and *Not Before Midnight* in the Sheriff Bud Blair Oregon Mystery Series. *Bitter's Run* and *Abiqua* are Rod's post-Civil War adventures.

What Do I Do When I Get There?: A New Manager's Guidebook is Rod's award-winning business reference guide.

Visit Rod at www.brightworkspress.com to learn more about his work.

www.ingramcontent.com/pod-product-compliance
Lightning Source LLC
LaVergne TN
LVHW091633070526
838199LV00044B/1051